SECOND SIGHT

Also by Amanda Quick in Large Print:

Dangerous
Deception
I Thee Wed
Mischief
Mystique
Ravished
Reckless
Rendezvous
Seduction
The Wicked Widow
With This Ring
Lie by Moonlight
The Paid Companion
Wait Until Midnight

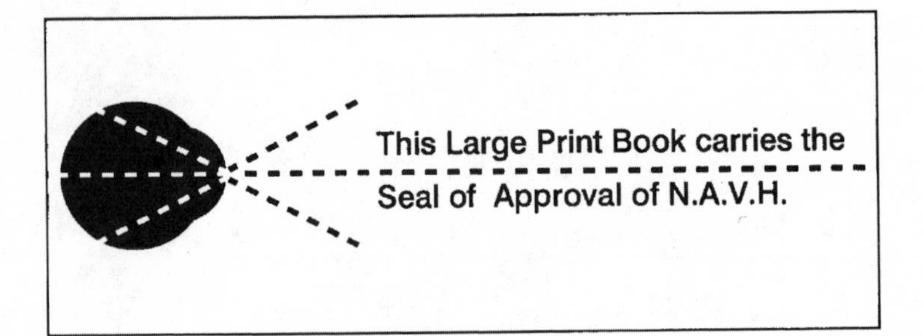

SECOND SIGHT

Amanda Quick

This is a work of fiction. Names, characters, places, and incidents either are the product of the author's imagination or are used fictitiously, and any resemblance to actual persons, living or dead, businesses, companies, events, or locales is entirely coincidental.

While the author has made every effort to provide accurate telephone numbers and Internet addresses at the time of publication, neither the publisher nor the author assumes any responsibility for errors, or for changes that occur after publication. Further, the publisher does not have any control over and does not assume any responsibility for author or third-party websites or their content.

Published in 2006 by arrangement with G. P. Putnam's Sons, a division of Penguin Group (USA) Inc.

Wheeler Large Print Hardcover.

The text of this Large Print edition is unabridged.
Other aspects of the book may vary from the original edition.

Set in 16 pt. Plantin by Ramona Watson.

Printed in the United States on permanent paper.

Library of Congress Cataloging-in-Publication Data

Quick, Amanda.
Second sight / by Amanda Quick.
p. cm.
ISBN 1-59722-232-1 (lg. print : hc : alk. paper)
1. Women photographers — Fiction. 2. Psychic ability — Fiction. I. Title.
PS3561.R44S4 2006b
813′.54—dc22 2006004437

For Cathie Linz:

Great Writer, Great Photographer,
Great Friend

National Association for Visually Handicapped
serving the partially seeing

As the Founder/CEO of NAVH, the only national health agency solely devoted to those who, although not totally blind, have an eye disease which could lead to serious visual impairment, I am pleased to recognize Thorndike Press* as one of the leading publishers in the large print field.

Founded in 1954 in San Francisco to prepare large print textbooks for partially seeing children, NAVH became the pioneer and standard setting agency in the preparation of large type.

Today, those publishers who meet our standards carry the prestigious "Seal of Approval" indicating high quality large print. We are delighted that Thorndike Press is one of the publishers whose titles meet these standards. We are also pleased to recognize the significant contribution Thorndike Press is making in this important and growing field.

Lorraine H. Marchi, L.H.D.
Founder/CEO
NAVH

* Thorndike Press encompasses the following imprints: Thorndike, Wheeler, Walker and Large Print Press.

Prologue

Late in the reign of Queen Victoria . . .

The skeleton lay on an elaborately carved and gilded bed in the center of the ancient laboratory that had become the alchemist's tomb.

The two-hundred-year-old bones were still draped in tattered robes that had been fashioned of what had surely been the most costly silks and velvets. Gloves and slippers embroidered with gold and silver thread shrouded the bones of the hands and feet, giving an eerie appearance of flesh and blood.

"His tailor must have loved him," Gabriel Jones said.

"Just because the client is an alchemist it doesn't follow that he cannot possess a keen sense of fashion," Caleb Jones remarked.

Gabriel glanced at his cousin's clothes and then surveyed his own attire. The trousers and linen shirts they wore were covered in dust and grime but the garments as well as their boots were handmade and fit to perfection.

"A family trait, it seems," Gabriel said.

"Makes for a nice addition to the Jones legend," Caleb agreed.

Gabriel moved closer to the bed and raised the lantern higher. In the flaring light he could make out the cryptic alchemical symbols for mercury, silver and gold that decorated the wide hem of the skeleton's robes. Similar designs were carved into the wooden headboard.

A heavy strongbox sat on the floor next to the bed. Two centuries of rust encrusted the sides of the box but the lid was covered with a thin sheet of some metal impervious to corrosion. *Gold,* Gabriel thought.

He leaned down and used a still-spotless handkerchief to wipe away a bit of the dust that coated the lid. The light glinted on a leafy, decorative design and some cryptic Latin that had been etched into the thin sheet of gold.

"It's astonishing that this place was never discovered and looted at some point during the past two hundred years," he said. "By all accounts, the alchemist had a number of rivals and enemies during his lifetime. To say nothing of all the members of the Arcane Society and the Jones family who have searched for it for decades."

"The alchemist had a well-deserved reputation for cleverness and secrecy," Caleb reminded him.

"Another family trait."

"True," Caleb agreed. There was a decidedly grim edge to his voice.

He and his cousin were different in many ways, Gabriel reflected. Caleb was inclined to brood and sink into long silences. He preferred to spend time alone in his laboratory. He had no patience with visitors, guests or anyone else who expected a modicum of civility and a few social graces from him.

Gabriel had always been the more outgoing and less moody of the two of them, but lately he found himself retreating into his personal library for extended periods of time. He knew that he was seeking not only knowledge but distraction, perhaps even escape, in his studies.

They were both running, each in his own way, from those aspects of their natures that could only be classified as *not normal,* he thought. He doubted that either of them would find whatever it was they were searching for in a laboratory or a library.

Caleb examined one of the old books.

"We'll need assistance packing up these relics."

"We can hire men from the village," Gabriel said.

Automatically he began formulating a plan of action to take care of the crating and shipping of the contents of the alchemist's laboratory-tomb. Formulating plans of action was something he did well. His father had told him on more than one occasion that his ability to craft strategy was closely related to his unusual psychical talents. Gabriel, however, preferred to think of it as a manifestation of the part of him that was *normal* rather than paranormal. He wanted desperately to believe that he really was a logical, rational man of the modern age, not some primitive, uncivilized throwback to an earlier stage of evolution.

He pushed the disturbing thoughts aside and concentrated on his scheme to transport the relics. The nearest village was several miles away. It was very small and no doubt owed its survival over the centuries to the smuggling business. It was a community that knew how to keep its secrets, especially when there was money involved. The Arcane Society could afford to buy the villagers' silence, Gabriel reflected.

The remote location on the coast that

the alchemist had chosen for his small fortress of a laboratory was desolate even today. Two hundred years ago it would have been even wilder and more isolated, he thought. The laboratory-tomb had been concealed underground beneath the remains of an ancient, tumbledown castle.

When he and Caleb had finally succeeded in opening the door of the laboratory a short while ago they had been met with a foul, dead-tasting wind. It had sent them both reeling back, coughing and gasping.

By mutual agreement, they had decided to wait for the atmosphere inside the chamber to be refreshed by the crisp ocean breeze before entering.

Once inside, they had discovered a room furnished in the manner of a scholarly study. Ancient leather-bound volumes, the spines cracked and worn, lined the bookshelf. Two candlesticks stood at the ready, awaiting tapers and a light.

The two-hundred-year-old apparatuses that the alchemist had used to pursue his experiments were neatly set out on a long workbench. The glass beakers were caked with dirt. The metal implements, burner and bellows were clogged with rust.

"If there is anything of great value in

here it will no doubt be in that strongbox," Caleb said. "I don't see a key. Shall we force the lock now or wait until we get it back to Arcane House?"

"We had better find out what we are dealing with," Gabriel said. He crouched beside the heavy chest and examined the iron lock. "If there is a fortune in gems or gold inside this box, it will be necessary to take extra precautions to protect the contents on the journey home."

"We'll need some tools to pry open that lid."

Gabriel looked at the skeleton. An iron object lay partially concealed beneath one gloved hand.

"I think I see the key," he said.

He reached down and carefully lifted the gloved fingers to remove the key. There was a soft rustling sound. The hand separated from the wrist. He found himself holding a glove filled with bones.

"Damn," Caleb muttered. "Talk about a chill of dread going down one's spine. Thought that sort of thing only happened in sensation novels."

"It's just a skeleton," Gabriel said, putting the glove and its morbid contents down on the old bed. "A two-hundred-year-old one at that."

"Ah, but it happens to be the skeleton of Sylvester Jones, the Alchemist, our ancestor and the founder of the Arcane Society," Caleb said. "From all accounts the man was both very cunning and very dangerous. He may not like having his laboratory discovered after all these years."

Gabriel lowered himself beside the strongbox again. "If he felt that strongly about his privacy he should not have left clues to the location of this place in that series of letters he wrote before he died."

The letters had sat moldering away in the society's archives until he had dug them out several months ago and succeeded in deciphering the alchemist's private code.

He tried the key in the lock and knew at once it was not going to work.

"Too much rust," he announced. "Get the tools."

Ten minutes later, working together, they managed to pry open the strongbox. The lid rose reluctantly. Harsh grinding groans emanated from the hinges. But there were no explosions, flashes of fire or other unpleasant surprises.

Gabriel and Caleb looked down into the box.

"So much for the notion of finding a hoard of gold and jewels," Caleb said.

"Fortunately we did not carry out this expedition with the hope of discovering a treasure," Gabriel agreed.

The only object inside the strongbox was a small leather-bound notebook.

He picked up the book and opened it with great care. "I suspect this will contain the formula that the alchemist hinted at in his papers and letters. He would have considered it vastly more important than gold or jewels."

The yellowed pages were filled with the alchemist's precise handwriting, all in cryptic Latin.

Caleb leaned forward for a closer look at the seemingly meaningless jumble of letters, numbers, symbols and words that covered the first page.

"It's written in another one of his damned private codes," he said, shaking his head.

Gabriel turned one of the pages. "A love of secrecy and codes is a tradition that the members of the Arcane Society have maintained with great enthusiasm for two centuries."

"I have never encountered a greater bunch of obsessive, reclusive eccentrics in my life than the members of the Arcane Society."

Gabriel closed the notebook with great care and met Caleb's eyes. "There are some who would say that you and I are just as eccentric if not more so than any of the members of the society."

"*Eccentric* is probably not the right word for us." Caleb's jaw tensed. "But I'd just as soon not try to come up with a more appropriate term."

Gabriel did not argue. When they were younger they had reveled in their *eccentricities,* taking their special sensitivities for granted. But maturity and adulthood had given them a different, far more cautious perspective.

Now, to make life even more difficult, Gabriel thought, he found himself dealing with a modern-thinking father who had become an enthusiastic supporter of Mr. Darwin's theories. Hippolyte Jones was determined to see his heir married off as soon as possible. Gabriel had concluded that his sire secretly wished to discover if the unusual sort of paranormal sensitivity his son possessed would prove to be an inheritable trait.

Damned if he would allow himself to be coerced into participating in an experiment in evolution, Gabriel thought. When it came to finding a wife, he preferred to do his own hunting.

He looked at Caleb. "Does it ever concern you that we are members of a society that is populated by secretive, reclusive eccentrics who are obsessed with the arcane and the uncanny?"

"Not our fault," Caleb declared, bending to study one of the old instruments on the workbench. "We were merely fulfilling our filial obligations when we allowed ourselves to be inducted. You know as well as I do that both of our fathers would have been outraged if we had refused to join their precious society. Besides, you are in no position to complain. You were the one who talked me into agreeing to go through with the damned ceremony."

Gabriel glanced down at the black-and-gold onyx ring that he wore on his right hand. The stone was embossed with an alchemical symbol for fire.

"I am well aware of that," he said.

Caleb exhaled heavily. "I realize that you felt an enormous amount of pressure to join the society, given the circumstances."

"Yes." Gabriel closed the heavy lid of the box and studied the cryptic words engraved on the gold sheet. "I certainly hope this isn't some alchemical curse. *He who dares open this strongbox will die a dreadful death by sunrise,* or something along those lines."

"It probably is a curse or at least a warning of some kind." Caleb shrugged. "The old alchemists were notorious for that sort of thing. But you and I are men of the modern age, are we not? We don't believe in that kind of nonsense."

The first man died three days later.

His name was Riggs. He was one of the villagers Gabriel and Caleb had hired to pack up the contents of the alchemist's tomb and see the crates safely aboard the wagons for transport.

The body was discovered in an ancient alley near the docks. Riggs had been stabbed twice. The first strike had pierced his chest. The second slashed open his throat. A great deal of blood had pooled and dried on the old stones. He had been killed with his own knife. It lay beside him, the blade darkly stained.

"I am told that Riggs was a loner who had a penchant for drinking, whoring and getting into tavern brawls," Caleb said. "As far as the locals are concerned, he was bound to come to a bad end sooner or later. The assumption is that he finally got into a fight with an opponent who was either faster or luckier than he was."

He looked at Gabriel; waiting, not speaking.

Resigned to the inevitable, Gabriel crouched beside the body. Reluctantly he picked up the knife by its hilt, focused his attention on the murder weapon and braced for the shock of icy awareness that he knew awaited him.

There was still a great deal of energy left on the knife hilt. The murder had been committed only a few hours ago, after all. Strong sensations still clung to the blade, enough to ignite a dark thrill deep inside him.

All of his senses sharpened. It was as if he was suddenly more alert in some indefinable metaphysical fashion. The disturbing part was the elemental desire to hunt that heated his blood.

He released the knife quickly, letting it clatter on the stones, and rose to his feet.

Caleb watched him intently. "Well?"

"Riggs was not killed by a stranger who was in the grip of a sudden rage or panic," Gabriel said. Absently he made a fist out of the hand he had used to grip the knife. The gesture was automatic, a futile attempt to exorcise the lingering stain of evil and the urge to hunt that it excited in him.

"Whoever met him in this alley came here with the deliberate intention of killing him. It was all very cold-blooded."

"A cuckolded husband or an old enemy, perhaps."

"That's the most likely explanation," Gabriel agreed. But he could feel the prickles of awareness raising the hair on the back of his neck. This death was no unconnected event. "Given Riggs's reputation, the authorities will no doubt come to that conclusion. I think, however, that we should inventory the contents of the crates."

Caleb's brows rose. "Do you believe that Riggs may have stolen one of the artifacts and attempted to sell it to someone who then murdered him?"

"Perhaps."

"I thought we agreed that there was very little in the alchemist's laboratory that was worth a lot of money, let alone a man's life."

"Let's notify the local authorities and then open the crates," Gabriel said quietly.

He turned and started swiftly toward the narrow mouth of the alley, wanting to put as much distance between himself and the spoor of violence as possible. The desire to hunt was still under control but he could feel it whispering darkly, urging him to open himself to that other aspect of his nature, the part of him that he feared was anything but modern.

It took some time to check each of the relics that had been carefully wrapped and prepared for shipment against the list of artifacts that Gabriel and Caleb had made. In the end only one item was found to be missing.

"He took the damned notebook," Caleb said, disgusted. "It will not be amusing to explain the loss to either one of our fathers, let alone the Council."

Gabriel contemplated the empty interior of the strongbox. "We made it easy for him because we had already pried the lid open. He didn't have to work very hard to retrieve the notebook. But why would anyone want it? At most it's merely an interesting scholarly artifact filled with the deluded ramblings of a mad old alchemist. It's of historical significance only to the members of the Arcane Society and then only because Sylvester was the founder of the society."

Caleb shook his head. "It would seem that there may be someone who actually believes that the formula will work. Someone who is willing to kill for it."

"Well, one thing is certain. We have just witnessed the start of a new addition to the legends of the Arcane Society."

Caleb winced. "The Curse of Sylvester the Alchemist?"

"It has a certain ring to it, don't you think?"

1

Two months later . . .

He was the man she had been waiting for, the lover who was destined to ruin her. But first she wanted to photograph him.

"No," Gabriel Jones said. He crossed the richly appointed library, picked up the brandy decanter and splashed a healthy dose of the contents into two glasses. "I did not bring you here to Arcane House to take my picture, Miss Milton. I employed you to photograph the society's collection of relics and artifacts. I may appear to be in my dotage to you, but I like to think that I am not yet ready to be classified as an antiquity."

Gabriel was no aged relic, Venetia thought. Indeed, she sensed in him the power and confidence of a man in his prime. He gave every appearance of being just the right age to sweep her off her feet into the thrilling fires of an illicit passion.

She had waited long enough to find the right man for the task, she thought. By

Society's standards she was past the age when a lady could reasonably expect to contract a marriage. The responsibilities thrust upon her a year and a half ago when her parents had been killed in the train wreck had sealed her fate. Few respectable gentlemen were eager to take to wife a woman in her late twenties who was the sole support of two siblings and a maiden aunt. In light of her father's behavior, she had grave misgivings about the institution of marriage, in any event.

But she did not want to live the rest of her life never knowing genuine physical passion. A lady in her situation, Venetia thought, had a right to engineer her own ravishment.

The project of seducing Gabriel had been a great challenge because she possessed no practical experience in the business. True, there had been a few minor flirtations here and there over the years but none had resulted in anything more than some experimental kisses.

The truth was, she had never encountered any man who was worth the risk of an illicit affair. Following the death of her parents, the need to avoid a disastrous scandal had become even more imperative. The financial security of her family was entirely dependent upon her career as a photographer. She must not do anything to jeopardize it.

But this magical time at Arcane House had been literally dropped into her lap; a gift that she had never expected to receive.

It had come about in the most mundane way, she reflected. A member of the mysterious Arcane Society had viewed her photographic work in Bath and recommended her to the society's official governing Council. The Council, it seemed, had determined to have the contents of their museum recorded in photographs.

The lucrative commission had offered her an unprecedented opportunity to live out her most secret romantic fantasies.

"I would not charge extra for taking your portrait," she said quickly. "The fee that was paid in advance will cover all expenses."

And a good deal more, she thought, trying not to reveal her satisfaction. She was still dazzled by the incredibly handsome sum the Arcane Society had paid into her account at the bank. The unexpected windfall was literally going to change her future and that of her small family. But she did not think it would be wise to explain that to Gabriel.

Image was everything in her profession, as Aunt Beatrice never hesitated to point out. She must give her client the impression that her work was worth every penny of the huge sum that had been paid.

Gabriel smiled his cool, mysterious smile and handed her one of the brandies. When his fingers brushed against hers, a little thrill tingled along her nerves. It was not the first time she had felt the sensation.

She had never met a man like Gabriel Jones. He had the eyes of an ancient sorcerer. They were filled with dark, unfathomable secrets. The flames that flared on the massive stone hearth cast a wash of golden light across the planes and angles of a face that had been carved by strong, elemental forces. He moved with a dangerous, predatory grace, and he looked incredibly masculine and elegant in his beautifully tailored black-and-white evening clothes.

All in all, she thought, he was quite perfect for what she had in mind.

"Cost is not the issue, Miss Milton, as I'm sure you're well aware," he said.

Embarrassed, she took a quick swallow of brandy and prayed that the shadowy lighting would conceal her blush. Of course cost was not the problem, she thought, chagrined. Judging by the furnishings that surrounded her, the Arcane Society was evidently sustained by a comfortable fortune.

She had arrived at the crumbling heap of stone named Arcane House six days ago, conveyed in a modern, well-sprung private carriage that Gabriel had dispatched to meet her at the train station in the village.

The massively built coachman had been a dour sort who had spoken very little after confirming her identity. He had hoisted the trunks that contained her clothes as well as her dry plates, tripod and developing chemicals as easily as though they contained nothing but feathers. She had insisted on carrying her camera herself.

The journey from the station had taken nearly two hours. Night had fallen and Venetia had been uneasily aware of the fact that she was being driven deeper and deeper into a remote, seemingly uninhabited landscape.

By the time the taciturn coachman had drawn up in front of an old mansion that had been built upon the ruins of an even more ancient abbey, it was all she could do to conceal the jittery sensations that coursed through her. She had even begun to wonder if she had made a great mistake by agreeing to take the exorbitantly lucrative commission.

All of the arrangements had been conducted by post. Her younger sister, Amelia, who worked as her assistant, had planned to accompany her. But at the last minute Amelia had contracted a bad cold. Aunt Beatrice had been anxious about Venetia going off on her own to complete the commission but in the end financial necessity had won out. Once the grand sum of money had been deposited into the bank, Venetia had never once considered declining the project.

The isolated location of Arcane House had generated more than a few doubts but her first encounter with Gabriel Jones had quelled all of her private concerns.

When she had been ushered into his presence by the near-silent housekeeper that first evening, she had been nearly overwhelmed by a rush of astonishing awareness. The sensation was so acute it had aroused and excited all of her senses, including the very special kind of vision that she kept secret from everyone except the members of her own family.

That was when the inspiration for her grand plan of seduction had struck.

This was the right man, the right place

and the right time. After she left Arcane House she was highly unlikely to ever again encounter Gabriel Jones. Even if by some chance they did happen to cross each other's path in the future, she sensed he would be gentleman enough to keep her secrets. She suspected that he had a few of his own.

Her family, clients and neighbors in Bath would never know what took place here, she thought. While she was at Arcane House she was free from Society's strictures in a way that she never would be again.

Until today she had dared to hope that, in spite of her lack of practical experience, the seduction of Gabriel Jones was going well. She knew from the occasional glimpses of heat that she surprised in his eyes and the exciting aura of energy that enveloped them when they were in the same room that he was attracted to her.

In the past few days they had sat down to long, intimate dinners and stimulating, wide-ranging conversations by the fire. They had breakfasted together in the mornings, served by the taciturn housekeeper, and discussed the day's photography plans at length. Gabriel seemed to enjoy her company as much as she did his.

There was just one problem. This was her sixth night here at Arcane House and thus far Gabriel had made no attempt to even take her into his arms, let alone carry her upstairs to one of the bedrooms.

True, there had been many small, fleeting, incredibly exciting little intimacies: his warm, powerful hand on her elbow when he guided her into a room, a casual, seemingly unintended touch, a sensual smile that promised more than it delivered.

All extremely tantalizing, to be sure, but not what one would call definitive indications that he desired her enough to make mad, passionate love to her.

She was starting to worry that she had fumbled the business. In a few more days she would depart Arcane House forever. If she did not do something soon, her dreams would remain unrealized.

"You have made excellent progress with your work here," Gabriel said. He went to stand in front of the windows, looking out into the moonlit night. "Do you feel that you will be able to finish on schedule?"

"Most likely," she admitted. *Unfortunately,* she added silently. She would have given a great deal for an excuse to linger. "With all the sun we have enjoyed these past few days I have had very few problems with the lighting."

"The light is always a photographer's greatest concern, is it not?"

"Yes."

"The word from the village is that the weather is expected to hold."

More bad news, she thought glumly. Poor weather was the only reason she could think of for prolonging her stay.

"How nice," she said politely.

Time was running out. A sense of desperation gripped her. Gabriel might feel some desire for her, but he appeared to be too much of a gentleman to act on it.

Her plans for at least one night of illicit passion appeared to be evaporating before her very eyes. She had to act.

Recklessly she tossed back the last of the brandy. It burned all the way down but the fire gave her the courage she needed to rise to her feet.

She set the glass aside with such determination that it made a decided *clink* when it hit the table.

It was now or never. Would he be appalled if she simply threw herself into his arms? Most certainly. Any true gentleman would be utterly shocked by such unseemly behavior. She was rather appalled at the thought, herself. What if he rejected her? The humiliation would be unbearable.

This situation called for subtlety.

She groped for inspiration. Outside, moonlight streamed down onto the terrace. It cast a very romantic spell, she thought.

"Speaking of atmospheric conditions," she said, striving for a light tone, "it has become a trifle warm in here, has it not? I believe I shall take some fresh air before retiring. Will you join me, sir?"

She moved toward the glass-paned doors that opened onto the terrace in what she hoped was a suitably sultry, inviting manner.

"Yes, of course," Gabriel said.

Her spirits soared. This just might work.

He followed her to the door and opened it for her. When she stepped out onto the stone terrace the chill night air struck her with unexpected force. Her optimism failed abruptly.

So much for her brilliant ploy, she thought. This brisk temperature was hardly likely to incline Gabriel toward a state of heated passion.

"I should have brought a wrap," she said, folding her arms beneath her breasts to warm herself.

Gabriel braced one booted foot on the low stone wall that surrounded the terrace and examined the starry night sky with an assessing expression.

"The crisp, clear weather tonight is another indication that we will, indeed, enjoy ample sunlight tomorrow," he said.

"Wonderful."

He glanced at her. In the moonlight she could see that he was smiling his cryptic smile.

Good grief, was he amused by her poor attempt at seduction? That was an even more distressing thought than the fear that he might reject her.

She hugged herself more tightly and imagined the photographic portrait she would have made of Gabriel if he had given her the opportunity. There would have been areas of intense, powerful shadow in the final image, she thought, reflections of the invisible dark energy that emanated from him.

That knowledge did not alarm her. She knew that the metaphysical darkness that flared around Gabriel was evidence of his strong will and self-mastery. It was not the sort of disturbing energy that emanated from a fevered brain. She had glimpsed those peculiar, dreadful hues occasionally among some who sat for their portraits. The chilling experiences never failed to leave her with a sick sense of revulsion and fear.

Gabriel Jones was very, very different.

She pondered the night and her failed attempt at seduction. There was nothing to be gained standing out here shivering. She might as well admit defeat and retreat back into the warmth of the library.

"You're feeling the cold," Gabriel said. "Allow me."

To her amazement, he unfastened his elegantly cut coat and peeled it off with fluid masculine grace. The next thing she knew, he was draping the heavy garment around her shoulders.

The fine wool carried the residual heat of his body, warming her instantly. She inhaled and caught the trace of his scent.

Do not read too much into this bit of gallantry, she thought. He was merely playing the gentleman.

Nevertheless the intimacy of the situation was incredibly exhilarating. She wanted to cling to the coat and never let go.

"I must tell you that I have found this photography commission quite interesting," she said, huddling deeper into his coat. "From both an artistic and an educational point of view. I had no idea that the Arcane Society even existed before I arrived here."

"As a general policy the members of the society shun any sort of public notice."

"You have made that clear," she said. "I know it is none of my affair, but I cannot help but wonder why the society is so intent on maintaining a cloak of secrecy."

"Blame it on tradition." Gabriel smiled again. "The society was founded some two hundred years ago by an alchemist who was obsessed with secrecy. Throughout the years, the members have maintained the same attitude."

"Yes, but this is the modern age. No one takes alchemy seriously these days. Even in the late sixteen hundreds it was considered to be one of the dark arts, not a genuine science."

"Science has always been dark at its edges, Miss Milton. The border between the known and the unknown is extremely murky, to say the least. Today, those who explore those obscure fringes call what they do psychical or metaphysical research. But in truth, they are merely modern-day alchemists sailing under a new flag."

"The Arcane Society is engaged in psychical research?" she asked, startled.

For a moment she thought he might not answer the question. But then he inclined his head, once.

"That is correct," he said.

Venetia frowned. "Forgive me, but in that case, the obsession with secrecy seems very odd, indeed. After all, psychical research is a perfectly respectable field of study these days. Why, they say that in London one can attend a séance any night of the week. And there are a vast number of learned journals dealing with psychical investigations published each month."

"The members of the Arcane Society view the majority of those who claim to possess psychical powers as frauds, charlatans and tricksters."

"I see."

"Arcane Society investigators and researchers take their work very seriously," Gabriel added. "They do not wish to be associated with impostors and deceivers."

It was clear from the tone of his voice that he held similar strong views, she thought. This was certainly not the time to announce that she could see auras.

She tugged the edges of his coat more snugly around herself and retreated into the safety and privacy of her own secrets. The last thing she wanted to do was leave her fantasy lover with the impression that she was a charlatan or a fraud. Nevertheless, she could not bring herself to drop the subject without some small protest.

"Personally," she said, "I prefer to keep an open mind. I certainly do not believe that all who claim to possess paranormal senses are liars and frauds."

He turned his head to look at her. "You misunderstand me, Miss Milton. The members of the society are more than willing to allow for the possibility that some individuals do possess paranormal senses and abilities. That possibility is the reason the Arcane Society is still in existence."

"If the society's focus is psychical in nature, why has it acquired the rather strange artifacts in the museum here at Arcane House?"

"The antiquities in the collection are all believed to have some metaphysical importance, either real or imaginary." He shrugged. "I think it is safe to say that in the majority of instances, the latter is the case. Either way, each relic has research and historical significance as far as the society is concerned."

"I must tell you that I found many of the artifacts exceedingly unpleasant, even disturbing in some manner."

"Did you, indeed, Miss Milton?" he asked very softly.

"My apologies, sir," she said hastily. "I did not mean to offend your taste or that of the other members of the society."

He was amused. "Never fear, Miss Milton, I am not so easily offended. As it happens you are a very perceptive woman. The artifacts here at Arcane House were not collected with a view toward preserving the elegant or the artistic. Each was brought here for purposes of scientific study."

"Why did the society decide to have the collection photographed?"

"There are many members throughout Britain and in other parts of the world who wish to examine the relics but are unable to make the journey to Arcane House. The Master of the society decreed that a photographer be employed to record the relics so that those who cannot view them in person will be able to study the pictures."

"The society plans to issue the photographs in the form of albums that can be dispersed to the members?"

"That is the intent, yes," he said. "But

the society does not want the pictures made available to curiosity seekers and the general public. That is why, by the terms of our agreement, I will take possession of the negatives. That way the number of prints produced can be strictly controlled."

"You do understand that our arrangement is most unusual. Until this commission, it has been my practice to retain possession of every negative that I create."

"I appreciate your reluctance to alter your customary mode of business." His brows rose slightly. "But I believe the society did make it worth your while in this instance."

She blushed. "Yes."

He shifted slightly in the shadows, taking his foot down off the low wall. It was the most casual of motions but it somehow closed the space between them, heightening the sense of intimacy in a way that made her pulse race.

He reached out with one hand and lightly gripped the lapel of the coat she wore. "I am pleased that you are satisfied with our financial arrangements."

She went very still, startlingly aware of his strong fingers so tantalizingly close to her throat. This was definitely not a casual sort of touch, she thought.

"I hope you will be equally satisfied with my work," she said.

"I have seen enough in the past few days to know that you are an excellent photographer, Miss Milton. The pictures you created are remarkably clear and detailed in every respect."

She swallowed hard, striving to project a woman-of-the-world image. "You did say that you wanted to be able to see every inscription and line of engraving on every artifact."

"Detail and clarity are critical."

He gripped both lapels of the coat and drew her closer. She did not even attempt to resist. This was what she had been yearning for these past few days and nights, she reminded herself. She was not about to lose her nerve at this juncture.

"I have found my work here quite . . . stimulating," she whispered, staring at his mouth.

"Did you?"

"Oh, yes." She could hardly breathe now.

He tugged her a little closer.

"Would it be presumptuous of me to conclude that you find me somewhat interesting, too?" he asked. "Or have I misread the situation between us?"

Excitement shot through her, brighter

than the glare of the magnesium ribbons she occasionally used to light her subjects. Her mouth went dry.

"I find you quite riveting, Mr. Jones."

She leaned closer, parting her lips a little, inviting him to kiss her.

He responded at last. His mouth closed on hers, slow and searching. She heard herself make a soft, urgent little sound and then, greatly emboldened, she put her arms around his neck, clinging as though for dear life.

The warm coat slid off her shoulders but she paid no attention. She no longer needed the garment. Gabriel was holding her tightly against him. The heat of his body and the invisible energy of his aura enveloped her.

The kiss was beyond her wildest dreams and fantasies. There was much about Gabriel that remained an enigma, but she knew at last that his desire for her was very real.

Her seduction plan was a blazing success.

"I think," Gabriel said against her throat, "that it is time to go back inside."

He picked her up in his arms as though she were weightless and carried her back through the open door into the inviting warmth of the fire-lit library.

2

He set her down on her feet in front of the fire. Holding her mouth captive with his own, he went to work unfastening the hooks at the front of the stiff bodice of her gown. She shivered again in spite of the warmth of the flames on the hearth and was suddenly very glad that she numbered herself among the many women who considered corsets unhealthful as well as uncomfortable. It would have been awkward, indeed, to stand here while Gabriel unlaced her, she thought.

Oddly disoriented and a little unsteady, she instinctively braced her hands against his shoulders. When she felt the sleek muscle beneath the fabric of his shirt an unfamiliar heat swirled inside her.

Impulsively she flexed her hands, sinking her nails into him.

Gabriel smiled slowly. "Ah, my sweet Miss Milton, I do believe that you will drive me mad tonight."

The heavy gown fell away before she even realized that he had gotten it open.

The dark crimson skirts pooled at her feet. She drew a sharp, unsteady breath when his hand cupped her breast. Through the fine linen of her underclothes she was intensely aware of his fingers moving gently, coaxingly across her nipple.

The next thing she knew her hair was tumbling down around her bare shoulders. He had removed the pins, she thought.

It dawned on her that in spite of the fact that this was her seduction, he was doing all the work now. Surely as a woman of the world she should be doing something more assertive.

She caught one end of his bow tie and yanked hard.

A little too hard.

Gabriel gave a husky laugh. "Do you mean to strangle me before we have concluded this business, Miss Milton?"

"I'm sorry," she whispered, horrified.

"Allow me."

He deftly unknotted the tie. It dangled briefly from his fingers and then, to her astonishment, he draped it lightly around her throat. In the firelight, his eyes darkened with an emotion she knew was desire.

In a matter of a few more moments, the length of black silk was all that she wore. She closed her eyes against the realization that she was nude in front of her dream lover.

"You are very beautiful," he said against her throat.

She knew that was somewhat short of the truth but she suddenly *felt* quite lovely, such was the power of his voice and the atmosphere of the room.

"So are you," she blurted, enthralled.

He laughed softly, picked her up and settled her on the velvet cushions of the sofa. Dazed from the waves of excitement and sensation pulsing through her, she closed her eyes. The end of the sofa gave beneath his weight. She heard one of his boots hit the floor and then the other.

He rose from the sofa. She opened her eyes in time to watch him strip off his shirt. In the golden light of the fire she could see that he was sleekly, powerfully made.

He stepped out of his trousers and tossed them aside.

When he turned back to her she froze at the sight of his aroused body.

He, too, went still.

"What is it?" he asked.

"Nothing," she managed. She could hardly tell him that this was the first time she had ever seen an adult man naked and erect. A woman of the world would be familiar with a sight like this, she reminded herself.

"Do you find the sight of me displeasing?" he asked, still not moving.

She drew a deep, steadying breath and gave him a tremulous smile.

"I find the sight of you very . . . stimulating," she whispered.

"Stimulating." He sounded as though he did not know what to make of that. Then he smiled his mysterious smile. "I believe you used that term to describe your work here at Arcane House. Does that mean that you would like to set up your camera before we proceed?"

"Mr. Jones."

He came to her in a low roar of masculine laughter. Lowering himself down on top of her, he slid one muscled thigh between her legs.

He breathed hot, seductive, shockingly wicked words against the bare skin of her breast. She responded impulsively, not with words because she could no longer speak, but with her body. She twisted and arched beneath his weight, clutching at him.

Very soon he ceased talking to her. His breathing became harsher. She could feel his muscles tightening beneath her hands. The dark thrills flashing through her were so intense that she could not even spare a second to be shocked anew when he reached down between them and caressed her sex.

She *needed* him to touch her like that. In fact, she needed more; much more.

"Yes," she whispered. "Please, yes."

"Anything," he got out hoarsely. "Anything you want. You have only to ask."

He stroked her until she pleaded with him for a release she could not describe, until she was clenched with need. When he slipped a finger inside her the sense of urgency became unbearable.

She realized that a similar sensation was riding him, too. He groaned, as though he ached somewhere deep inside. He was no longer touching her with the exquisite tenderness of a gentlemanly lover. Instead he was fighting her for the embrace, tormenting her, challenging her. She fought back, glorying in the sensual battle.

"You were made for me," he said suddenly, as though the words had been ripped from him. "You are mine."

It was a statement, not an endearment. A declaration of indisputable fact.

He caught her face between his hands. "Say it. Say that you are mine."

"I am yours." *For tonight,* she added silently. She raked her nails across his back.

Energy swirled around them. Her aura, she thought in some distant part of her mind, somehow it had infused with his to create an invisible metaphysical storm that engulfed them both.

When she narrowed her eyes slightly she realized that her paranormal vision was flashing in and out of focus. Light and shadow reversed and reversed again.

Gabriel used one hand to fit himself to her. He probed once and then he drove deep with a single, relentless thrust.

Pain snapped through her, shattering the sensual trance.

Gabriel froze, every muscle rock solid.

"Sweet hell," he muttered. He raised his head and looked down at her with eyes that were as dangerous as his dark aura. *"Why didn't you tell me?"*

"Because I knew you would stop if I did," she whispered. She speared her fingers through his hair. "And I didn't want you to stop."

He groaned. *"Venetia."*

But the energy they had generated between them was rising once more. Gabriel lowered his mouth to hers in a kiss that had all the hallmarks of a stamp of possession as well as passion.

When he freed her she drew in an unsteady breath, wriggling a little in an effort to adjust to the intimate invasion.

"Don't," Gabriel said. "Move." He sounded as though he was having trouble breathing.

She smiled a little, put her arms around his neck and pulled him more tightly to her.

"You do realize you will pay for this," he said.

"I certainly hope so."

He started to withdraw very slowly.

"No." She tightened herself around him, trying to hold him deep inside.

"I'm not going anywhere," he said.

The words were both a promise and a delicious threat.

He drove back into her, filling her, stretching her to the limit. She wanted this desperately but she could not take any more of it, she thought.

Without warning the great tension inside her was released in compelling waves, a pleasure so intense that it bordered on pain.

With an exultant roar, Gabriel surged

into her one last time. His climax caused the psychical fire to leap with such potent force that she was amazed it did not set the whole of Arcane House ablaze.

3

She felt Gabriel stir a long time later. He sat up slowly, his hand resting on her breast. He studied her for a long time in the firelight before he bent his head, kissed her lightly and got to his feet.

He picked up her underclothes and handed them to her. Then he reached for his trousers.

"I think," he said, "that you owe me an explanation."

She crushed the fine linen of her chemise between her fingers. "You are annoyed because I did not tell you that I had never done this sort of thing before."

He looked thoughtful, almost amused. "*Annoyed* is not the right word. I am delighted to know that you have not done this sort of thing before with any other man. But you should have made that clear at the outset."

She struggled into the chemise. "If I had, would you have gone forward with the project?"

"Yes, my sweet. Without a doubt."

She looked up, startled. "Is that true?"

"It's true." He smiled slightly. "But I like to think that I would have employed rather more finesse."

"I . . . see."

He watched her face in the firelight. "Does that shock you?"

"I'm not sure. Yes, I think it does."

"Why? Did you believe me to be such a proper gentleman, then?"

"Well, yes," she admitted.

"And I believed you to be a lady with some experience of the world. It seems that we were both under some minor misconceptions."

"*Minor* misconceptions?" she repeated coolly.

"Not that they matter now." He fastened his trousers. "Tell me, what made you decide to seduce me?"

So much for her powers of subtlety. She was embarrassed that she had been so obvious.

"Given my age and circumstances, it has become clear that I am unlikely to ever marry," she said. "Frankly, sir, I saw no reason on earth why I should feel obliged to deny myself a taste of passion for the rest of my life. If I were a man, no one would expect me to remain celibate forever."

"You are correct, of course. When it comes to certain things, Society sets down a different set of rules for men than it does for women."

"Nevertheless, there are rules." She sighed. "One flaunts them at one's peril. I have certain responsibilities to my family. I must be careful to avoid any scandal that could ruin my photography career. It is our only source of income."

"But when you arrived at Arcane House it occurred to you that the situation offered an opportunity to conduct a grand experiment with illicit passion, is that it?"

"Yes." She had her dress on now. She busied herself with the hooks. "You did not appear to object, sir. In fact, you seemed quite willing to go along with my *experiment.*"

"I was, indeed, quite willing."

"Well, there you have it." Relieved that her logic had proven sound, she managed a smile. "There is no need for either of us to be concerned about what happened here tonight. We will soon go our separate ways. When I return home to Bath, it will be as though it was all a dream."

"I don't know about you," Gabriel said, suddenly quite grim, "but I think I need some fresh air."

"No offense, sir, but are men always this moody after making love?"

"I happen to possess rather delicate sensibilities."

He took her hand and led her back out onto the terrace. The evening coat that he had given her to wear earlier lay in a crumpled heap on the stone. He picked it up and draped it once more around her shoulders.

"Now," he said, gripping the lapels to hold her where he wanted her. "About this theory of yours that what happened here tonight will soon be nothing more than a dream."

"What of it?"

"I have news for you, my sweet. The situation between us is somewhat more complicated than you believe it to be."

"I don't understand," she whispered.

"Trust me, I am all too well aware of that. But I do not think that tonight is the right moment for a full explanation. Tomorrow will be soon enough."

He bent his head to kiss her again. But this time she could not abandon herself to the embrace. Uncertainty was clawing at her. Perhaps she had made a terrible mistake, after all.

Gabriel's temper seemed uncertain, even

volatile. All in all, he was behaving in an extremely odd manner for a man who had just been engaged in an act of passion. Then again, what did she know of how men acted after such events?

His mouth covered hers. She opened her eyes, braced her hands on his shoulders and pushed hard. It was like trying to shove aside a mountain. Gabriel did not move but he did raise his head.

"Will you deny me a good-night kiss?" he asked.

She did not answer him. She wanted to view his aura first. It might give her some clue to his true emotions.

For a second or two her vision wavered between normal and paranormal. Light and shadow reversed. The night took on the aspect of a photographic negative.

Gabriel's aura became visible. But so did someone else's.

Startled, she looked out into the dark woods beyond the garden.

"What is it?" Gabriel asked quietly.

She realized that he had immediately understood that something was wrong.

"There is someone out there in the woods," she said.

"One of the servants," he suggested, turning to look.

"No." There were very few servants at Arcane House. Over the past few days, her curiosity about the place had prompted her to view all of their auras. Whoever was out there in the thick trees was a stranger to her.

A second aura appeared, trailing swiftly behind the first.

There was no point trying to describe what she saw to Gabriel. Let him think that her vision was especially keen. That was, in a sense, the truth.

"There are two of them," she said softly. "They are keeping to the shadows. I think they are making for the conservatory door."

"Yes," he said. "I can see them."

She glanced at him, astonished. The intruders' auras were visible to her paranormal senses but she could not believe that Gabriel could make out the two men using only his normal vision. Very little moonlight penetrated the woods that bordered the grounds of Arcane House.

There was no time to question him. He was already in motion.

"Come with me." He swung around, seizing her arm.

Automatically, she clutched his coat to keep it from sliding off her shoulders. He drew her swiftly back through the French doors into the warmth of the library.

"Where are we going?" she asked a little breathlessly.

"There is no way of knowing who those two are or what they are after. I want you away from this place at once."

"My things —"

"Forget them. There is no time to pack."

"My camera," she said, trying to dig in her heels. "I cannot leave it behind."

"You can buy another with the money you were paid for this commission."

That was true but she did not like the thought of leaving her precious equipment behind, let alone her clothes. The gowns she had brought with her to Arcane House were her best.

"Mr. Jones, what is going on here? Surely you are overreacting. If you alert the servants they will be able to make certain that those housebreakers do not get inside."

"I doubt very much that those two are ordinary, garden-variety thieves." Gabriel paused beside the desk and gripped the velvet bell pull. He gave it three short, sharp tugs. "That will alert the servants. They have their instructions for this sort of emergency."

He opened the bottom drawer of the desk and reached inside. When he straightened Venetia saw that he held a pistol in his hand.

"Follow me," he ordered. "I will see you safely out of here and then I will deal with the intruders."

A hundred questions leaped to mind but there was no ignoring the unequivocal air of command. Whatever was going on here, Gabriel obviously believed that it amounted to more than a common house burglary.

She grabbed fistfuls of her heavy skirts and hurried after him. She assumed that they would make for the door that opened onto the long, central hall. But to her amazement, Gabriel went to a classical statue of a Greek god that stood near a bookcase and moved one of the stone arms.

The muffled groan of heavy hinges emanated from somewhere inside the wall. A section of the wooden paneling swung ponderously outward to reveal a narrow staircase. She could see only the first few steps. The rest plunged downward into darkness.

Gabriel hoisted a lantern that had been left at the top of the staircase and struck a light. The yellow glare of the lamp spilled into the pool of midnight below the steps. He waited until she had stepped gingerly onto the top step before pulling the wall closed behind them.

"Have a care," Gabriel said, starting down into the depths. "These steps are very old. They date back to the most ancient portion of the abbey."

"Where do they lead?"

"To a concealed tunnel that once served the abbey as an escape route in the event of attack," he said.

"What makes you think that those two intruders are more than ordinary ruffians?"

"Very few people outside the members of the society are even aware that Arcane House exists, let alone its precise location. You will recall that you were driven here at night in a closed carriage. Could you find your way back again?"

"No," she admitted.

"When visitors are brought to Arcane House they always arrive in a similar manner. Yet those two villains obviously know where they are going and what they are about. Therefore I must assume that they are more than simple burglars who happened to stumble upon a likely looking household to rob."

"I take your point."

Gabriel reached the bottom of the steps. Venetia barely avoided stumbling into him.

The flaring lantern light illuminated a stone-walled corridor. The smell of damp earth and decayed vegetation was heavy. There was an unpleasant rustling and skittering at the edges of the shadows. The light gleamed briefly on small, malevolent eyes.

Rats, Venetia thought. Just the added touch needed to complete the scene of gothic horror. She raised her skirts a little higher so that she could see precisely where she was putting her feet.

"This way," Gabriel ordered.

She followed him along the low, vaulted tunnel, running to keep up with him. Gabriel had to keep his head low to avoid a nasty encounter with the unyielding stone.

A fresh wave of unease washed across her senses. The passageway seemed to constrict around her. She fought the panic, forcing herself to concentrate on following Gabriel.

"Are you all right?" he asked.

"It is very close in here," she said tightly.

"Not much farther," he promised.

She could not answer. She was too busy managing her skirts and the shifting weight of the small bustle that threatened to unbalance her.

The tunnel twisted and turned several times. Just when she was sure that she would start screaming mindlessly, the corridor dead-ended in a solid wall of stone.

"Dear heaven," she whispered, slamming to a stop. "I had better warn you that I do not think I can make a return trip through that dreadful tunnel."

"There is no need to go back," Gabriel said. "We have arrived at our destination."

He reached out and grasped a heavy iron lever embedded in the stone. When he pulled it down a section of the wall slid aside.

Cool night air flowed into the passageway. Venetia breathed deeply, shivering with relief.

Gabriel stepped through the opening, gun in hand.

"Willard?" he called softly.

"Here, sir." A bulky figure loomed in the shadows.

Venetia recognized the coachman who had collected her from the train station and driven her to Arcane House. She had seen him several times during the past few days.

"Excellent," Gabriel said. "Do you have your pistol?"

"Yes, sir."

"Mrs. Willard is safe?"

"She is in the carriage, sir. Scanton and Dobbs are waiting for you at the entrance to the Great Vault, according to the plan you gave us."

"You will take Miss Milton and Mrs. Willard to the village. Stay with Miss Milton until she boards the morning train."

"Yes, sir."

Gabriel turned back to Venetia and lowered his voice. "Goodbye, my sweet. I will find you when this business is finished. Remember what you said to me tonight when you lay in my arms. You are mine."

She could scarcely believe her ears. He intended to see her again? Dumbfounded, she opened her mouth to ask when and where they would meet.

But Gabriel did not give her an opportunity to speak. He kissed her once, very hard. It was the kiss of a man who is staking a claim.

Before she could recover, he was turning away, heading toward the blackness of the tunnel entrance. She concentrated briefly. The world became a negative image. She caught one last glimpse of Gabriel's dark, powerful aura, and then he was gone.

Before she could collect herself, the wall of stone resealed itself, leaving her alone with Willard.

"This way, Miss Milton," Willard said.

She looked at the solid stone wall. "Will he be safe?"

"Mr. Jones knows how to take care of himself."

"Perhaps you should accompany him."

"Mr. Jones doesn't like it when folks fail to follow his orders, Miss Milton. I've worked for him long enough to know that it's best to do as he says. Come along now. It's a long drive back to the village."

Reluctantly she allowed him to assist her into the sleek carriage. The housekeeper was already inside. She did not speak when Venetia sat down across from her.

Willard slammed the door shut and bounded up onto the box. The vehicle swayed beneath the weight of his bulk. She heard the slap of the leathers.

The horses leaped forward, jolting Venetia back into the depths of the cushioned seat. Pulling aside the curtain, she watched the stone wall through which Gabriel had disappeared until it was lost from sight. It was not long before the carriage rounded a corner, cutting off her view.

Some time later it dawned on her that she was still wearing Gabriel's coat. She sank deeper into it, comforting herself with his lingering scent.

Talk about extraordinarily poor timing, Gabriel thought. Irritation compounded the icy anticipation of the hunt as he moved back through the ancient tunnel. The evening had been going very well, indeed. He had enjoyed his seduction enormously, even though there had been a few surprises in the course of events. If there had been even a modicum of justice in the universe, he would have been escorting Venetia Milton upstairs to a cozy bedroom about now.

He regretted having to send her away, but given the seriousness of the situation, he'd had no choice. He did not know yet what the intruders were after or just how dangerous they might prove to be. But the very fact that they had found Arcane House and seemed to know their way around was a very bad sign.

He reached the hidden staircase and climbed it swiftly. At the top he paused to listen before opening the secret panel.

All of his senses were fully open now. In

this heightened state of awareness he could detect his prey and anticipate its actions in the way that only a true predator can.

It chagrined him to realize that he had been so intent on trying to decide how and when to tell Venetia the full truth about their situation that he had not immediately sensed the intruders. The fact that she had noticed them first was embarrassing, to say the least. Obviously his attention and his concentration had been elsewhere.

Nevertheless, it was astonishing that she had been able to see them at all in the dark woods that ringed Arcane House. He would have to ask her about that the next time they met.

The psychical side of his nature would no doubt prove quite useful in dealing with whatever was about to happen here tonight. But it was an unpleasant reality that he could not make use of his paranormal senses without succumbing to the chilling fever of the hunt. It was already upon him, igniting his blood.

His father was convinced that psychical senses represented a new, more advanced development in humans. But Gabriel secretly wondered if in his case the reverse might be true. Perhaps he was in reality some sort of throwback.

When he was in this state his deepest fear was that beneath his expensive clothes and the gloss of a fine education and drawing room manners, he was actually something quite the opposite of a truly modern man. He wondered if, in fact, he was exhibiting traits and characteristics that could only be described as primeval.

If Mr. Darwin's theories were correct, what did that make him? he wondered.

There were two reasons he had wanted Venetia safely away from this place tonight. The first was to ensure her safety as well as that of the only other woman on the premises, Mrs. Willard.

But the second reason was to prevent Venetia from seeing him while the fever was upon him.

It was not the sort of thing that would make a good impression on one's future wife.

4

Bath: One week later . . .

"Mr. Jones is dead." Venetia stared, horrified, at the small notice in the newspaper. She felt as though she had been turned inside out. "Impossible. It can't be true."

Her aunt, Beatrice Sawyer, her sixteen-year-old sister, Amelia, and her nine-year-old brother, Edward, all looked up from their breakfasts.

It was just a small item buried next to the shipping news. Venetia realized that she had almost missed it entirely.

Shaken, she read it again, this time out loud for the benefit of the others at the table.

FATAL FIRE AND ACCIDENT
IN THE NORTH

The body of a man named Gabriel Jones was discovered following a devastating fire in a mansion known locally as the Abbey. The tragic events occurred on the 16th of the month.

Mr. Jones was found dead amid a collection of ancient relics, evidently having been killed when one of the heavy artifacts toppled over and struck him on the head.

It is believed that at the time of his death the victim was attempting to save the antiquities from the fire that swept through the premises. Many of the objects were destroyed in the blaze.

The body was identified by the housekeeper and her husband. The pair told the authorities that Mr. Jones had taken up residence at the Abbey shortly before the dreadful fire that took his life. Neither servant knew much about their employer. Both stated that he was exceedingly secretive and eccentric in his ways.

Stunned, Venetia lowered the paper and looked at her companions. "The sixteenth was the night I left Arcane House. It isn't possible. He said that we would meet again. He said there were things we needed to discuss."

"Indeed?" Amelia was clearly intrigued. Her pretty face brightened with curiosity. "What was it he wished to talk to you about?"

Venetia brought herself back to the moment with an act of will. "I don't know."

Beatrice frowned at her through her spectacles. "Are you all right, dear?"

"No," Venetia said. "I am in a state of shock."

"Get ahold of yourself, dear," Beatrice said. Her round face crinkled with concern and a hint of reproof. "True, it is a bit of a jolt to lose a wealthy, exclusive client. But you were only acquainted with the gentleman for a few days. And he did pay in advance."

Venetia folded the paper with great care. Her fingers were shaking.

"Thank you, Aunt Beatrice," she said quietly. "As always, you do have a way of putting matters into perspective."

Beatrice had come to live with Venetia's family upon her retirement as a governess and had immediately devoted herself to an endless series of artistic endeavors. She had been in the household when Venetia, Amelia and Edward had gotten word of the terrible train wreck that had taken the lives of their parents. Beatrice's presence had steadied them all through the tragedy and the financial disaster that followed.

"You never said that you developed some strong feelings for Mr. Jones," Amelia exclaimed, eyes widening. "You were only in his company for a few days, not quite a week. You assured us that he had been a complete gentleman."

Venetia elected not to respond to that.

"From what you have told us," Beatrice said, "those two servants mentioned in the newspaper account were correct. Mr. Jones appears to have been secretive to the point of eccentricity."

"I would not employ the term *eccentric* to refer to him," Venetia said.

Edward looked interested at that. "What term would you use?"

"Extraordinary. Intriguing." Venetia paused, searching her brain. "Compelling. Mysterious. Fascinating."

It was only when she saw the startled expressions on the faces of the others that she realized how much she had revealed.

"Really, dear." Beatrice's voice sharpened with unease. "You make Mr. Jones sound like one of those odd relics that you say you photographed in his museum."

Edward reached for the jam. "Was Mr. Jones covered with unreadable inscriptions and cloaked in inscrutable codes like the antiquities you described?"

"In a manner of speaking, yes," Venetia said. She seized the coffeepot, which stood next to the teapot. She greatly preferred tea but when she felt anxious or uneasy, she drank coffee on the theory that it would fortify her nerves. "He was certainly a man of mystery."

Amelia frowned. "I can see you are upset by this news but Aunt Beatrice is correct. Do keep in mind that Mr. Jones was only a client, Venetia."

"That may be true, but I will tell you this much," Venetia said, pouring coffee into her cup. "If he truly is dead, it is most likely because he was murdered, not because he was the victim of an accident. I told you about the two intruders who were trying to enter the house the night I left. I suspect they were responsible for the fire and, quite likely, for the death of Mr. Jones. There ought to be a thorough investigation."

Beatrice hesitated. "There was nothing about intruders mentioned in that news account, only a fire and a fatal accident involving an antiquity. Are you quite certain that the two people you saw in the woods that night were burglars?"

"They were certainly bent on mischief, I can tell you that much," Venetia said quietly. "What is more, Mr. Jones concluded the same thing. In fact, he was even more concerned about those men than I was. That is why he insisted I be escorted off the premises via the secret tunnel."

Edward munched his toast. "I would like to have seen that tunnel."

Everyone ignored him.

Beatrice looked thoughtful. "Surely the local authorities would have conducted proper inquiries if there had been any indication of violence or burglary."

Venetia absently stirred cream into her coffee. "I don't understand why there was no mention of the intruders in the paper."

"And what of the servants who identified Mr. Jones's body?" Edward asked with a shrewd expression. "Surely they would have said something about the villains to the authorities." He paused for emphasis. "*If* there really were villains involved, that is."

They all looked at him.

"Hmm," Venetia said. "That is a very good point, Edward. I wonder why the servants neglected to mention the intruders."

Beatrice gave a soft, ladylike snort. "Remember, you have only a small news account of the events. Given the nature of the press it is quite likely that there are a number of inaccuracies in that report."

Venetia sighed. "In which case, we will probably never know for certain what really did happen that night."

"Well, I think it is safe to say that we do know that Mr. Jones is no longer in this world," Beatrice declared. "That is probably the one thing the press got right. I doubt that there will be any more lucrative photography commissions coming from that quarter."

Gabriel Jones could not be dead, Venetia thought. She would know it if he were.

Wouldn't she?

She started to drink some of the strong coffee. A sudden thought made her pause, her cup in midair.

"I wonder what happened to the negatives and the prints that I made for Mr. Jones while I was at Arcane House?"

Amelia shrugged. "They were probably destroyed in the fire."

Venetia thought about that. "Another thing. There is no mention in the paper about a photographer having been in the mansion on the night that Mr. Jones was killed."

"For which we can only be extremely grateful," Beatrice said with a visible shudder of relief. "The very last thing we need is for you to be dragged into a murder investigation, especially now that our financial situation is starting to appear solid and stable at long last."

Venetia placed the cup very precisely down on the china saucer. "Thanks to Gabriel Jones and the fees he saw to it were paid in advance."

"Indeed," Beatrice allowed. "Venetia, I understand that the news concerning Mr. Jones has come as a blow to you. But you must put the matter behind you. Our future lies in London. Our plans are in place. We must go forward with them."

"Of course," Venetia said absently.

"Clients come and clients go, Venetia," Amelia added helpfully. "A professional photographer cannot allow herself to become too attached to any of them."

"Besides," Beatrice said, cutting straight to the heart of the business, "the man is dead. Whatever the truth of the events at Arcane House, it no longer concerns us. Now then, let us get on to more pressing matters. Have you decided upon the name you will adopt when we open the gallery in London?"

"I am still quite taken with *Mrs. Ravenscroft,*" Amelia said. "It is ever so romantic don't you think?"

"I prefer *Mrs. Hartley-Pryce,*" Beatrice

announced. “It has a more established ring to it.”

Edward grimaced. “I still say that *Mrs. Lancelot* is the best name of all.”

Amelia wrinkled her nose. “You have been reading too many Arthurian tales.”

“Hah,” he retorted. “You’re a fine one to talk. I know perfectly well that you got that silly Mrs. Ravenscroft name out of that sensation novel you are reading.”

“The thing is,” Venetia said, interrupting firmly, “I can’t quite see myself living with any of those names. For some reason they don’t seem to fit, if you see what I mean.”

“You’ll have to make a decision and soon,” Beatrice said. “You cannot call yourself Mrs. Milton. Not when your brother and sister are also named Milton. People would think Amelia and Edward were your children, rather than your siblings. That would not do.”

“We have discussed this at some length,” Amelia pointed out. “You have no choice but to go into business as a widow.”

“Quite true,” Beatrice said. “An unmarried lady not yet past thirty will have a great deal of trouble attracting the right sort of clientele. In addition, it will be difficult for you to conduct business with men without projecting the wrong impression.

Your status as a widow will endow you with a certain respectability that will otherwise be impossible to attain."

"I understand," Venetia said. She straightened in her chair. "I have been giving the matter of my new name a great deal of consideration and I have made a decision."

"Which name did you choose?" Edward asked.

"I will call myself Mrs. Jones," Venetia said.

Amelia, Beatrice and Edward stared at her, mouths agape.

"You are going to adopt the name of your deceased client?" Beatrice asked, amazed.

"Why not?" Venetia said. A sad, wistfulness rose up inside her. "Who will ever guess that a certain Mr. Gabriel Jones was my inspiration? After all, Jones is an exceedingly common name."

"That's true," Amelia said thoughtfully. "Why, there must be hundreds, if not thousands of Joneses in London."

"Precisely." Venetia warmed to her own idea. "No one will ever think to make a connection between me and the gentleman at Arcane House who was once, quite briefly, a client. In fact, to make quite certain of that, we shall invent an exciting little story to explain why our Mr. Jones is no longer among the living. We shall see to it that he expired in some distant, foreign clime."

"I suppose it is rather fitting, in a way," Beatrice mused. "After all, had it not been for Gabriel Jones and those enormous fees that were paid in advance, we would not now be plotting our new financial venture."

Venetia felt the dampness gathering behind her eyes. She blinked hard, several times, but the burning sensation returned.

"You must excuse me," she said brusquely. She got to her feet and started around the table toward the door. "I just remembered that I want to place an order for a new supply of dry plates."

She could feel the worried eyes of her family upon her but no one tried to stop her.

She hurried upstairs to the tiny bedroom of the rented cottage and let herself inside. She closed the door behind her and looked at the wardrobe on the far side of the room.

Slowly she crossed the space, opened the wardrobe door and took out the gentleman's evening coat she had stored inside.

She folded the coat over one arm and smoothed the expensive fabric in a way she had done many times since the flight from Arcane House.

She carried the coat to the bed, lay down and let the tears fall.

Some time later, her emotions drained to the point where she no longer felt much of anything, she got up and dried her eyes.

Enough was enough. She could not afford useless sentiments and romantic daydreams. She was the sole support of her family. Their futures depended entirely on her ability to forge a career as a photographer in London. She could not allow herself to be distracted from the daring plans she and the others had made. Success would require a great deal of hard work, cleverness and attention to detail.

Aunt Beatrice was right, she thought, picking up the tear-stained coat. There was no reason to become overly sentimental about a dead client. She had known Gabriel for only a few days after all; made love with him only once.

He was a midnight fantasy, nothing more.

She put the coat back into the wardrobe and closed the door.

5

Three months later . . .

"I don't pretend to comprehend how it has come about," Gabriel said, "but I appear to have acquired a wife."

"The devil, you say." Caleb crossed the library in a few long, impatient strides and came to a halt on the other side of the desk. "Is this your idea of a joke, cousin?"

"I think you know me well enough to realize that I do not make jokes when it comes to the subject of my future wife."

Gabriel had been leaning forward, both hands braced on the desktop, to read the article. He straightened and reversed the newspaper so that Caleb could see the small notice.

Caleb picked up the paper and read the item aloud.

PHOTOGRAPHIC EXHIBITION
HELD IN NOCTON STREET

On Thursday evening a large crowd filled the new photographic exhibition halls in Nocton Street. The pictures displayed were widely held by those present to be among the finest and most striking examples of the photographer's art. Various traditional categories were represented, including landscape, still life, architecture and portraiture.

All were works of exceptional beauty and power, fully deserving to be hailed as High Art. But in this reviewer's opinion, the pictures that most riveted the eye were the four photographs listed in the catalog as being the first in a series titled *Dreams.*

Although exhibited in the architecture category, the photographs are remarkable in that they combine portraiture, architecture and a metaphysical quality that can only be described as dreamlike. One of the pictures took first prize and deservedly so.

Mrs. Jones, the photographer responsible for the winning picture, was to be seen in the crowd. She is quite new on the photography scene in London and she has met with nothing short of great success. Her list of clients already includes some of the most discerning members of Society.

The elegant widow was dressed in

deepest mourning, as is her custom. Her elegant black gown accentuated her lustrous dark brown hair and amber-colored eyes. Indeed, it was remarked by several of those present that the photographer is as dramatic as any of her photographs.

Mrs. Jones's touching devotion to the memory of her late husband, who perished tragically while the couple was on their honeymoon in the Wild West, is well known in photographic circles. The lady has made it clear that, having lost the great love of her life, she will never love again. All of her attention, sensibilities and emotions are now employed in the perfection of her art to the great benefit of connoisseurs and collectors.

"Damnation." Caleb looked up from the article. His already stern features hardened further. "Do you really believe that this is the same photographer that you employed to record the collection at Arcane House?"

Gabriel crossed the library and came to a halt in front of the Palladian windows. He clasped his hands behind his back and studied the rain-drenched garden. "It could be a coincidence."

"I know how you feel about coincidence."

"I must be realistic. What are the chances that three months after Miss Milton was hired to photograph the collection at Arcane House, another lady with the same color hair and eyes has set herself up in the photography business in London? I knew Miss Milton was very excited by the size of the fee she received from the Council. I could see that she had plans for the money, big plans, although she did not confide in me."

"You can't be sure it is the same photographer."

Gabriel glanced at the newspaper over his shoulder. "You read those comments. The critic called her work striking and powerful. He said it had a metaphysical quality. That describes Miss Milton's pictures quite accurately. She is a brilliant photographer, Caleb. And then there is the business of the name."

"If you're right, what would have induced her to change her name to Jones?"

Perhaps she was pregnant with his child, Gabriel thought.

The thought staggered him, triggering a surge of possessiveness and arousing protective instincts he had not even realized he had until that moment.

On the heels of the possibility came another realization that made him deeply uneasy. If Venetia had taken his name to lend respectability to a pregnancy, she must be terrified.

He decided not to mention that potential problem to Caleb.

"I can only assume that she concluded that she would be better off carrying on her career in the guise of a widow," he said instead. "You know how difficult it is for any woman to conduct business or make a living in a profession. It is even harder for a single, attractive female."

There was a short silence behind him. Gabriel turned around to find Caleb watching him with a considering expression.

"Miss Milton is attractive?" Caleb asked neutrally.

Gabriel raised his brows. "She is nothing short of riveting."

"I see," Caleb said. "You still have not answered my question. Why do you think she chose to use the last name of Jones when she decided to pass herself off as a widow?"

"Very likely because it was convenient."

"Convenient," Caleb repeated.

"I expect she must have seen the notice that appeared in some of the newspapers following the events at Arcane House," Gabriel explained. "Evidently she concluded that, as I no longer had any use for the name Jones, she would borrow it."

Caleb looked down at the newspaper. "That is unfortunate under the circumstances."

"It is more than unfortunate." Gabriel turned away from the window. "It is a potential disaster. At the very least it throws all of our carefully laid plans into chaos."

"It is not as though our scheme was proceeding all that well, in any case," Caleb pointed out. "We have not yet turned up any trace of the thief."

"The trail has, indeed, gone cold," Gabriel agreed. A faint tingle of energy went through him. "But I think that is about to change."

Caleb narrowed his eyes faintly. "Will you be able to deal with this on your own, cousin?"

"I don't see much choice."

"If you can wait for a month or so I might be able to assist you."

Gabriel shook his head. "This cannot wait. Not now that Venetia is involved. You have your own responsibilities to attend to. We both know that they are every bit as important as this matter."

"I fear that may, indeed, be the case."

Gabriel started toward the door. "I shall leave for London at dawn. I wonder what my grieving widow will say when she discovers that her late husband is very much alive."

6

There was nothing like having a dead husband return from the grave to ruin a fine spring morning.

Venetia gazed, transfixed, at the headlines of *The Flying Intelligencer.*

NOTED PHOTOGRAPHER'S HUSBAND,
FEARED DEAD, RETURNS
by Gilbert Otford

This correspondent is delighted to be the first to report that Mr. Gabriel Jones, believed to have perished while on his honeymoon in the American West, has returned unharmed to London.

Readers will be thrilled to learn that Mr. Jones is none other than the husband of the renowned Society photographer Mrs. Venetia Jones.

Mr. Jones spoke briefly with your humble correspondent shortly after his safe arrival in our fair city. He explained that, having suffered a severe bout of amnesia following his unfortunate accident in the Wild West, he wandered for several months. During that time he was unable to make his identity known to the authorities. But now, his memory and his health fully restored, he declared with the most fervent enthusiasm that he could scarcely wait to be reunited with his beloved bride.

The eminent Mrs. Jones, who has caught the attention of connoisseurs of photography, has been sunk in the sad gloom of widowhood for nearly a year. Her devotion to the memory of the husband she believed to be dead has touched the hearts of all of her clients and those who admire her work.

One can only imagine the magnitude of the joy and delight that will ignite the lady's heart when she discovers that her husband is alive and has come back to her.

"There has been a dreadful mistake," Venetia whispered, aghast.

Beatrice paused in the act of buttering a slice of toast. "Whatever is the matter, dear? You look as if you have just seen a ghost."

Venetia shuddered. "Please do not use that word."

"What word?" Amelia asked.

"Ghost," Venetia said.

Edward paused in mid-chew. "You saw a ghost, Venetia?"

"Edward, do not speak with your mouth full," Beatrice said absently.

Edward dutifully swallowed the last of his buttered toast. "Describe the ghost, Venetia. Was it transparent? Could you see straight through it? Or was it solid, like a real person?"

"I did not see a ghost, Edward," Venetia said firmly. She was well aware that she had to squelch the notion immediately if there was to be any hope of restraining her brother's boundless curiosity. "There is a mistake in the morning papers, that's all. Errors are quite common in the press."

That was all it was, she thought, an appalling error. But how could such a thing happen?

Amelia watched her expectantly. "What did you see in the papers that disturbed you so?"

Venetia hesitated. "There is a reference to the recent return of a Mr. Gabriel Jones."

Amelia, Beatrice and Edward stared at her, stunned.

"What on earth?" Beatrice managed, going rather pale.

Amelia looked very worried. "Good heavens, are you certain of the name?"

Venetia handed her the paper across the table. "Read it for yourself."

Amelia snatched the newspaper from her.

"Let me see." Edward hopped out of his chair and went to stand behind Amelia's shoulder.

Together they studied the notice in the paper.

"Oh, dear," Amelia said. "Oh, my. This is, indeed, very disturbing."

Edward's expression crumpled into severe disappointment. "It doesn't say anything about a ghost. It says that Mr. Gabriel Jones, who was supposed to be dead, is actually alive. That's not the same thing as being a ghost at all."

"No." Venetia reached for the coffeepot. "It's not." *Unfortunately,* she added under her breath. A situation involving a ghost would have been a good deal easier to handle.

"It is very odd, is it not?" Edward continued thoughtfully. "It says that this Mr. Jones died in the Wild West. That is just like the story that we invented for our Mr. Jones."

"Very odd, indeed," Venetia said, gripping the coffeepot.

Beatrice reached for the paper. "Let me see that, please."

Amelia handed it to her without a word.

Venetia watched her aunt read the dreadful little announcement of a living, breathing, *fervently enthusiastic* Gabriel Jones having recently returned to London.

"Good heavens," Beatrice said when she finished. She handed the paper back to Venetia. Evidently unable to come up with any additional comment, she repeated herself. "Good heavens."

"It must be a mistake," Amelia said forcefully. "Or perhaps some bizarre coincidence."

"It may be a mistake," Venetia allowed. "But it is certainly no coincidence. All of Society knows how I became a widow."

"Do you think that, by some astonishing chance, it is the real Mr. Jones?" Beatrice asked uneasily.

They all looked at her. Venetia's sense of gathering dread intensified.

"If it is the real Mr. Jones," Beatrice observed, "he will likely be quite annoyed to discover that you are posing as his widow." She paused, frowning. "Have a care with the coffee, dear."

Venetia looked down and saw that she had just overfilled her cup. Coffee had spilled over the rim and splashed into the saucer. Gingerly she set the pot aside.

"Only think of the scandal that will ensue if it gets out that you have been pretending to be the widow of a gentleman who was never your real husband," Amelia said. "It will be worse than it was when we discovered the truth about Papa. At least we were able to keep that a secret. But this situation will create a terrible sensation in the newspapers if it gets out."

"The business will be ruined," Beatrice said in sepulchral tones. "We shall be plunged back into poverty. Venetia, you and Amelia will be forced to become governesses."

"Stop." Venetia held up a hand, palm out. "Do not go any further in such speculation. Whoever this man is, he cannot be the real Mr. Jones."

"Why not?" Edward asked with predictable logic. "Perhaps the notice in the newspaper saying that Mr. Jones was killed trying to save a relic in a house fire was wrong."

The initial shock was fading. Venetia found that she could once again think clearly.

"The reason I am certain that it cannot be the real Mr. Jones," she said, "is because in the time that I spent with him at Arcane House I learned that he was a very reclusive gentleman. For heaven's sake, he even belonged to a society whose members are obsessed with secrecy."

"What do his eccentricities have to do with this?" Beatrice asked blankly.

Venetia sat back in her chair, satisfied with her own reasoning. "Trust me when I tell you that having a casual chat with a member of the press, especially a reporter from a gossipy rag such as *The Flying Intelligencer*, is the very last thing the real Mr. Jones would do. Indeed, the gentleman I met at Arcane House would go out of his way to avoid such a meeting. Why, he refused to even let me photograph him."

Amelia pursed her lips. "If that is the case, then we must assume that someone else has chosen to pose as our Mr. Jones. The question is why?"

Beatrice frowned. "Perhaps one of your competitors has concocted this tale thinking it will create an embarrassing sensation that will hurt the business."

Amelia nodded quickly. "We all know that your success has not set well with every member of London's photographic community. It is a very competitive profession and there are those who would not hesitate to reduce the competition."

"Such as that very unpleasant little man named Burton, for example," Beatrice said grimly.

"Yes," Venetia said.

Beatrice peered over the rims of her spectacles. "Do you know, now that I think upon it, I would not put it past Harold Burton to plant an outrageous tale in the press simply to start up gossip about you."

"Aunt Beatrice is right," Amelia said. "Mr. Burton is a dreadful creature. Every time I think of those pictures that he left on our doorstep, I want to strangle him."

"So do I," Edward declared fiercely.

"We do not know for certain that Mr. Burton was the person who left those photographs," Venetia said. "Although I must admit one of them certainly bears his stamp. He is a very good photographer, after all, and he does have a rather unique style."

"Odious little man," Beatrice muttered.

"Yes," Venetia said. "But somehow I do not see him engaging in a scheme of this nature."

"What do you believe is going on?" Beatrice asked.

Venetia drummed her fingers lightly on the table. "It occurs to me that whoever has decided to pose as Mr. Gabriel Jones may have blackmail in mind."

"Blackmail." Beatrice stared at her in horror.

"What on earth will we do?" Amelia asked.

"What is blackmail?" Edward asked, searching each of their faces in turn. "Does it refer to a letter written on black paper?"

"It has nothing to do with paper and ink," Beatrice said briskly. "At least, not directly. Never mind, I will explain later." She turned back to Venetia. "We do not have enough money to pay an extortionist. We have invested everything in this house and the gallery. If this is a blackmail attempt, we are ruined."

That was quite true, Venetia thought. They had used almost every penny of the generous advance that the Arcane Society had paid her to rent the small town house here in Sutton Lane and to outfit the gallery on Bracebridge Street.

Venetia took another sip of coffee, hoping for inspiration.

"It occurs to me that this may be one of those situations in which one must fight fire with fire," she said at last. "Perhaps I should go to the press, myself."

"You must be mad," Amelia said, astonished. "Our goal should be to squelch the rumors, not fuel them."

Venetia checked the paper again, memorizing the name of the correspondent who had written the outrageous piece. "What if I were to inform this Mr. Gilbert Otford that an impostor is perpetrating a terrible hoax on a devoted widow?"

Beatrice blinked twice and then turned abruptly thoughtful. "Do you know, that is a rather brilliant notion, Venetia. Who can challenge you? You are Gabriel Jones's widow, after all. You knew him better than anyone. Unless this fraudulent person can prove his identity, the public will be on your side."

Amelia contemplated that for a moment. "You may be right. Handled well, the notoriety could be turned to our advantage. I can foresee the possibility of generating a great deal of public interest and sympathy for Venetia. Why, curiosity alone will bring many potential customers into the gallery. Everyone loves a sensation."

Venetia smiled slowly as the plan took shape. "It just might work."

The muffled clang of the door knocker echoed from the front hall. Mrs. Trench's footsteps sounded in response.

"Who on earth would call at this hour?" Beatrice asked. "The post has already arrived."

Mrs. Trench's sturdy frame appeared in the doorway of the breakfast room. Her broad face was uncharacteristically flushed with excitement.

"There's a gentleman at the door," she announced. "He says his name is Mr. Jones. Asked to see his wife, if you can believe it. Said her name is Mrs. Venetia Jones. I didn't know what to do. The only thing I could think of to say was that I would see if the lady was at home."

Venetia was dumbfounded. "How bold he is. I cannot believe he has the nerve to turn up on our doorstep like this."

"Good heavens," Amelia whispered. "Shall we summon the police?"

"The *police?*" Mrs. Trench's red-faced excitement transformed into alarm. "See here, when I agreed to take this post there was no mention of dangerous callers."

"Calm yourself, Mrs. Trench," Venetia said quickly. "I'm sure it will not be necessary to summon a constable. Please show the gentleman into the study. I will be in shortly."

"Yes, ma'am." Mrs. Trench hurried away.

Amelia waited until the housekeeper was

gone before she leaned forward and said in low tones. "Surely you do not intend to confront this blackmailer, Venetia?"

"How can you possibly even consider such a thing?" Beatrice demanded.

"We must discover as much as possible about what we are dealing with," Venetia said, trying to strike a note of calm authority. "It is always important to know the enemy."

"In that case, we will accompany you to meet this man," Amelia stated, starting to rise from her chair.

"Of course," Beatrice agreed.

"I will also come along to help protect you, Venetia," Edward said.

"I think it would be best if all three of you wait here while I interview our visitor," Venetia said.

"You cannot go in there alone," Beatrice insisted.

"I am the one who brought this problem down upon our heads by choosing to use Mr. Jones's name." Venetia crumpled her napkin and got to her feet. "It is my responsibility to discover a solution to it. Besides, this impostor will no doubt reveal more of his true intentions if he thinks that he has to deal with only one person."

"There is that," Beatrice admitted. "In

my experience, a man who finds himself alone with a woman is generally inclined to believe that he has the upper hand."

Edward frowned. "Why is that, Aunt Beatrice?"

"I have no idea, dear," Beatrice said absently. "I suppose it is because they are often somewhat larger in size. Very few appear to understand that it is intelligence, not muscle, that matters most."

"The thing is," Amelia said anxiously, "this particular man may present a threat to your person, Venetia. And in that sort of situation, size does, indeed, matter."

"I don't think he will try to harm me," Venetia said. She shook out the black skirts of her gown. "Whoever he is and regardless of his plans, he is highly unlikely to murder me in this house."

"What makes you so certain of that?" Edward asked curiously.

"Well, for one thing, there would be no profit in such an act." Venetia made a face. "One can hardly collect blackmail from a dead woman." She rounded the table and went toward the door. "In addition, there would be far too many witnesses to his crime."

"There is that," Beatrice agreed reluctantly.

"Nevertheless, you must promise to scream if you sense that he is about to do you some harm," Amelia said.

"I will fetch one of the knives from the kitchen, just in case," Edward said, rushing toward the swinging door that separated the breakfast room from the kitchen.

"Edward, you are not to pick up any knives," Beatrice called after him.

Venetia sighed. "I trust it will not come down to the use of knives."

She went quickly along the hall, anger, fear and determination pounding through her. The last thing she needed was a blackmailer, she thought. It was not as though she did not have enough problems to deal with at the moment. The chilling photographs that had been sent to her anonymously were keeping her awake at night, as it was.

She paused at the closed door of the small study. Mrs. Trench hovered uneasily.

"I showed him into the room, ma'am."

"Thank you, Mrs. Trench."

The housekeeper opened the door for her.

Venetia drew a deep breath, focused her mind and the part of her that allowed her to see beyond the normal range of human vision and swept into the study.

7

In the negative-image world in which she now moved, she saw the man's aura far more clearly than she saw his face.

She stopped, stunned.

Auras were unique and none more so than that of Gabriel Jones.

Controlled, intense and powerful, the dark energy flared around him.

"Mrs. Jones, I presume," Gabriel said. He stood near the window, his face in shadow.

The sound of his voice made her lose her faltering concentration. Venetia blinked. The world reverted to its normal hues and colors.

"You're alive," she whispered.

"Yes I am, as a matter of fact," Gabriel said. "I can see that the news has come as an unpleasant shock to you. Forgive me, but speaking personally, I must admit to being somewhat relieved under the circumstances."

Everything in her was urging her to throw herself into his arms, to touch him and inhale his scent; to revel in the glorious knowledge that he really was alive. But she was paralyzed by the enormity of the disaster that loomed.

She swallowed hard. "The notice in the press —"

"Contained some factual errors. Never believe everything you read in the papers, Mrs. Jones."

"Dear heaven." Pulling herself together with an effort of will, she managed to reach the desk. She sat down hard in the chair. She could not take her eyes off him. *He was alive.* "I must tell you, sir, that I am delighted to learn that you are in good health."

"Thank you." He remained where he was, silhouetted against the window. "Forgive me, madam, but I feel that, under the circumstances, I must ask if you are . . . well?"

She blinked. "Yes, of course. I, too, am quite fit, thank you."

"I see."

Was that disappointment she heard in his voice?

"Did you expect to find me unwell?" she asked, baffled.

"I was concerned that there might have been some repercussions from our earlier association," he said gravely.

Belatedly it dawned on her that he had wondered if she was pregnant. She turned very warm and then quite cold.

"I suppose you are wondering why I borrowed your surname," she mumbled.

"I can certainly understand why you decided to set up in business as a widow. It was a shrewd decision, given Society's attitudes toward unmarried females. But yes, I will admit to some curiosity concerning precisely why you chose to use my last name. Was it simply a matter of convenience?"

"No."

"Was it because you concluded that Jones was such a common name no one would notice the connection?"

"Not entirely." She gripped a pen very tightly in her right hand. "Actually, I made the choice for sentimental reasons."

His dark brows rose. "Indeed? But I thought you just implied that there was no need to conceal anything of a personal nature."

"It was your decision to employ me to photograph the collection at Arcane House. The generous fee that I received for that project allowed us to open our gallery here in London. I thought that taking your name would be a fitting tribute, as it were."

"A tribute."

"A very private, very personal tribute," she emphasized. "No one outside the family knows about it."

"I see. I can't recall that anyone has ever before seen fit to honor me for merely having seen to it that a bill was paid in advance."

His low, dark, resonant voice sent a chill of awareness through her. He did not sound amused.

She put the pen down on the blotter, sat forward and folded her hands. "Mr. Jones, please believe me when I tell you that I sincerely regret this entire situation. I am very much aware that I had absolutely no right to appropriate your surname."

"*Appropriate* is an interesting word under the circumstances."

"However," she said, plowing on, "I must point out that the problem that appears to have arisen here would never have occurred in the first place if you had refrained from giving a somewhat detailed interview to that correspondent from *The Flying Intelligencer*."

"Otford?"

"May I ask why you spoke with him? If you had kept quiet, we could have passed this off with no one being the wiser. There are a number of Joneses in the world. No one would have made a connection between the two of us."

"Unfortunately I fear we cannot depend upon that assumption."

"Don't be ridiculous." She unclasped her hands and spread them wide. "If you had not spoken to the press no one would have paid the least attention to a coincidence in names. Unfortunately, you saw fit to declare to that reporter that you were looking forward with *fervent enthusiasm* to being reunited with your wife, the *photographer.*"

He nodded. "Yes, I believe I did say something to that effect."

"No offense, sir, but I must ask you why, in the name of all that is sane and reasonable, you did such a featherbrained, mutton-headed, doltish thing? Really, what were you thinking?"

He studied her for a moment. Then he crossed the room to stand directly in front of her, looming over the desk in a most unsettling manner.

"I was thinking, Mrs. Jones, that you have greatly complicated my life and in the process quite possibly put yourself in mortal danger. *That* is what I was thinking."

She sat back very quickly. "I don't understand."

"Is it the word *complicated* or the word *danger* that defeats you?"

Her cheeks burned. "I fully comprehend the meaning of the word *complicated,* especially given the context."

"Excellent. We are making some progress."

She frowned. "What is this about my being in danger?"

"That aspect of the matter is also complicated."

She flattened her shaking hands on the blotter. "Perhaps you would be so good as to explain yourself, sir."

He exhaled heavily, turned and walked back toward the window. "I will try, although it will take some time."

"I suggest you go straight to the heart of the matter."

He stopped and looked out into the tiny garden. "Do you recall the night you departed Arcane House via the secret tunnel?"

"I am hardly likely to forget the incident." A thought struck her. "Which reminds me, since you are obviously alive, who was the man whose body was found in the museum? The one the housekeeper and gardener identified as Gabriel Jones."

"He was one of the intruders you spotted moving through the woods that night. I regret to say the other one got away, although he did not succeed in making off with the relic that he and his companion had planned to steal. The artifact was quite heavy, you see. It would have required two men to carry it."

"The notice in the newspaper mentioned that there was an accident in the museum," she ventured. "Something to do with a heavy stone artifact falling on the unfortunate victim, as I recall."

"I believe that was the way the death was reported, yes."

"I don't understand. Why did the Willards identify the dead intruder as you?"

"The staff at Arcane House is very well trained," Gabriel said expressionlessly. "And very well paid."

The servants had lied, she thought. Another icy shiver trickled down her spine. She felt as though she were wading into very deep, very dark waters. She did not really want to know any more about the secrets of the Arcane Society. But in her experience, blissful ignorance of a potential problem had a variety of unpleasant consequences.

"Can I assume that there was no fire and that no artifacts were destroyed, either?" she asked.

"There was no blaze and the relics are all in excellent condition, although many have been moved into the Great Vault for safekeeping."

"What did you hope to accomplish by letting it be known in the press that you were the one who was killed?" she asked.

"The intent was to buy some time and confound the villain who sent those two men to Arcane House. It is an ancient strategy."

"I would have thought that going after villains was a job for the police."

He turned his head and gave her his cryptic smile. "Surely you learned enough about the eccentricities of the Arcane Society to realize that the very last thing the members would wish to do is involve the police in the society's affairs. Tracking down the villain is my task."

"Why would the society select you to perform such an investigation for them?" she demanded suspiciously.

His mouth twisted in a humorless smile. "You could say that I inherited the problem."

"I don't understand."

"Believe me, Mrs. Jones, I am very aware of that fact. Unfortunately, in order to bring you to a full realization of the danger you may be facing, I am going to have to tell you some of the Arcane Society's most closely guarded secrets."

"Frankly, sir, I would rather you didn't."

"Neither of us has any choice. Not now that you have elected to call yourself Mrs. Jones." He studied her with his sorcerer's eyes. "We are man and wife, after all. There should be no secrets between us."

She felt as if the breath had been knocked out of her lungs. It took her a few seconds to collect herself and find her voice.

"This is not an appropriate moment in which to indulge your obviously warped sense of humor, sir. I want an explanation and I want it immediately. I deserve that much."

"Very well. As I said, I more or less inherited this situation."

"How did that come about?"

He began a slow prowl of the room, halting in front of one of the two framed photographs that hung on the wall. He examined the picture of the dark-haired woman first and then turned to the portrait of the robust, larger-than-life man.

"Your father?" Gabriel asked.

"Yes. He and my mother died a year and a half ago in a train accident. I took both pictures shortly before they were killed."

"My condolences."

"Thank you." She paused meaningfully. "You were saying?"

He resumed his prowl. "I told you that I was in pursuit of the individual who sent the intruders into Arcane House."

"Yes."

"I did not tell you what it was those men went there to steal."

"One of the more valuable artifacts, I assume."

He stopped, turned and looked back at her. "The exceedingly odd aspect of this affair is that the relic those men tried to take was not considered particularly valuable in either a scholarly or a monetary sense. It was a heavy, two-hundred-year-old strongbox. Perhaps you remember it. The lid was inset with a sheet of gold inscribed with a design of herbal leaves and a passage in Latin."

She sifted through her recollections of the many disturbing items in the society's collection that she had photographed. It was not difficult to recall the strongbox.

"I remember it," she said. "You said that it wasn't considered particularly valuable but what about the gold in the lid?"

He shrugged. "It is only a thin sheet."

She cleared her throat. "No offense, Mr. Jones, but such things are relative. Gold is gold, after all. The box may have appeared far more valuable to a poor, hungry thief than it does to you or the other members of the society."

"A thief intent only on financial gain would have tried to take one of the smaller, gem-encrusted artifacts, not a box so heavy it requires two men to lift it."

"I see what you mean," she said slowly. "Well then, perhaps the thief assumed there was something of great value inside the strongbox."

"The box was empty and unlatched because the object that had once been housed inside was stolen several months ago."

"Forgive me, Mr. Jones, but it would seem that the society has a rather serious problem guarding its antiquities."

"I must admit that lately that does appear to be the case whenever I'm involved."

She elected to ignore that strange remark. "What was originally stored in the strongbox?"

"A notebook."

"That's all?"

"Believe me, I am as puzzled as you are,"

he said. "Let me explain. The box and the notebook it protected were part of the contents of a secret laboratory built by a notorious alchemist who lived in the latter part of the seventeenth century. The alchemist died inside his hidden room. The location was lost for two centuries. Eventually the laboratory was discovered and excavated."

"How was it discovered?" she asked.

"Two members of the society succeeded in deciphering some coded letters that the alchemist wrote shortly before he disappeared into his laboratory for the last time. In the letters there were hints and clues that were eventually pieced together."

"These two members of the society you just mentioned," she said. "Were they the ones who excavated the laboratory?"

"Yes."

"One of those two people was you, wasn't it?" she guessed.

He stopped his restless prowling and looked at her. "Yes. The other man is my cousin. We were inspired to carry out the project because the alchemist is a family ancestor. He also happens to be the founder of the Arcane Society."

"I see. Go on."

"The alchemist was convinced that he

possessed some psychical talents. He spent years working on a formula to enhance those abilities. He was, in fact, obsessed with his research. He indicated in some of his last letters that he was close to perfecting his formula." Gabriel moved one hand slightly. "My cousin and I suspect that was what was in the notebook that was stolen out of the strongbox."

"For heaven's sake, what person with any common sense would be so foolish as to believe that an alchemist who lived two centuries ago had actually developed a formula for enhancing psychical talents?"

"I don't know," Gabriel said. "But I can tell you this much. Whoever he is, he was willing to kill for that damned formula."

Another chill iced her spine. "Someone was murdered because of this ancient notebook?"

"One of the workmen who helped pack the crates containing the contents of the laboratory was evidently bribed to take the notebook out of the strongbox and deliver it to someone. The workman's body was later found in an alley. He was killed with a knife."

She swallowed hard. "How dreadful."

"My cousin and I spent a considerable amount of time trying to find out who had bribed the workman and murdered him but the trail went cold almost immediately," Gabriel continued. "Then, three months ago those two men came to Arcane House and attempted to steal the strongbox."

"I don't understand. If the thief already possesses the alchemist's notebook, why would he take the risk of sending men into Arcane House to steal the box in which it had been stored?"

"That, Mrs. Jones, is an excellent question," Gabriel said. "One to which I do not yet have the answer."

"There appear to be a great many unanswered questions here, sir."

"There are, indeed. And I fear that if I do not find the answers soon, someone else may die."

8

The news had a pronounced effect upon her vivid, expressive face. Venetia was clearly appalled. Gabriel regretted the necessity of frightening her, but it was for her own good. He had to make her understand that the situation was extremely serious.

Her brows snapped together. "Where is your cousin, the person who assisted you in the excavation?"

"Caleb was called back to his ancestral home on vital family business. I'm afraid it is up to me to finish the task of tracking down the notebook and the person who stole it."

She cleared her throat. "No offense, sir, but have you had any experience in this sort of thing?"

"Not a great deal. This sort of problem doesn't come up much at Arcane House. I am a scholar and researcher by training, not a detective."

She sighed. "I see."

It was so exquisitely satisfying to be in her presence again, he thought. She was even more spectacularly compelling than she had been in his dreams these past months. The fashionably cut black gown she wore was no doubt meant to throw up a forbidding barrier to intimacy, but to his mind it created a startlingly sensual effect instead.

The tight bodice of the gown was cut in a square that framed her graceful breasts. The snug fit emphasized the sleek, enticing curves of her waist and hips. The skirt was hooked up, revealing a glimpse of ankle. The dainty bustle added a discreetly provocative touch.

He realized that, for all her photographer's sensibilities, she was blissfully unaware of the exotic, seductive challenge she posed dressed in the colors of night.

Some men might be put off by the feminine resolve and determination that she radiated, he thought. But those characteristics aroused him as surely as the sight of that shapely little ankle.

"What progress have you made in tracking down the thief?" she asked.

She was obviously suspicious of the extent of his abilities in that line, he thought.

"I regret to say that I am not much closer to a resolution now than I was on the night the thieves attempted to steal the box from Arcane House," he admitted.

She closed her eyes briefly. "I was afraid of that."

"For the past three months my cousin and I have been operating under the theory that the attempted theft was engineered by a member of the Arcane Society who has managed to conceal his identity. But I am starting to question even that basic assumption. Unfortunately, if someone outside the society is involved, I am dealing with a much larger pool of potential suspects."

"It cannot be too large. I doubt if there is a vast number of people who even know about your alchemist, let alone that his laboratory was discovered and excavated. Even fewer would give a penny for a two-hundred-year-old notebook."

"I can only hope you are right." He held her eyes, willing her to comprehend the severity of the situation. "Venetia, I must tell you that I am not at all happy with the knowledge that you have become involved in this affair."

"I am not greatly enchanted by the information, myself. As you will have noticed, I have a business to pursue, Mr. Jones. I cannot afford to become enmeshed in a scandal involving alchemy, murder and a dead husband who has shown the extremely poor taste to come back from the grave. I could be ruined. If I am ruined, my family will also be ruined. Do you comprehend me, sir?"

"Yes. I give you my word that I will do my best to protect your reputation until this matter is concluded, but do not ask me to walk away from you or this household. There is too much danger involved."

"Why, precisely, am I in danger?" she asked, clearly exasperated.

"Because you chose to present yourself to Society as the widow of Gabriel Jones."

"If you had not spoken with that reporter —"

"Venetia, I talked to the reporter because I had to move quickly. Once I realized what you had done, I had no choice but to take immediate steps to protect you."

"From whom?" she demanded.

"From the person who stole the formula and tried to steal the strongbox."

"Why would the villain be interested in me?"

"Because," Gabriel said with careful precision, "if the villain becomes aware of you and if he connects you to me, he will likely suspect that all is not as it appears. He will no doubt start to wonder if he is still being hunted."

Her brows came together in a delicate frown. "Hunted? That is an odd choice of words."

Gabriel felt his jaw clench. "The word is not important. My point is that we must assume that sooner or later you will likely attract the villain's attention. It is only a matter of time. There are too many clues."

"What would he want with me? I'm just a photographer."

"The photographer who recorded the relics at Arcane House," Gabriel said deliberately. "The photographer who claims to have been married to me."

Her eyes widened. "I still do not understand."

But she was beginning to comprehend, he thought. He could see it in her eyes.

"The villain wants the strongbox for some reason," he continued. "He knows that after the failed attempt to steal it from Arcane House, it will likely now be secured in the Great Vault. He must realize that he cannot possibly get his hands on it now. But he will also know that it is possible that a photograph of the box exists."

She cleared her throat. "I see."

"Once he concludes that you were the

photographer who took the pictures of the relics, he might also conclude that you possess the negatives. Most photographers, as you once pointed out, do keep the negatives of their own work."

"Dear heaven."

"Do you see why you may well be in danger now, Mrs. Jones?"

"Yes." She tightened her grip on the pen. "But what do you propose?"

"If the thief has decided to stalk you, as I suspect, he will likely be hanging about somewhere in your vicinity, trying to determine if you really are my widow and if I am still alive."

"How can you know that?"

"It is what I would do in his place."

Her eyes widened.

He ignored her startled expression. "In any event, if my reasoning is correct, I may be able to identify the villain before he does any more mischief."

"What will you do, sir? Post guards at the front and back doors? Interrogate every client who wants his portrait taken? For heaven's sake, surely you can see that such actions would lead to the wildest sort of rumors and speculation. I simply cannot afford that kind of notoriety."

"I intend a more subtle approach."

"You call announcing your startling return and *fervent enthusiasm* at the prospect of being united with your bride to a member of the press an example of a subtle approach?"

"I would remind you that you were the one who precipitated this situation in which we now find ourselves."

"Hah. Do not attempt to pin this on me, sir. How was I to know that you had faked your own death?" She shot to her feet, confronting him across the desk. "You never bothered to send me so much as a letter or telegram letting me know that you were alive and well, did you?"

It dawned on him that she was furious.

"Venetia —"

"How do you think I felt when I picked up that newspaper and read that you were dead?"

"I did not want to get you involved in this affair," he said steadily. "I did not contact you because I thought you would be safer that way."

She straightened her shoulders. "That is a very poor excuse."

He felt his temper start to slip. "You were the one who said that you did not want anyone to know of our night together at Arcane House. Your plan, as I recall, was to have a brief affair and never look back."

Her mouth thinned. She sank back down into her chair. "This is ridiculous. I cannot believe we are arguing over the fact that you are alive."

He hesitated, wary of her mood. "I understand that you are in shock."

She folded her hands and looked at him. "What, precisely, do you want of me, Mr. Jones?"

"Play the role that you have invented for yourself. Present me to the world as your husband."

She said nothing. She just sat there, watching him as if he were quite mad.

"It is a simple, straightforward plan," he assured her. "Nothing complicated about it. The word is already out in the press that I have made an astonishing return. You need only support that story. As your husband, I will be in an excellent position not only to protect you, but to hunt the thief who may be circling in your vicinity."

"Nothing complicated about it at all." She winced. "Tell me, sir, just how does one go about pretending to have a live husband when one has gone to great pains to ensure the world that he is dead?"

"Quite simple. I will take up residence

here with you and your family. No one will question our association."

She blinked. "You intend to move into this household?"

"Believe it or not, there are those who would find it quite unusual, shocking, in fact, if you insisted that your husband take lodgings in another part of town."

She turned pink. "Yes, well, under the circumstances, I don't see any other course of action. You cannot move in here, sir."

"Be sensible, Mrs. Jones. You know how it is, a man's home is his castle and so on and so forth. Society would be appalled if you forced me to live somewhere else."

"This house is hardly a castle," she said. "Indeed, we are quite crowded as it is. Every bedroom is occupied."

"What of the servants? Where do they sleep?"

"There is only one, the housekeeper, Mrs. Trench. She has the small sitting room off the kitchen. You cannot ask me to make her abandon it. She would give notice on the spot. Do you know how difficult it is to find a good housekeeper?"

"There must be someplace I can sleep. I assure you, I am not particular. I have spent a good deal of my life traveling in foreign climes. I am accustomed to living rough."

She contemplated him for a very long moment.

"Well, there is one room that is not occupied," she said eventually.

"I'm sure it will do." He looked at the door. "Now then, perhaps you should introduce me to the other members of your family. I believe they are out there in the hall. They are no doubt quite anxious to know what is happening in here."

She frowned. "How did you know they were out there? Never mind."

She got up, rounded the desk and crossed the room. When she opened the door Gabriel saw a small cluster of concerned faces. The housekeeper, an older woman who had the look of a maiden aunt, a pretty young lady of about sixteen and a boy who appeared to be nine or ten.

"This is Mr. Jones," Venetia said. "He will be staying with us for a while."

The crowd in the hall fixed Gabriel with expressions that ranged from astonishment to curiosity.

"My aunt, Miss Sawyer," Venetia said, making introductions. "My sister, Amelia, my brother, Edward, and our housekeeper, Mrs. Trench."

"Ladies." Gabriel bowed politely. Then he smiled at Edward, who was clutching a wicked-looking kitchen knife in both hands. "Ah, a lad after my own heart."

9

"You consigned him to the attic?" Amelia set down a tray of retouching tools. "But he is your husband."

"There appears to be a grave misunderstanding here." Venetia grasped the edge of the large metal stand that held the painted backdrop of an Italian garden. "Mr. Jones is not my husband."

"Yes, of course, I know that," Amelia said, impatient. "The thing is, people are supposed to *believe* that he is your husband."

"That circumstance," Venetia said, hauling the backdrop into position behind the sitter's chair, "is not my fault."

"A matter of opinion, if you ask me." Amelia began to sort through the large selection of props. "What will the neighbors think if they discover that you have stashed Mr. Jones in the attic?"

"It is not as though I had a great deal of choice." Venetia released the backdrop stand and stood back to survey the results. "I am certainly not about to give up my bedroom and take up residence in the attic. Nor will I allow you or Edward or Aunt Beatrice to be shifted upstairs. It would not be right."

"I doubt that Mr. Jones would want you to inconvenience any of us to that extent in any event," Amelia said. She selected an Italianate vase from the assortment of props. "He seems very much the gentleman."

"When it suits him," Venetia muttered darkly.

She was still feeling the mix of angry tension and crushing dismay that had settled upon her following the initial joy at discovering that Gabriel was alive. It had not taken long for her to realize that he had not come back to her because he wanted to be in her company again. Oh, no, she thought, he had landed on her doorstep that morning only because he was convinced that she had interfered with his scheme to catch a thief.

This time around their association was a straightforward business affair as far as Gabriel was concerned, a matter of strategy. She must not forget that. She would not allow him to break her heart a second time.

Amelia grew thoughtful. "I do not suppose that there is any need for the neighbors to discover that your husband is living in the attic. They are hardly likely to take a tour of the house."

"Of course not." Venetia crossed the studio to where her camera was mounted on a tripod. She checked to see how the scene appeared.

Thanks to Beatrice's expertise as a painter, the Italian garden backdrop looked impressively real, right down to the classical statue of Hermes and the graceful ruins of a Roman temple. A few additions such as the vase would complete the desired effect.

The rent on the gallery, which was located within walking distance of Sutton Lane, was higher than that of the house in which they all lived because it was in a far more fashionable street. Venetia and the others had agreed that the cost was worth it. Location was crucial to the stylish image they wished to present to the world.

The premises they had chosen had originally been an elegant little two-story town house. The owner of the property had converted it into space for two businesses. The upper floor, accessed by a separate entrance, was vacant at the moment.

Venetia, Beatrice and Amelia had chosen

the front rooms on the ground floor for the sales gallery. The walls were lined with samples of Venetia's photographs for clients to examine and purchase.

The darkroom, a storage room and the dressing rooms for the clients occupied the remaining space.

The studio itself had originally been a small greenhouse. The glass walls and roof allowed a flood of natural light in good weather. When she was faced with having to do portraits on foggy or overcast days, Venetia augmented the poor light with gas lamps and the burning of magnesium ribbons.

Lately she had given some thought to investing in a small, gas-fueled dynamo so that she could experiment with the new electric lights. Thus far she had not been at all impressed with the weak light given off by the small bulbs, however, and they were quite expensive.

In the meantime, she considered herself extremely fortunate to have found the little house with the glass-walled room. Many of her colleagues were forced to work in dark, converted parlors, sitting rooms and other poorly illuminated spaces that made it impossible to conduct business in bad weather.

In desperation, a number of photographers resorted to the use of explosive pyrotechnic powders made of magnesium mixed with other ingredients. Unlike the steady burn one could achieve with a strip of pure magnesium, however, the powder concoctions were dangerously unpredictable. The photography journals were routinely filled with notices of the destruction of homes, serious injury and deaths due to the use of such flash powders.

To control the natural light in the greenhouse, Venetia, Amelia and Beatrice had designed a complicated system of drapery operated by cords and pulleys. Several large, parasol-shaped devices covered with various colored cloths and a variety of backdrops helped diffuse the light. Mirrors, and a number of polished reflective surfaces made it possible to create interesting artistic effects.

Two sittings were scheduled for that day. Both of the clients were wealthy ladies who had been referred by another satisfied customer, Mrs. Chilcott. In spite of the unsettling events of the morning, Venetia was determined to give satisfaction. Her reputation as a fashionable photographer was building swiftly. There was nothing like a referral from a well-connected member of

Society to ensure future business.

"Is the ladies' dressing room ready?" Venetia asked.

"Yes." Amelia carried the vase across the room and positioned it beside the chair. "Maud cleaned it this morning."

The ladies' dressing room had required a staggering investment but the marble-topped table, velvet curtains, carpets and mirrors had been well worth it. Venetia knew that several of her new clients had booked portraits on the basis of the gossip about the small jewel of a room.

"I wonder how long it will take Mr. Jones to find this villain he is seeking," Amelia mused.

"Left to his own devices, I fear it could take forever," Venetia said. "He admitted that he has had very little experience in this sort of thing. He also said that he has had no luck thus far, even though he has been searching for the thief for three months. It appears that I shall have to assist him."

Amelia's head snapped up. "You are going to help him with his investigation?"

"Yes." Venetia made a small adjustment to the tripod. "If I don't, we shall never be rid of him. We cannot have him living in the attic indefinitely."

"Is Mr. Jones aware that you plan to aid him in finding this dangerous individual?"

"I haven't spoken to him about my plans yet," Venetia said. "What with one thing and another today, we haven't had an opportunity to discuss the matter in depth. I will mention it to him later this evening, after the exhibition is concluded. He insists upon accompanying me to the event."

Amelia looked at her. "Hmm."

"What is it now?"

"I will admit that I have only just made Mr. Jones's acquaintance," Amelia said. "But it strikes me that he may not be enthusiastic about taking advice and guidance."

"That is too bad." Venetia moved one of the parasols into position. "It was his choice to take up residence in our household. If he wishes to live with us, he will be obliged to listen to my opinions."

"Speaking of the photographic exhibition this evening," Amelia said, "I expect that there will be a very large crowd. Everyone will be extremely curious about the miraculous return of the late Mr. Jones."

"I am well aware of that," Venetia said.

"What of your dress? Your entire wardrobe is black because you were supposed to be a widow. You do not have any fashionable gowns in other colors."

"I shall wear what I had planned to wear this evening." Venetia made another slight adjustment to the parasol. "The black gown with the black satin roses at the neckline."

"A long-lost husband returns and takes up residence in the attic and his widow continues to wear black." Amelia shook her head. "It all seems rather odd, if you ask me."

"Mr. Jones is rather odd," Venetia said.

Amelia surprised her with a knowing grin. "There are those who, if they were aware of your unusual abilities, sister dear, would no doubt conclude that *you* are quite odd."

Venetia tweaked the tripod one last time. "At least I have the common decency and good manners to conceal my oddities from polite company."

10

"I hope you won't take this personally, sir." Puffing a little from the long climb to the top of the house, Mrs. Trench opened the attic door. "I'm certain that the only reason Mrs. Jones put you in this dreadful little room is because she is not herself at the moment. She'll change her mind once she recovers."

"That is an interesting observation, Mrs. Trench," Gabriel said. Together with Edward, he maneuvered one of the traveling trunks into the small, cramped space. "When I spoke with Mrs. Jones in her study a short time ago, I found her to be exactly as I remembered her, entirely in command of herself." He looked at Edward, who was at the other end of the heavy trunk. "Let's set it down here."

"Yes, sir," Edward said. He carefully lowered his end of the trunk to the floor, obviously pleased to have been asked to assist in the manly task.

Mrs. Trench opened the faded curtains on the single window. "I'm sure Mrs.

Jones's nerves have been quite shattered by the shock of your return, sir. As I understand the situation, she was a very new bride on her honeymoon when you were taken from her. That sort of thing is bound to have a profound effect upon a lady's delicate sensibilities. Just give her some time to adjust."

"I appreciate the advice, Mrs. Trench." Gabriel dusted off his hands and nodded at Edward. "Thank you for your assistance."

"You're welcome, sir." Edward beamed shyly. "Don't worry about being up here in the attic. There are no spiderwebs or mice. I know because I come up here sometimes to play on rainy days."

"You relieve my mind." Gabriel hung his long gray overcoat on a peg.

Mrs. Trench snorted. "Of course there are no spiderwebs or mice, nor will there be so long as I am in charge of keeping this household clean."

"I have every confidence in you, Mrs. Trench," Gabriel said.

"Thank you, sir." She planted her large, work-worn hands on her hips and surveyed the narrow bed. Then she switched her gaze to Gabriel, giving him an appraising, head-to-toe examination. "I was afraid of this."

"Afraid of what, Mrs. Trench?"

"That bed is much too small for you, sir. You won't be at all comfortable on it."

"It'll do for now, Mrs. Trench."

She heaved a disgruntled sigh. "I expect the former tenants put the governess in this room. Not right to lodge the head of the household up here."

"I like this room." Edward went to the window and waved a hand to indicate the array of rooftops visible through the glass. "From here you can see all the way to the park. On windy days there are lots of kites in the air, and sometimes there are fireworks at night."

Gabriel spread his hands and smiled at Mrs. Trench. "There you have it on the best authority, Mrs. Trench. This is clearly the finest bedroom in the entire house."

Mrs. Trench shook her head. "It's not at all suitable, but as there's nothing to be done about it, we'll let the matter drop for the time being. Now then, breakfast is usually served sharply at eight so that Mrs. Jones can get an early start at the gallery. Mrs. Jones likes the morning light for her work. In the evening we dine at seven, so that Master Edward can join the family. Does that schedule suit you, sir?"

"That will be fine, Mrs. Trench." He did

not care to contemplate Venetia's reaction if he were to change something so basic to the household routine as the time of meals.

"Very well." Mrs. Trench headed for the door. "Let me know if there's anything you need."

"Thank you, Mrs. Trench."

The housekeeper departed, leaving Gabriel alone with Edward.

When the door closed, Edward said quietly, "I know you're not really my brother-in-law, sir. Venetia explained everything to me."

"Did she?"

Edward nodded quickly. "She says that we are going to play a game of pretend while you are here."

"Do you mind?"

"Not at all," Edward said. "It will be fun to have you here for real."

"For real?"

"Yes. I helped Venetia get rid of you, you see. Now that you are actually here, it is as if you have become real."

"I think I've got the gist of it." Gabriel crouched to unlock the trunk. "What parts of my history did you invent?"

"I made up the bit about you tumbling off the cliff in the Wild West and getting swept away by a raging river," Edward said, shoulders straightening with pride. "Did you like it?"

"Very clever."

"Thank you. Venetia wanted to say that you were shot dead by a gang of outlaws during the course of a train robbery."

"Charming. Tell me, did I die a true hero of the Wild West, fighting on until my gun was empty of bullets?"

Edward frowned. "I don't recall that you had a gun."

"She intended to send me off to face the outlaws unarmed?" Gabriel opened the trunk. "She must have wanted to be quite certain that I did not survive."

"I thought it was an excellent story but Aunt Beatrice told her it was much too grisly for polite company. Then Venetia came up with the idea that you had been trampled by a herd of wild horses."

"That sounds exceedingly unpleasant. What saved me from that fate?" Gabriel asked.

"Amelia said that since you and Venetia were supposed to be on your honeymoon, you should die in a more romantic fashion."

"That is when you invented the notion of having me fall off the cliff?"

"Yes. I'm very glad you like it."

"It was quite brilliant." Gabriel reached into the trunk to remove the leather kit that contained his shaving things. "If I'd been shot dead by outlaws or trampled by wild horses it would have been somewhat more difficult to explain my presence in the household now."

Edward hurried across the small room to examine the contents of the trunk. "I expect that we would have thought of something. We always do."

Gabriel rose and set the shaving kit on the washstand. He turned to contemplate Edward. It could not have been easy for a boy, no matter how intelligent, to maintain the fiction that his older sister was a widow.

"You seem to be quite expert at playing games of pretend," Gabriel said.

"I am."

"Perhaps you can give me some tips on how to go about it."

"Certainly, sir." Edward looked up from his perusal of the interior of the trunk. "It's hard sometimes, though. You have to be very careful when there are other people around, especially Mrs. Trench. She's not supposed to know our secrets."

In his experience, Gabriel thought, it was usually impossible to prevent the servants from learning a family's secrets. It was astonishing that Venetia and the others had managed the feat for the three months they had been living in London. He doubted they would be able to maintain the fiction indefinitely.

"I will be very careful," he promised.

He reached into the trunk again and took out a stack of neatly folded shirts. Ducking to avoid the low, sloping ceiling, he placed the shirts in the old, battered wardrobe.

Edward watched his every move, fascinated. "Perhaps someday when you are not too busy we could go to the park and fly a kite."

Gabriel looked at him. "I beg your pardon?"

"That is what a boy and his brother-in-law might do, isn't it?" Edward was starting to look anxious.

Gabriel braced one hand against the sloped ceiling. "When was the last time you went to the park?"

"I go there sometimes with Aunt Beatrice or Venetia or Amelia but I have never flown a kite. Once some of the other boys asked if I would like to play a game with them but Aunt Beatrice said I mustn't."

"Why not?"

"I am not to talk to people very much, especially other children." Edward made a face. "They are all afraid that I might forget and tell someone our secrets."

Every time Edward used the word *secret,* he employed the plural. How many confidences was the boy keeping?

"It must have been difficult pretending that your sister was a widow for the past few months," Gabriel said.

"Master Edward?" Mrs. Trench's voice sounded from the foot of the attic stairs. *"Your aunt sent me to tell you that you are not to bother Mr. Jones. Come down to the kitchen. I'll cut you a slice of plum tart."*

Edward rolled his eyes but he went obediently, if reluctantly, toward the door. When he reached it he paused and looked back at Gabriel.

"Actually, it hasn't been very hard pretending that Venetia is a widow," he said. "She wears black every day, you see."

Gabriel nodded. "I can understand how her attire would constitute a daily clue."

"I think it is the other secret that they all worry about the most," Edward explained. "The one about Papa."

He turned and vanished through the doorway.

Gabriel stood for a while, neckties in hand, and listened to the sound of Edward's footsteps on the stairs.

This is, indeed, a house of secrets, he thought. But then, what house didn't have a few?

11

Two more fish had died.

They floated just beneath the surface, pale bellies gleaming a dull silvery color in the light of the gas lamp.

The new aquarium was massive compared to the previous tanks. The size and depth of three bathtubs placed side by side, it was fashioned of wood and glass supported by a sturdy metal frame. The front of the tank was made of glass. An underwater jungle of aquatic plants had been installed to provide nutrients and natural concealment for prey and predator alike.

The killer picked up a net and scooped out the dead fish. An examination of the bodies would be necessary to rule out illness or some other natural cause but from the looks of things, the new species of plants were evidently not producing enough oxygen. Half the fish in the tank had died in the past two days.

Reproducing a Darwinian world in miniature was proving to be far more complicated than one would have thought. The laws of nature seemed so dazzlingly clear and straightforward when one considered them in the abstract but in practice there were so many variables. Temperature, weather, disease, the food supply, even coincidence and chance came into play when one was dealing with the real world.

But regardless of the variables, the laws were immutable. And overarching all others was the greatest law of all: Only the fittest survived.

The killer took particular satisfaction in the obvious corollary: Only the fittest *deserved* to survive and prosper.

Nature had, of course, taken care to make certain that prey enjoyed some protections. It was necessary to maintain a balance, after all. Where would all the predators be if there was no prey?

But there could be no doubt whatsoever about which group had been designed and refined by the relentless, implacable forces of natural selection to rule.

The knowledge that nature had ordained that there be predators and prey was vastly pleasing. It was self-evident that the strong had every right, indeed, a *responsibility,* a *destiny,* to dominate and control the weak.

To show compassion or mercy was to deny the natural order.

The fittest also had a duty to pass on the strong traits with which they had been endowed. Finding a suitable mate, a healthy female who also possessed superior characteristics, was an imperative.

His first choice of mates had proven to be a disappointment, the killer reflected. But he was now quite certain that there was another, more appropriate selection available: a woman who was in all likelihood endowed with the unique talents he wanted in the mother of his offspring.

The long-standing traditions of the Arcane Society were well known within the society. He knew that Gabriel Jones would not have chosen an unimportant female like the photographer — a woman with no money or social connections — unless she possessed strong psychical powers of her own.

The killer placed the dead fish on the examination table and reached for a knife.

Eyes that gleamed with a nerveless, inhuman lack of emotion watched him from inside the fern-choked, glass-fronted Wardian cases that lined one wall of the room.

The insect, reptilian and aquatic worlds provided the ultimate examples of the great forces of natural selection in their purest form, the killer thought. There was no sentiment, no emotion, no family bonds, no passion or politics in those spheres. Life was reduced to its most basic elements. Kill or be killed.

He went to work on the fish. Failed experiments were always disturbing but they were not without some interest.

12

"Christopher Farley is no doubt greatly indebted to you this evening, Mr. Jones." Adam Harrow swirled the champagne in his glass with a lazy movement of one gloved hand. "Mind you, I'm certain there would have been an excellent turnout even without your presence on account of the excellence of your wife's photographs. Nevertheless, I strongly suspect that the news of your astonishing return did much to enhance the size of the crowd."

Gabriel turned his attention away from the framed photograph he had been examining and surveyed the thin, languidly graceful young man who had come up beside him.

Venetia had introduced him to Harrow shortly after their arrival at the exhibition hall. She had then been swept up by a throng of individuals who appeared to be evenly divided between colleagues, admirers and the just plain curious. She was now holding court on the other side of the room. Gabriel had soon discovered that he would be on his own tonight. The exhibition was a social affair on the surface but beneath the earnest conversations about the art of photography and the latest gossip, his *wife* had business to conduct.

Fortunately Harrow had proved to be an interesting companion. His voice was low and cultured. He projected the cool, amused air that marked him as a gentleman accustomed to the best in everything from clubs and mistresses to art and wine. His trousers and wing-collared shirt were in the latest style. His light brown hair was brushed straight back from his forehead and gleamed with a judicious application of pomade.

Harrow's features were finely, almost delicately, molded. They put Gabriel in mind of one of the ethereally handsome knights in a Burne-Jones painting. Recalling the name of the painter made Gabriel realize yet again just how common the name Jones was. No wonder Venetia had concluded that no one would notice one more Jones in London.

"I take it that Farley is the person responsible for staging this exhibition?" Gabriel asked.

"Yes." Harrow took a sip of champagne and lowered the glass. "He is a gentleman of means who has become something of a patron to the photographic community. He is known to be generous to those who are starting out in the profession. He even maintains a well-stocked darkroom here on the premises for photographers who cannot afford their own equipment and chemicals."

"I see."

"Farley has contributed greatly to the notion that photography deserves to be considered a true art." Harrow arched a delicate brow. "Unfortunately, that view is still quite controversial in some circles."

"One wouldn't know it by the crowd here tonight," Gabriel said.

The brightly lit exhibition hall was crammed with well-dressed visitors. The guests promenaded around the room, glasses of champagne or lemonade in hand, and made a great show of scrutinizing the photographs that hung on the walls.

The pictures in the exhibition were the work of a number of different photographers and had been arranged by competition categories: Pastoral Views, Portraits, Monuments of London, and Artistic Themes. Venetia had entered photographs in both the Portraits and Monuments divisions.

It occurred to Gabriel that Harrow could be a useful source of information. If the thief was moving in Venetia's business circles, he might be here tonight.

"I would appreciate it if you would enlighten me as to the identities of some of those present tonight," Gabriel said. "My wife appears to be mingling with a rather elevated lot."

Harrow gave him a speculative glance and then shrugged. "My pleasure. I don't know everyone, of course, but I can point out some of the highfliers." He angled his chin toward a distinguished, middle-aged couple. "Lord and Lady Netherhampton. They consider themselves connoisseurs of art. The fact that they are here tonight gives this exhibition considerable cachet."

"I see," Gabriel said.

Harrow smiled fleetingly. "I am told that years ago Lady Netherhampton was an actress. Everyone in Polite Society has conveniently forgotten her origins due to the fact that she is now married to Lord Netherhampton."

"I'm sure that the craft of acting made excellent training for moving in the Polite World."

Harrow laughed. "No doubt. It is, indeed, a world of masks and false facades, is it not?" He nodded toward another woman. "The overdressed female in pink on the far side of the room is Mrs. Chilcott. Her husband obligingly dropped dead two years ago, leaving her a fortune. She was one of your wife's first clients and has since sent several of her friends to her."

"I must remember to be very polite to the lady if we are introduced."

Harrow swept the crowd with an assessing glance and paused. "Do you see the elderly gentleman with the cane? The one who looks like he might fall over at any moment? That is Lord Ackland."

Gabriel shifted his gaze to a stooped, gray-haired, heavily bewhiskered man in the company of a much younger, strikingly attractive woman. In addition to the cane, Ackland gripped the lady's arm in a manner that suggested he needed it for additional support. The couple was admiring a photograph in the Portraits division.

"I see him," Gabriel said.

"Ackland retired to the country years ago. Never produced an heir. The fortune will go to some distant relatives, I believe."

"Unless the lovely lady who is propping him up can persuade him to marry her?" Gabriel said.

"That is the speculation, of course. Ackland was said to be slipping into senility and in very poor health but it seems that he has been pulled back from death's door by the lovely creature at his side."

"Astonishing what a beautiful woman can do for a man even when his doctors have given up all hope," Gabriel said.

"Indeed. The lady with the remarkable therapeutic powers is Mrs. Rosalind Fleming."

Harrow's tone had altered, Gabriel noticed. The underlying note of mocking amusement was gone. In its place was a cold, flat quality.

"What happened to Mr. Fleming?" Gabriel asked.

"An excellent question," Harrow said. "The lady is, of course, a widow."

Gabriel did his own survey of the room, the hunter in him searching not for prey but for the competition; others who looked as if they might be predators under their civilized facades.

"What about the man standing by himself near the potted palm?" he asked. "He does not appear to be here with the intention of making casual conversation."

The man next to the plant seemed to occupy a remote, separate space in the room.

It was clear to Gabriel that one encroached on that space at one's peril.

Harrow glanced in that direction, frowning a little. "That is Willows. I cannot tell you much about him. Appeared on the scene a few months ago. He is a collector of art and antiquities. Keeps to himself but he evidently commands a fortune. I believe he has acquired some of Mrs. Jones's pictures for his private museum."

"Married?"

"No," Harrow said. "At least, we don't think so."

Gabriel wondered about the *we* but his instincts told him not to inquire.

He made a mental note of the name and went back to searching the room, seeking others who projected the same aloof, potentially dangerous air.

Over the course of the next several minutes he added three more names to his private list as Harrow continued his commentary. He paid particular attention to persons Harrow said collected Venetia's work.

"I congratulate you on your knowledge of Society gossip," he said when Harrow eventually wound down.

"One hears things at one's club." Harrow took another swallow of champagne. "You know how it is."

"I have been out of town for some time," Gabriel reminded him. "I fear I am out of touch."

That much was true enough, he thought. Almost no one in the reclusive Jones family took an interest in Society. That fact served him well now because he could move through the Polite World with very little risk of being recognized.

"Yes, of course," Harrow said. "And then there was that dreadful case of amnesia that you suffered after your accident. It can't have helped your memory."

Gabriel realized that he had pushed the questioning a little too far. Harrow was starting to grow curious. That was not good.

"No," he agreed.

"When did you first recall that you had a wife?" Harrow asked.

"I believe the memory came to me one morning when I was sitting down to breakfast in a hotel in San Francisco," Gabriel said, improvising. "It suddenly dawned on me that there was no wife around to pour my tea. It seemed to me that there ought to be one about somewhere. I got to wondering if I had misplaced her. And then it all came back to me in a blinding flash of memory."

Harrow's brows rose. "It would have taken a very severe blow to the head to make a man forget Mrs. Jones."

"Indeed," Gabriel said. "Plunging head-first into a canyon will have that effect, I'm sorry to say."

He looked across the room to where Venetia stood in the center of a knot of people. Her *Dreaming Girl*, the newest picture in the *Dreams* series, hung on the wall behind her.

The photograph was a moody, atmospheric picture of a sleeping girl gowned in billowing, diaphanous white. Earlier Gabriel had taken a closer look and recognized Amelia as the model. A first-place ribbon dangled from a pin next to the picture.

Harrow followed his gaze. "I cannot help but notice that Mrs. Jones is still wearing black, in spite of your return to the land of the living."

"She mentioned something about not having any fashionable gowns in other colors," Gabriel said. "There was no time to purchase a new dress for tonight's event."

"She will no doubt look forward to replacing all that mourning with more colorful gowns."

Gabriel let that remark pass without comment. He had a hunch that Venetia was not going to rush out straightaway to a dressmaker to celebrate his return.

At that moment one of the men in the crowd around Venetia leaned in a bit closer to her and murmured something in her ear that made her smile.

Gabriel had a sudden urge to cross the room, seize the man by the throat and toss him out into the street.

Harrow glanced at him. "You must have been vastly disappointed to discover that Mrs. Jones had a prior engagement planned for this evening."

"I beg your pardon?" Gabriel said absently, his attention still on the man who was leaning so close to Venetia.

"I doubt very much that any husband who had been parted from his bride for such a lengthy period of time would have looked forward to spending his first night home enduring an exhibition of photographs."

Harrow was turning the tables, Gabriel thought. The younger man was now the one asking the questions.

"Fortunately for me, my wife's photographs are stunning," Gabriel said.

"Indeed. Pity the same cannot be said for most of the other pictures on display here tonight." Harrow turned back to the photograph on the wall. "Mrs. Jones's work exerts a certain, subtle power over the viewer, doesn't it? Her pictures compel one to look deeper into the scene."

Gabriel studied the photograph that Harrow was admiring. It had been entered in the Architecture category. Unlike the other pictures hanging next to it, there was a human figure in the scene. A woman — Amelia again, her hat clutched in one gloved hand — stood in the vaulted stone entrance to an ancient church. The scene evoked a haunting effect.

"It is as though the lady we are viewing is a ghost who has chosen to make her presence known to us," Harrow observed. "She enhances the eerie gothic quality of the architecture, don't you agree?"

"Yes, she does," Gabriel said, turning away from the picture to watch Willows head toward the front door.

"Mrs. Jones manages to endow all of her photographs with some indefinable sensibility," Harrow continued. "Do you know, I have looked at her work hundreds of times and I still cannot identify the aspect that captivates me. I once asked her how she achieves her deeply emotional effect upon the viewer."

Willows disappeared. Gabriel turned back to Harrow.

"What did she say?" he asked.

"Only that it has something to do with the lighting," Harrow said.

"A reasonable answer." Gabriel shrugged. "The art of the photographer is about the business of capturing light and shadow and preserving them on paper."

Harrow's fine mouth twisted wryly. "Every photographer will tell you that and I will admit there is a great deal of truth to the statement. I comprehend that lighting is an extremely difficult and complex task, requiring intuition and an artistic eye. But in the case of Mrs. Jones's work I am inclined to believe that there is some other talent involved."

"What sort of talent?" Gabriel asked, suddenly intrigued.

Harrow regarded the photograph of the ghostly lady. "It is as if she first sees something unique in her subjects, something that is not at all obvious. She then employs every aspect of the science and art of photography to hint at that quality in the finished picture."

Gabriel took another look at the picture of Amelia in the church doorway.

"Her pictures are about secrets," he said.

Harrow gave him a veiled look. "I beg your pardon?"

Gabriel thought about the photographs Venetia had taken at Arcane House; how she had captured some element of the mystery of each artifact, even while she had created a detailed pictorial record.

"My wife's pictures reveal even as they conceal," he said. It was astonishing how easily the words *my wife* came to his lips. "That is what draws the eye. People, after all, are always most intrigued by what they have been forbidden to know."

"Ah, yes, of course," Harrow said softly. "The lure of the forbidden. There is nothing more interesting than a closely guarded secret, is there?"

"No."

Harrow inclined his head in a thoughtful manner. "That is it, precisely. I should have hit upon it sooner. Your wife photographs secrets."

Gabriel took another look at the photograph and shrugged. "I thought it was obvious."

"On the contrary. You need only read some of the reviews written by the critics to discover that words fail time and again when it comes to describing the appeal of your wife's photographs. In fact, she has been criticized in the press precisely because her themes are not painfully clear."

"She has critics?"

Harrow laughed. "You sound quite annoyed. You may as well save your time and energy. Where there is art, it follows that there will be critics. It is the nature of things." He glanced across the room. "There is an example of the breed over there by the buffet table."

Gabriel followed his gaze. "Ah, yes, Mr. Otford of *The Flying Intelligencer.* We have met."

"Yes, he did that inspiring story of your startling return in the morning paper, didn't he? You will be able to read his overwrought review of Mrs. Jones's work in tomorrow's edition, I'm sure."

"I shall look forward to reading his observations," Gabriel said.

"Bah." Harrow's disgust was clear. "Do not waste your time. I assure you that you possess more insight in your little finger than that man does in his entire brain. In fact, I would go so far as to say that you have more artistic intuition than most of the collectors I know." He paused a beat. "To say nothing of the vast majority of husbands."

"Thank you, but I have the impression that I am missing your point."

"My point, sir, is that most gentlemen in your position who returned home to discover that their wives had set themselves up in business would be less than pleased."

It was true, Gabriel thought. Venetia, Beatrice and Amelia were walking a very fine line with their gallery. The world had changed considerably in the past fifty years but some things were slower to change than others. There were still very few professions open to women. Operating a business was not considered appropriate for a lady who had been reared in polite, respectable circles. And there was no doubt but that Venetia and her family had come from such circles.

"My wife is an artist," he said.

Harrow stiffened. "I say, there is no need to threaten me, sir. No offense intended, I assure you. I am a great admirer of your wife's art."

Gabriel drank some of the champagne from the glass in his hand and said nothing.

"Please believe me when I tell you that I am sincere, sir." Harrow moved cautiously closer again. "Indeed, I am struck by your modern notions. So few husbands are as advanced in their thinking as you are."

"I do like to consider myself a man of the modern age," Gabriel said.

13

Venetia caught another glimpse of Harold Burton just as she excused herself from the group of amateur photographers that had gathered around her.

She tried to follow his progress through the crowd. It wasn't easy. She lost track of him for a moment and then spotted him again. He was on the far side of the exhibition hall, near a side door.

She saw him glance furtively around two or three times before scuttling out the door.

Oh, no you don't, Venetia thought. *You're not going to escape me this time, you annoying little man.*

She whisked up a handful of her black skirts and prepared to make her way as unobtrusively as possible to the door through which Burton had just disappeared.

Agatha Chilcott materialized in her path. She was enveloped in pink. The heavy folds of several layers of tied-back pink skirts cascaded from a bustle that was broad enough to hold a vase of flowers. A massive necklace of pink stones filled in the expanse of bosom exposed by the neckline of the dress.

The color of the elaborately coiled braid that sat like a crown atop Agatha's head was a much darker shade of brown than the rest of her graying hair. The false piece was firmly anchored with a number of gem-set hairpins.

Agatha was a wealthy and well-connected woman with a great deal of time on her hands. She whiled away the hours collecting and dispensing the juicier tidbits of gossip that floated around in London's better circles.

Venetia felt a great deal of gratitude toward her. Agatha had been one of her first important clients. The lady had been so impressed with the portrait of herself as Cleopatra that Venetia had created that she had happily recommended her to her friends.

"My dear Mrs. Jones, I read the astonishing news of your husband's return in the morning papers." Agatha came to a halt in front of Venetia, effectively barring her path. "You must have been quite overcome with an excess of emotion when you learned that Mr. Jones was alive."

"It was an extremely startling incident,

to be sure," Venetia said, trying to edge politely around Agatha.

"I am positively amazed that you felt able to attend the exhibition this evening," Agatha continued with an air of grave concern.

"Why on earth would I miss it? I am in excellent health." Venetia went up on her toes, trying to peer above the heads of the crowd to see if Burton had returned to the room. "There was never any doubt but that I would be able to attend."

"Indeed?" Agatha cleared her throat in a meaningful manner. "One would have thought that after sustaining such a shock to the nerves as you did today that one would feel the need to take to one's bed for a day or two in order to recover."

"Nonsense, Mrs. Chilcott." Venetia snapped her black silk fan a couple of times and tried to keep an eye on the side door. "One certainly cannot allow a case of shattered nerves to keep one from fulfilling one's commitments."

Agatha glanced across the hall to where Gabriel stood talking to white-haired, bespectacled Christopher Farley, the sponsor of the exhibition.

"I admire your fortitude, my dear," Agatha said.

"Thank you. One does what one must. I hope you will excuse me, Mrs. Chilcott."

Agatha's heavily drawn brows rose. "But even if you did feel strong enough to carry on with your appointments, one would have thought that Mr. Jones might have had other notions concerning how to pass this evening."

Venetia paused, baffled by the remark. There was no way that Agatha could possibly be aware of Gabriel's plans to track down a thief.

"I beg your pardon?" she said cautiously. "Why would Mr. Jones have other ideas?"

"One would have expected that such an obviously healthy, evidently *virile* gentleman who had been forced to forgo the natural affections of a loving spouse for an extended period of time would have experienced a strong desire to spend his first evening here in London at home."

"At home?"

"In the *bosom* of his family, so to speak." Agatha clasped her gloved hands together in front of her own impressive bosom. "Renewing his *intimate connection* with his wife."

Understanding finally struck Venetia with the force of a jolt of electricity. She could feel the sudden heat in her cheeks.

Dread lanced through her. Was everyone in the room speculating on the status of her *intimate connection* with Gabriel and wondering why they were not spending the evening together in bed?

She had been concentrating so intently on the many and varied difficulties that confronted her that she had not even considered the possibility that people would be fascinated by the romantic implications of her situation.

"No need to worry on that account, Mrs. Chilcott." She summoned up the same bright, reassuring smile that she had bestowed on Agatha when she had assured the lady that the large mole on her chin would not appear in the finished Cleopatra portrait. "Mr. Jones and I had a lovely chat earlier today. We caught up on all the news."

"A chat? But my dear, the account in *The Flying Intelligencer* indicated that Mr. Jones was looking forward to being reunited with you with the most fervent enthusiasm."

"Come now, Mrs. Chilcott. You are a woman of the world. I'm sure you are aware that even the most fervently enthusiastic reunions need not consume a great deal of one's time."

"Be that as it may, Mrs. Jones, I couldn't help but notice that Mr. Jones has spent most of the evening on the other side of this hall."

"What of it?"

"One would have thought that he would have been reluctant to leave your side tonight."

"I assure you, Mr. Jones is quite capable of keeping himself occupied."

Agatha gave her a steely look. "Indeed?" Abruptly her expression softened. "Ah, I think I understand the problem."

"There is no problem, Mrs. Chilcott."

"Nonsense, my dear. No need to be shy. It is perfectly reasonable to expect that a certain natural awkwardness might exist between married persons who have been forced apart for so long."

"Yes, of course." Venetia seized on the explanation. "Very awkward."

"Especially under the circumstances," Agatha added delicately.

"Circumstances?"

"I seem to recall hearing that Mr. Jones disappeared on your honeymoon."

"Quite right," Venetia said. "Disappeared without any notice, mind you. Walked off a cliff. Fell into a deep canyon. Raging river. Body never found. Presumed dead. Very tragic but these things happen, you know. Especially in places like the Wild West."

"Which means that you had very little opportunity to become accustomed to your marital duties, my dear."

Venetia's mouth went dry. "My marital duties?"

Agatha patted her gloved hand. "You are no doubt quite tense and anxious this evening."

"You have no idea, Mrs. Chilcott."

"Why, I wouldn't be surprised to discover that you are experiencing some of the same trepidation that you no doubt felt on your honeymoon."

"Yes, indeed." Venetia summoned up her brightest smile. "Fortunately, Mr. Jones is very respectful of my delicate sensibilities."

"I'm delighted to hear that, Mrs. Jones. Nevertheless, I hope you will take some advice from an older and perhaps wiser woman."

"I don't think the situation calls for advice, thank you very much."

"I assure you, my dear, a healthy, virile gentleman who has been reunited with his bride after a lengthy absence will have certain natural urges."

Venetia stared at her, thunderstruck. "Urges?"

Agatha leaned in very close and lowered her voice. "I advise you to attend to those entirely natural urges without delay, my dear. You would not want Mr. Jones to seek relief elsewhere."

"Good heavens." Venetia felt her brain go quite blank.

"I can see from the expression on your face that you did not have much of an opportunity to become accustomed to your marital duties before Mr. Jones suffered that dreadful fall." Agatha tapped Venetia's wrist with her fan. "You must trust me when I tell you that a wife's conjugal obligations are not nearly as objectionable as some would have you believe." She winked. "Not when her husband is as healthy and virile as Mr. Jones appears to be."

Smiling benignly, Agatha turned and swept off into the throng.

Venetia finally managed to get her mouth closed. With an effort of will she pulled herself together and continued toward her objective.

But she was now very conscious of the veiled glances and curious stares aimed in her direction. People were, indeed, speculating about the intimate aspects of her relationship with Gabriel, she thought. Her face burned.

The irony of her predicament was enough to make her grind her teeth. She could not bear to contemplate the many long, lonely, sleepless nights she had spent reliving the memory of her one night in the arms of her fantasy lover and quietly mourning the loss of what might have been.

Now she knew that Gabriel Jones had blithely gone about his Arcane Society business, never for one moment considering what the news of his death might have done to her nerves.

Really, men could be so thoughtless.

When she reached the side door through which Burton had vanished, she paused to look back to where Gabriel had been standing a few minutes ago, talking to Christopher Farley. She could no longer see him. Perhaps he had gone outside for some fresh air. She could use some of that commodity, herself.

Unfortunately she had a more important task to accomplish. She could only hope that Burton had not left the exhibition hall altogether while she had been obliged to discuss her marital duties with Mrs. Chilcott.

She opened the door and slipped out of the brightly lit hall into a darkened corridor.

She closed the door and stood quietly for a moment, waiting for her eyes to adjust to the deep shadows. There was just enough moonlight seeping through the high windows above the staircase at the end of the passageway to reveal a row of closed doors.

She tried to listen for Burton's footsteps but all she could hear was the faint, muffled noise of the crowd on the other side of the wall.

She started forward slowly, wondering why Burton had come this way.

This was not her first visit to Farley's exhibition rooms. She had been here, behind the scenes, on several occasions in recent weeks to discuss business. Christopher Farley had taken an interest in her work right from the start when she had brought him some of her pictures to examine. He had advised her regarding the financial side of the profession and introduced her to some of her first important clients. In return, she had given him some of her photographs to exhibit and sell.

Because of the meetings with Farley, she had a general knowledge of how the rooms and offices were arranged on this floor.

The corridor in which she was standing was intersected by another passage midway along the hall. Farley's large office was in the other corridor.

She went quietly to the corner and looked down the second, even darker hall. No gaslight showed through the glass panes of the door to Farley's office. The glow of the moon from the windows inside the room caused the opaque panel to gleam a dull gray against the deeper shadows. The room next to the office was the one used by Farley's two clerks. It, too, was unlit.

She turned back to the main hallway. She knew that there were three offices, a large storeroom and a darkroom in that direction.

The firm's clerks used the darkroom to make additional prints of some of the photographs that were offered for sale in the showrooms. Farley was also known to invite talented but impoverished photographers to make use of the facilities. She could not imagine why Harold Burton would enter either the storeroom or the darkroom. He had his own small gallery and possessed his own equipment.

It was possible, of course, that Burton had chosen to depart the exhibition via the stairs at the end of the hall. But if he had wished to leave it would have been a good deal faster to go out through the main entrance, which descended to a gracious lobby and the busy street.

The staircase at the end of the corridor in which she stood led to the alley.

If Burton had left the building via these stairs she might as well abandon any effort to confront him tonight.

But there was another possibility. Burton's ethics were not of the highest caliber, she reminded herself. Perhaps he had let himself into Farley's office to have a look around. There was no doubt a good deal of information on the firm's clients locked up in that room. Burton was not above helping himself to something that might offer a potential profit.

Moving as quietly as possible so as not to provide a warning, she started along the hallway that led to Farley's office.

Two steps into the darkness she heard the faint sound of a door opening in the other corridor.

She turned quickly, intending to rush back out into the other passageway to intercept Burton. But a flash of icy intuition made her hesitate.

If that was Burton, he was behaving in what could only be described as a furtive manner. It might pay to see if she could discover what he was about. She needed whatever small advantage she could obtain.

She tiptoed back to the intersection of the two halls and stopped just short of the main corridor.

The muted voices of the crowd in the exhibition galleries suddenly seemed very far away. She felt unnervingly alone in the darkness.

Footsteps sounded in the other hallway. Burton was not coming in her direction. He was going toward the rear stairs. In another few seconds he would be gone. If she did not act now, he would escape.

But something held her back. She was not afraid of Burton, she told herself. She was angry because of what she was sure he had done but she was not frightened. Why was she hesitating?

She gathered her nerve and her skirts, took another step forward and leaned ever so slightly out into the other hall.

The murky moonlight illuminated the silhouette of a man in a long overcoat and a tall hat. He was moving swiftly away from her, striding purposefully toward the stairwell.

Not Burton, she decided. This man was taller. He did not scuttle along in the manner that characterized Burton's walk. Instead, he moved with a smooth, co-ordinated, surprisingly graceful ease that suggested strength and power. *Not unlike the way Gabriel moves,* she thought.

She concentrated intently, looking at the moving figure as though he were a sitter she was about to photograph, trying to catch a glimpse of his aura.

Light and shadow reversed. The corridor became a negative image. A pulsing aura appeared around the man at the end of the hall. Hot and cold shades of energy flashed in the darkness.

Fear lanced through her. Over the years she had seen many different auras, but none had alarmed her the way this one did.

She knew in that moment that she was viewing an erratic, raging energy given off by some strange, abnormal lust. She sensed intuitively that no woman could ever satisfy that unwholesome desire. She prayed that she would never learn the nature of whatever it was that the beast required to sate its terrible hunger.

To her overriding relief the figure plunged down the stairs and disappeared.

For a few more seconds she remained in the sanctuary of the connecting hall, too shaken to move.

Then she remembered Harold Burton.

A sick dread rose within her.

She made herself move out of the hallway and down the corridor to the darkroom.

"Mr. Burton?" She knocked once on the door.

There was no response.

"Are you in there?"

The silence raised the small hairs on the nape of her neck.

There was no point delaying any longer. She knew deep down that something terrible had occurred inside the darkroom. She also sensed that no matter how hard she knocked, Harold Burton was probably not going to answer.

She twisted the knob and opened the door very slowly.

Someone had pulled aside the heavy drape that usually covered the small window of the darkroom. The slanting triangle of moonlight illuminated Burton's sprawled, unmoving figure. He lay faceup on the floor, staring emptily at the ceiling.

"Dear heaven."

She crouched beside him, her skirts pooling around her, and felt for a pulse with shaking fingertips. No life beat at the base of Burton's throat. His skin was already growing unnaturally cold.

Then she saw the brandy bottle and the overturned glass on the counter. Liquid dripped over the edge and splashed onto the floor. She could smell brandy fumes.

"What the devil is going on here?" Gabriel's voice was low and dangerous.

She leaped to her feet and swung around, barely managing to stifle a small scream.

"What are you doing here?" she gasped.

"I noticed that you had left the hall. When you did not return in a reasonable length of time I decided to see what was keeping you."

She saw that he had one hand clenched very tightly around the doorknob. Something odd was happening. She concentrated briefly and saw the pulse of dark energy in the atmosphere around him.

"Are you all right?" he asked.

When she did not respond immediately, he released the doorknob and seized her wrist.

"Answer me," he said softly. "Are you all right?"

"Yes." She pulled herself together with an effort. Her normal vision snapped back into focus. "Yes, I'm fine."

He turned up the gas lamp on a nearby

table and looked down at the body.

"Tell me who this man is," he said.

"Harold Burton. He was a photographer."

"You came here to meet him?"

The question was ice cold.

"No," she said, shivering a little. "Well, yes. Not exactly. Not like this." She abandoned the explanation. "I just walked into the room and found him."

"Is there a wound?"

"I don't think so. There is no blood."

"He did not die of natural causes," Gabriel said.

She wondered how he could be so certain of that.

"I don't think so," she agreed.

He looked at her. "What do you know of this business?"

"Someone left this room just before I arrived. I think he may have had something to do with this. At the very least he will likely know what occurred in here."

"You saw this person?" Gabriel asked, his voice sharpening.

"I got only a fleeting glimpse as he went down the stairs."

"Did you recognize him?"

"No."

"Did he see you?" The question was far more urgent than the previous one.

She shook her head. "I'm sure he did not notice me. As I said, he was moving away from me. I was in the other hallway, watching him from around the corner. No, I'm certain he did not see me. He never even paused."

Gabriel took a step toward the counter where the spilled brandy dripped.

"Don't touch that liquid," she said quickly. "Or the glass, either, for that matter."

He stopped and looked back at her.

"Why not?" he asked.

Most men would have been annoyed at the notion of a woman giving orders under such circumstances. Ladies were expected to succumb to hysteria and the vapors when they were confronted with situations involving dead bodies.

But Gabriel was not questioning her common sense or good judgment, she realized. He simply wanted to know why she had warned him away from the spilled brandy.

She drew a deep breath. "There are only two possibilities here." She looked at the empty glass and then at Burton's sprawled body. "I suppose it could have been suicide. That is certainly the usual explanation in cases like this. But from what I know of Harold Burton, I find it hard to believe that he took his own life."

"What do you mean, the usual explanation in cases like this?"

"I suspect that the authorities will find that Mr. Burton drank a glass of brandy laced with cyanide."

Gabriel tightened one hand into a fist and then opened it again in a small, quick gesture, as though trying to rid himself of something unpleasant that clung to his fingers. It struck her as a curiously restless movement for a man who was usually so well controlled.

"I think," he said, "that you had better tell me exactly what you are doing in this room."

"It is a somewhat complicated story."

"I suggest you tell it quickly, before we send for the police."

"Oh, heavens. The police. Yes, of course." She would worry about the potential scandal later, she thought.

She explained, very briefly, about the two photographs that had been sent to her anonymously.

"I'm not sure what Burton intended but it occurred to me that he was either attempting to frighten me into abandoning my business or worse."

"Worse?"

"I did wonder if he intended the photographs as a prelude to blackmail," she admitted.

"Were the photographs of a compromising nature?"

"No. They were just . . . unnerving. You would have to see them to understand."

"You will show them to me later. In the meantime, we will not mention those pictures to the police."

"But they may be clues."

"They are also potential motives for murder, Venetia."

The implications of what he had just said stunned her. She suddenly felt a little light-headed.

"Do you think the police might conclude that I killed Burton because I believed that he was the one who sent me those awful pictures?" she whispered.

"Do not concern yourself, Mrs. Jones. We are going to take steps to ensure that you do not become a suspect in this affair."

Anxiety knotted her stomach. "But even if we do not tell the police about the pictures, there is no getting around the fact that I was alone in the hallway for some time. I am the one who discovered the body. I cannot prove that there was anyone else in here before I arrived. What is to prevent the authorities from suspecting that I gave Burton the cyanide to drink?"

"Even if the police do decide that this is a case of murder and not suicide, I think it is safe to say that they will not question your innocence."

She was starting to grow annoyed with his attitude of cool authority. "What makes you so certain of that, sir?"

"Because there is someone who can provide you with an excellent alibi," Gabriel said patiently.

"Indeed? And just who is that person?"

He spread his hands. "Why, your beloved, recently returned-from-the-grave husband, of course."

"But I don't have a —" She broke off abruptly. "Oh. You."

"Yes, Mrs. Jones. Me. We found the body together when we stepped out of the overheated exhibition hall to find a bit of privacy. I'm sure everyone will understand."

"They will?"

"This is my first night home after the unfortunate accident that I suffered on our honeymoon, if you will recall. I have it on good authority that a man in my circumstances would go to great lengths to have even a few minutes alone with the bride he had been parted from for such a great length of time."

14

"There is a reason why photography has long been known as one of the black arts." Venetia sank down onto a chair in front of the hearth and slowly stripped off her gloves. "Two reasons, actually."

"The use of cyanide being one of them?" Gabriel tossed his overcoat across the corner of the desk. He did not remove his evening coat but loosened his tie and unfastened the top of his shirt.

Venetia was remarkably calm, given the ordeal she had just endured, but he could see the anxiety and tension that stiffened her shoulders.

"Yes," she said. "For years the photographic journals have railed against the practice of using potassium of cyanide as a fixing agent." She placed the black kid gloves very neatly, very precisely, on a small end table. "It is not as though there is not a perfectly acceptable and safe alternative available."

"The chemical that you used at Arcane House? I believe you called it hypo."

"Hyposulphite of soda. It has been around since the earliest days of the medium but there have always been those who insisted that cyanide was better suited to the task. In addition, before the new dry plates became available a few years ago, cyanide was very useful for removing the black stains on carpets and hands and everything else created by the silver bath drippings."

"The staining problem being the other reason why photography is known as a black art?"

She nodded somberly. "Until quite recently it was said that you could tell a photographer by his fingers. They were frequently blackened from the use of the silver nitrate that was used to prepare the old collodion wet plates. I did not begin my career until after the advent of commercially made dry plates so I have not had to deal with the problem of silver stains."

"There are those who still routinely use cyanide?"

"Unfortunately, yes. It remains a staple in many darkrooms. Certainly no one will think it odd that it was conveniently on hand in Mr. Farley's establishment tonight."

Gabriel crouched in front of the hearth and got a small blaze going. "I have noticed the occasional items in the papers concerning the deaths of photographers by cyanide."

"Not just photographers. Very often the victim is someone else in the household. A child who drinks it out of curiosity, for instance, or a young maid despondent over a failed love affair. Sometimes it is the family dog that is killed. There is no knowing how many people have expired either by accident or design because of the poison."

Gabriel rose to his feet and went to the table that held a decanter of brandy. "One would think that if Burton had been looking for a quick exit from this mortal plane he would have taken the cyanide straight. Instead, he drank it mixed with strong spirits."

She hesitated. "There are those who will say that he probably thought it would be easier to get down that way."

"True." Gabriel reflected briefly on the strong, disturbing frissons of violent intent that had clung to the glass knob of Farley's darkroom door. "But as I said earlier, I am in complete agreement with your conclusion concerning events tonight. Burton was murdered."

"It would have required only a single swallow," she said quietly. "A strong dose of cyanide kills very quickly."

He picked up the bottle of brandy and splashed the contents into two glasses. When he had completed the task, he contemplated the glasses for a few seconds.

"That thought does give one pause, doesn't it?" he asked, picking up the glasses.

She looked at the brandy that he was holding out to her. "Yes, it does."

She unclasped her hands and took the brandy from him. He could see that her fingers trembled ever so slightly.

He lowered himself into the other armchair and swallowed some of the contents of his glass. Venetia took a deep breath, wrinkled her nose and tossed back some of the brandy with a bit of a flourish.

He was amused. "Wouldn't want to develop a phobia about good spirits."

"Goodness, no."

"Staff of life on occasion."

"Absolutely."

They sat together for a while, contemplating the fire. Gabriel absorbed the silence of the household. It was well after midnight. When he and Venetia arrived home a short time earlier they had discovered that everyone else had gone to bed, including Mrs. Trench. It was just as well. There would be time enough for explanations in the morning.

He tilted his head against the back of the chair and thought about the conversation with the police.

"I got the impression that the detective is leaning heavily toward the theory that Burton committed suicide," he said.

"It certainly is the simplest explanation. But it does not account for the person I saw leaving the room shortly before I discovered the body."

"No," he said. "It does not."

The detective had questioned Venetia quite closely about the figure she had seen on the staircase but she had not been able to provide him with anything useful by way of a description.

For his own part, Gabriel thought, he could hardly claim that he had picked up emanations of violence off a doorknob. The detective would have considered him quite mad. The sensations were useless as a means of identification, in any event. They were quite strong but they could have belonged to anyone who had gone to that room with murder in mind.

He looked at Venetia. "You said you

followed Burton out of the exhibition hall this evening because you wanted to confront him about some disturbing photographs that you believe he sent to you?"

"Yes."

"Any idea why he would have done such a thing?"

She sighed. "I assumed it was because he was envious of me."

"He was jealous of your success?"

"That was the only motive I could come up with." She took another small sip of the brandy. "Mr. Burton was a very bitter man. His talent as a photographer was never properly appreciated or recognized. This is a very competitive business, you see."

"I did get that impression this evening."

"The ability to take good pictures is only part of what is required to establish a reputation that attracts fashionable clients. Those who move in polite circles tend to be extremely fickle. A successful photographer must project a certain style and a sense of exclusiveness. One must give the impression that one is not actually in trade, as it were, but rather providing the client with the benefit of one's artistic talents."

"Let me hazard a guess here," Gabriel

said. "Burton did not project that sort of image."

"No."

"There must be a great many other successful photographers who do a better trade than he did. Why did he fix on you as the object of his envy?"

"I think it was because I am a woman," she said quietly. "In his mind it was bad enough that he was outdone by other men. To have a lady arrive on the scene and meet with immediate success enraged him. He confronted me on one or two occasions and informed me quite bluntly that this was no profession for a female."

"When did the unpleasant pictures arrive?"

"The first photograph was left on my doorstep earlier this week. The second one came two days later. I suspected Burton straight off. I knew he would be at the exhibition tonight. I was determined to demand an explanation from him." She closed her eyes and rubbed her temples. "Now, I do not know what to think. He was obviously involved in some sinister dealings with the man who murdered him."

Gabriel stretched his legs out toward the fire. "Do you have any notion of who might want to kill him?"

She opened her eyes and made a face. "Aside from myself, do you mean? No. I can only tell you that Burton was not the most likable man. He was a conniving, unethical schemer who moved in the lower ranks of the photographic community. He had a small gallery in an unfashionable part of town but I don't know how he managed to make a living, to tell you the truth."

Gabriel cradled his glass in both hands. "I would like to see the photographs that he sent to you."

"They're in my bottom desk drawer. I'll get them."

She set the brandy glass aside, rose and crossed the carpet to the desk.

Gabriel watched her remove a small key from the dainty chatelaine bag that dangled from the waist of her gown. She used the key to open the drawer and remove two photographs.

Without a word, she walked back across the room, sat down and handed him one of the pictures.

He held the photograph facedown for a few seconds, *feeling* with the part of him that could perceive things that his other senses did not. There were faint whispers of anger and outrage but he was almost certain they had been left by Venetia. There was a sensation of self-control about them.

Beneath those emanations were even fainter traces of another fierce emotion, one that could only be described as obsessive rage. He was almost certain that sensation had been left by the person who had arranged for the photograph to be left on Venetia's doorstep.

He turned the picture over and examined it in the firelight.

"Is this the one that arrived first?" he asked.

"Yes."

The photograph was innocuous enough at first glance, if decidedly morbid. It showed the somber scene of a funeral cortege headed by a black funeral coach equipped with a team of black horses. The vehicle stood in front of the iron gates of a cemetery. A gloomy array of monuments, crypts and headstones was visible through the bars of the high fence that surrounded the graveyard.

It was only when one examined the picture closely that one noticed the woman dressed in a fashionable black gown and a wide-brimmed black hat standing to one side of the scene.

A cold sensation settled in Gabriel's gut.

"You?" he asked quietly.

"Yes. The cemetery in that picture is located a short distance from this street. I pass it every day when I go to the gallery." She held out the second photograph.

He took it from her, pausing briefly once again to see if he could detect any strong sensations. The remnants of Venetia's anger and outrage ruffled his senses but this time there was something else. Fear.

Beneath that layer of emotion was the same unwholesome obsession that had clung to the first picture.

He turned the picture over. This time he was looking at a photograph of an ornate funeral monument. For a few seconds he could not make any sense of the scene. Then he saw the name inscribed on the stone. The chill in his insides turned to ice.

" 'In memory of Venetia Jones,' " he read aloud.

Venetia grimaced. "An excellent example of what can be accomplished by a person who is skilled in the art of retouching photographs. After the picture arrived, Amelia and I went to the cemetery to see if that particular monument was located there."

"Did you find it?"

"Yes." She clasped her fingers tightly together. "The name engraved on the stone, however, is Robert Adamson."

"Whatever else he was, Harold Burton was a nasty son of a bitch."

She drank some more brandy. "That was certainly my opinion."

He looked at the first photograph again. "Was this one retouched also?"

"No. I was there in front of the cemetery that day, returning from my customary walk in the park. I happened to pass the gates just as the funeral cortege arrived." She hesitated. "I know this will sound as though I am quite paranoid but I have had the feeling that Burton has been following me about lately."

Gabriel put the photographs on the table next to the chair. "You're quite certain these were taken by him?"

She glanced at the pictures. "As certain as I can be without absolute proof. There is something about the style and composition. Burton was actually a very skilled photographer. I have seen some of his work. He had a particular talent for architectural themes. The first picture, the one of the cortege, was obviously taken on the spur of the moment. I could not have identified him as the photographer given just that single shot. But the second photograph was taken with great care."

Gabriel studied the picture of the headstone. "I see what you mean. The angle he used is quite dramatic."

"The lighting is also striking and very much in his style. As for the inscription, well, Burton is quite a skilled retoucher." Venetia shook her head. "I think that he was trying to impress me as well as frighten me with that second photograph. He wanted to show me that he was more expert with a camera than I am."

"You said you felt Burton was following you?"

"I didn't see him that day when the picture of the funeral cortege was taken but I did notice him a number of times over the course of several days. He appeared to be lurking in my vicinity."

"Describe the occasions when you saw him."

"I noticed him at least twice in the park not far from here. He always kept his distance and pretended not to see me. Then, the other morning Amelia and I went shopping in Oxford Street. I am certain that I spotted Burton there, too. He was lounging in the doorway of a shop. When I tried to approach him to ask what he was doing, he disappeared into the crowd. At first I assumed the various incidents were accidental. But in the past few days I vow I started to feel like a deer that is being stalked by the hunter." Her mouth tightened. "It was becoming quite unsettling, to tell you the truth."

And perhaps another motive for murder in the eyes of Scotland Yard, Gabriel thought.

"If the police question us again about Burton's death, we will not mention that he may have been following you," he said aloud. "Is that quite clear?"

She contemplated him with a steady gaze. "Do you mind if I ask you a question, Mr. Jones?"

"It depends upon the question, of course."

"There does appear to be some evidence" — she paused to hold up one finger — "not a great deal, mind you, but a few bits and pieces that would seem to point toward me as a possible suspect in this situation."

"I noticed that."

"You are aware that I disappeared several minutes before you found me with Burton's body tonight, ample time in which to pour a glass of brandy and lace it with cyanide. What makes you so certain that I did not kill him?"

He thought about how much to tell her. A murky mix of intense psychical spoors had marked the door of the darkroom and the space inside. He had sensed obsession, unwholesome excitement and fear, all swirled together in a seething brew that had been impossible to sort out. He knew that what he had sensed were several layers of recent emotions. Burton had no doubt touched the doorknob at least once. The killer had also touched it. So had Venetia. Between the three of them, they had left a chaotic soup of emotions.

But he was certain of one thing: Venetia was not the killer. He had been too close to her during their time together at Arcane House, too intimate. He would have known if she was capable of such vicious, cold-blooded violence.

"You told me that someone else left the room before you arrived," he said. "I believe you."

"Thank you. I appreciate your trust. But may I ask why you are so certain that I told you the truth?"

"Let's just say that after our time together at Arcane House, I think I know you well enough to place great faith in your integrity." That was the truth as far as it went.

"I'm delighted to know that I left you with such a good impression of my character," she said dryly.

She did not believe him, he realized. Fair enough, he knew that she was keeping secrets, too.

"Indeed, madam," he said. "And while I will have absolutely no difficulty whatsoever in sticking to the version of events that we gave to the police and which will no doubt appear in the morning papers —"

"The *papers.* I have not even considered that aspect of the situation. Mr. Otford of *The Flying Intelligencer* was at the exhibition this evening. There is no telling how this business will look in the press."

"We shall deal with that later. At the moment, I am far more interested in finding out why you lied to me and to the police tonight when you said that you did not recognize the man you saw on the stairs."

15

The question caught her completely by surprise, as he had intended. She turned her head very quickly to look at him, the expression in her eyes one of astonishment and alarm. It was as though he had startled her out of some secret hiding place.

"But I did not recognize him," she said a little too swiftly. "I told you, I did not even get a close look at him. I most certainly did not know him."

Gabriel got to his feet, picked up an iron poker and prodded the fire.

"You saw something," he said mildly.

"A man wearing a long overcoat and a tall hat. I told you that much." She paused and then added reflectively, "At least I think it was a man."

That observation got his attention. "You are not certain?"

"All I can say with any great assurance is that the person I saw was dressed in the manner of a gentleman. As I told the detective, I could tell that the individual was slender and of above medium height. But the light was too poor for me to notice any other details."

"I find it interesting that you would even allow for the possibility that the killer might have been female," he said, setting the poker aside. "Given his masculine attire, few would question the assumption that the person you saw was a man."

"When you consider the matter closely it is obvious that one of the easiest ways to disguise oneself is to adopt the clothing of the opposite gender."

He contemplated that. "And there is an old theory which holds that poison is a woman's choice of murder weapon."

"Under the circumstances, I do not think that we can place much credence in that notion. In this instance, the victim was a photographer and, quite frankly, the cyanide was an obvious choice on the part of the killer."

"I take your point." He rested one arm on the mantel. "You are certain that the fleeing figure did not notice you?"

"Positive," she said. "He did not glance back while I was watching him. Even if he had done so he could not have seen me."

"Why not?"

"Because I was in the darkest part of the corridor, peering around a corner. There was almost no light behind me. The killer was the one who was illuminated and then only minimally."

"You sound very certain."

Her mouth curved wryly. "I would remind you that I am a photographer, sir. I assure you, I have made a close study of the effects of light and shadow."

"I do not doubt your professional expertise, madam." He met her eyes. "But I must ask you again, what was it you saw tonight that you did not tell the police?"

She laced her fingers tightly together. "You are very insistent. What makes you think that I saw more than I told you or the detective?"

"Call it masculine intuition. During our all too brief interlude at Arcane House I learned a few things about you, Mrs. Jones. One is that when it comes to taking pictures, you often perceive what others do not. And I am still wondering how you spotted those two men in the woods that night."

"I noticed them when they went through a patch of moonlight."

"No moonlight penetrated those trees, but we'll let that go for now. Given the seriousness of our situation, however, I cannot let this other matter drop so easily.

I would very much appreciate the truth, so I ask again, what did you see tonight?"

Her reply was so long in coming that he began to think she was going to refuse to tell him. He could not blame her, he thought. She owed him nothing. But it disturbed him for some reason that she did not consider him a worthy confidant. He realized that he wanted her to trust him again, the way she had seemed to trust him at Arcane House.

"Nothing I perceived about the fleeing man would be of any use to the police," she said quietly.

He stilled. "But you did notice something about the killer?"

"Yes." She met his eyes. "You will no doubt think me either excessively imaginative or delusional if I tell you the truth. At best, you will conclude that I am a great fraud."

He took two steps toward her, closed his hands around her shoulders and raised her to her feet. "I assure you that nothing you could say would lead me to either of those conclusions."

"Indeed?" Wry skepticism flashed across her face. "What makes you so certain of that?"

He tightened his grip on her arms. "You

seem to forget that we spent several days in each other's company some three months back."

"No, Mr. Jones, I have not forgotten. Not for one moment."

"Neither have I. I have already told you that I have no doubts about your character. The same is true when it comes to the matter of your sanity."

"Thank you."

"But there is another reason why I would very likely believe anything you chose to tell me," he said.

"And what reason would that be, sir?"

"I want you far too much to permit myself to have any doubts where you are concerned."

Her lips parted. *"Mr. Jones."*

The questioning would have to be continued later. It had been too long. He could no longer resist temptation.

He lowered his head and took her mouth captive.

16

The shock of the embrace set her senses ablaze. After all the weeks and months of uncertainty over his fate and despair at the knowledge that if Gabriel was alive he had not come for her, he was kissing her again.

The effect of his embrace was even more stimulating than she had remembered. The heat of his body, the sensual taste of his mouth, the exhilarating strength of his arms incited a thrilling excitement deep within her.

"Do you have any notion," Gabriel whispered, "how many nights I have lain awake, imagining what it would be like to kiss you again?"

"How do you think it was for me? I was devastated when I got word of your so-called accident. I could not bring myself to believe it. I was convinced that you were alive. I told myself that if you were dead, I would somehow know it. But there was no word from you."

"I am sorry, my sweet." He used one hand to gently tilt her head back so that he could have access to her throat. "I swear, I never meant for you to hear the news of my death. How was I to know that you would see such a small story in the London papers? I thought you were safely tucked away in Bath."

"You should have contacted me," she insisted.

"Forgive me," he said into her ear. "I thought this damned business would be finished weeks ago and I would be able to come to you without trailing danger in my wake."

He eased his fingers through her hair. Pins plopped softly on the carpet. The intimacy of the situation made her shiver. She clutched his shoulders, aware of the crisp white linen of his shirt and the firm swell of muscle beneath the fabric.

Her hair tumbled down around her shoulders. The next thing she knew his fingers were at the fastenings at the front of her gown. The knowledge that he was about to undress her elicited a flicker of panic.

Everything was happening too fast, she thought. Gabriel acted as if he wanted her but she must not forget that he had come back to her for reasons other than passion. Furthermore, this was not remote, secluded Arcane House, where no one would know what happened between her and Gabriel. Gabriel himself was no longer a safe fantasy that she could savor without courting disaster.

They were in her personal study, for heaven's sake. Amelia and Beatrice and Edward were upstairs. Mrs. Trench was asleep in her little room off the kitchen. If any of them awakened they might hear sounds and come to investigate.

They were in the real world, she reminded herself. Things were different here.

But Gabriel was unfastening the bodice of her gown. His mouth was on hers, distracting and disorienting. She trembled, closed her eyes and clung to him to keep her balance.

"I was not mistaken, was I?" he rasped. The question was roughened by desire.

"About what?" she managed.

"That last night at Arcane House. You wanted to be in my arms. You wanted me."

Uncertainty spiraled through her. That night had been perfect, or nearly so. But tonight was not perfect. The setting was all wrong and Gabriel was no longer her mysterious, secret lover who could be conveniently hidden from sight. He was living right upstairs in the attic, for goodness sake. She would have to face him at breakfast tomorrow morning. In front of the entire household, no less.

"Yes," she whispered. "But that was then and this is now."

He stilled. "Is there someone else? I told myself that you would not lose interest in me in such a short period of time. Although I must admit that tonight when you disappeared from the exhibition hall, I wondered if I had miscalculated."

Miscalculated seemed an unusual choice of word, she thought. *Miscalculated* was a term one employed when one had plotted a strategy that had gone wrong. *Miscalculated* was not a word a lover used. At least she didn't think it was that sort of word.

She withdrew her arms from around Gabriel's neck and flattened her palms on his chest.

"Is there anyone else?" he asked again, without inflection. In the firelight his eyes were dangerously enigmatic.

"No," she confessed. "For heaven's sake, in the past three months I have been overwhelmed with the move to London and the establishment of my business here. I haven't had time to find anyone else. That is not the problem."

He smiled. She could feel the tension leave his muscles.

"I understand," he said, caressing her throat with his finger. "The events of the day have no doubt rattled your nerves."

That was as good an excuse as any, she decided.

"Yes, quite so." She took a deliberate step back. "My apologies, sir. A great many startling incidents have, indeed, occurred today. Why, one might say that events seem to have rained down upon me like a great waterfall. The shock of your return. This strange mystery involving the alchemist's formula. The discovery of Burton's body tonight. It is all simply too much. I do not believe that I am thinking as clearly as one should in these circumstances."

Amusement curved his mouth. "On the contrary, Mrs. Jones, this is one of those rare situations in which one should not depend entirely upon logic and clear thinking." He gently eased the edges of the gown's bodice together. "Nevertheless, I would not press you under such circumstances. You need time to recover from what has clearly been a series of shocks."

"Precisely, sir." She clutched the bodice of her gown, not knowing whether to be relieved or hurt by his consideration. If his passions had truly been fiercely aroused a moment ago would he not try to be just a bit more convincing? "I appreciate your sensitivity."

He leaned forward slightly and brushed his mouth across hers. "I am not being sensitive so much as pragmatic, my sweet," he said as if he had read her mind. "When we do eventually make love again, I would not wish you to harbor any doubts or regrets afterward."

She was not sure how to take that, either. Tonight everything involving their relationship seemed suddenly extremely murky. Things had been so much simpler when he had been just a fantasy.

"I will bid you good night, sir." Holding the bodice of her gown together in one hand, she hurried toward the door. "In addition to a problem with my unsettled nerves, I am quite exhausted."

That last was very true, she thought. She did feel strangely weary. But she also had a feeling that sleep would be hard to come by tonight.

"One more thing before you go, Mrs. Jones."

The coolly spoken, subtle command caused her hand to freeze on the doorknob. She looked back at him, deeply wary. He stood silhouetted against the firelight, darkly sensual and compelling in his open shirt and unknotted tie. A fresh wave of unease swept through her.

"Yes?" she said politely.

"You have not answered my question." He crossed to the small table that held the brandy, picked up the decanter and refilled his glass. "What was it you saw tonight when the killer fled down the stairs?"

He was not going to give up on that front, she realized. She had a feeling that, once he had determined upon an objective, Gabriel Jones rarely abandoned any quest. *Like a hunter that has sighted prey,* she thought. The image was disturbing. It was also, unaccountably, thrilling. It was as if he had issued some sort of elemental challenge.

She pondered her answer, strongly tempted to evade a direct reply. He was unlikely to believe her if she tried to explain her unusual talent, she thought. But she was intrigued by the fact that he was astute enough to realize that she had perceived something beyond the ordinary. Few people of her acquaintance, male or female, would have guessed that much.

Part of her was also suddenly curious to

know how he would respond to the truth.

"I doubt that you will credit this," she said, readying herself for instant skepticism, "but I saw an aura of psychical energy around the fleeing man."

The glass in his hand stopped halfway to his mouth.

"Damnation," he finally said, very softly. "I suspected as much, but I couldn't be certain."

"I beg your pardon?"

"Never mind. Tell me about these auras you see."

She had been prepared for disbelief, not a reasonable question. It took her a moment to adjust.

"They appear in the form of waves of energy that pulse around the individual," she said.

"You see these auras around everyone you meet? That must be somewhat disconcerting."

"I do not see them unless I concentrate and make an effort to distinguish them. Then, it is like looking at a negative image of the world. In that state, I can make out auras."

"Interesting."

"I do not expect you to understand what I am trying to tell you but I assure you that if I were to encounter the killer again and if I knew to look at him with my second sight I would very likely recognize him."

"Would you now?" he asked softly.

She did not know what to make of that response so she forged ahead, anxious to complete her explanation.

"You see why I did not say anything about any of this to the man from Scotland Yard," she said. "I doubt very much that he would have believed me. You saw how he treated me. He assumed that I was a victim of shock and that I was teetering on the verge of hysteria."

"True." Gabriel lounged against the edge of her desk. "He did aim most of his questions at me, didn't he?"

"Because you are a man."

"And because he believed me to be your husband."

"That, too." She made a face. "Even if I had volunteered the information about the fleeing man's aura, it would not have done the detective any good. There is no point describing a person's psychical energy pattern to someone who cannot perceive it."

Gabriel studied her for a moment. "You say auras are distinctive?"

"Yes. They definitely vary from one person to another. There are colors involved but I cannot tell you the names of the hues and shades that I see because they do not correspond to those that I see with my normal vision. I have invented my own, private vocabulary to describe them but it would be meaningless to you. There is also something about the intensity and the pattern of the psychical energy that is particular to each person."

"Can you determine a person's sex from his aura?"

"No. That is why I cannot say for certain that the fleeing figure was male or female."

"What of an individual's character or inclinations?"

That, she thought, was a very perceptive question. "Sometimes those aspects, if they are strong enough, are often startlingly vivid, yes."

"What did you learn about the nature of the person you saw in the hallway tonight?" he asked.

She drew a deep breath. "If that person had been an animal, I would have said that he was a predator, a creature that kills when death suits its purposes. In the animal kingdom, such beasts have a rightful place. They kill only to live. But among humans, we would label such an individual a monster."

Gabriel went motionless. All expression evaporated from his face.

"I see," he said. "A monster."

"That is how the fleeing figure appeared to me. Cold-blooded and very frightening. Quite frankly, I hope I never have occasion to see him or her again."

He did not speak.

Something about the dark stillness that emanated from him made the hair stir again on the nape of her neck, just as it had earlier when she had seen the killer flee the scene of his crime.

"Good night, Mr. Jones," she said.

"Good night, Venetia."

She stepped out into the hall, closed the door and hurried toward the staircase. She flew up the stairs as if she were being chased by the sort of predator that she had just tried to describe to Gabriel.

When she reached the safety of her bedroom she was breathless. The sight of herself in the dressing table mirror shocked her. Her hair was down, her gown was open and her eyes were dark pools of shadows.

The haunting sensuality of her own image shook her to the core of her being. *This is what Gabriel saw,* she thought.

She whirled away from the mirror and hastily undressed.

A few minutes later, garbed in her nightgown, she slipped between the covers and turned down the lamp. She waited, listening tensely to the quiet sounds of the house.

She never did hear Gabriel climb the stairs to the attic. But eventually she heard some faint noises overhead and knew that he had gone to bed.

It was not until she was sliding away into a dark, restless dream that she asked herself the question that had been troubling her ever since Gabriel had arrived on her doorstep.

He had made it plain that he needed her cooperation in his venture. Would he attempt to use seduction to achieve his ends?

In that instant the jumbled mix of confused emotions that she had been experiencing dissolved into sharp-as-crystal clarity.

The situation between herself and Gabriel Jones had become confounding and unsettling precisely because she was no longer in full control of it.

At Arcane House she had established all the unwritten rules that had governed their association. She had set out to seduce Gabriel to fulfill her very private dream of a perfect romantic interlude.

But now Gabriel was establishing all the rules. She would have to be very careful, indeed.

17

Footsteps sounded on the attic landing. Gabriel wiped the last of the shaving lather from his face, tossed the towel aside and crossed the small, cramped space to open the door.

Edward stood in front of him. The boy's hand was raised in preparation for a polite knock.

"Good morning," Gabriel said.

"Good morning, sir." Edward gazed up at him, openly curious. "You haven't finished dressing."

"Not quite."

"Mrs. Trench sent me to tell you that breakfast will be ready in a few minutes."

"Thank you. I am looking forward to a good home-cooked meal. I'll only be a moment."

He turned away from the door and took a clean shirt off one of the wall pegs.

"I'll wait for you," Edward volunteered, edging into the room. "I can show you the way to the breakfast room."

"I'd appreciate that," Gabriel said. "It

will save me wandering all over the house."

He watched Edward in the mirror while he fastened his shirt.

The boy looked around, studying each of the items that Gabriel had unpacked. He seemed particularly taken with the shaving things arrayed on the washstand.

"Papa kept his shaving items in a leather kit very similar to yours," Edward said.

"Did he?" Gabriel finished buttoning the shirt and pondered whether or not a tie was called for. When he was at home he always went down to breakfast in the comfort of his shirtsleeves. But his was a bachelor household.

"Yes," Edward said.

"You must miss your father a great deal."

Edward nodded. For a moment he fell silent. Gabriel slung his tie around his collar and knotted the silk in a four-in-hand.

Edward watched the knotting process very closely.

"Papa was an investor," he blurted out.

"Was he?"

"He traveled to America a lot. But when he was home he took me fishing and showed me how to do lots of things."

"That's what fathers are supposed to do," Gabriel said.

"A brother-in-law can do that sort of thing, too, can't he?"

Gabriel looked at him. "Yes," he said. "He can."

Edward brightened. "I know it's supposed to be a secret, about you not really being my brother-in-law and all. But as long as we're pretending, I thought perhaps you could show me some of the things that Papa did not have a chance to show me."

"I don't see why not," Gabriel said.

"Excellent." Edward grinned. "You needn't worry. As I explained, sir, I'm very good at keeping secrets."

"Yes, I know."

"I've had a lot of experience since Mama and Papa went to heaven," Edward said with a touch of pride. "In a way, pretending that you are my brother-in-law is very much like the secret that I have to keep about Papa."

"I see."

"Papa was a big mist."

Gabriel went blank. "A big mist?"

"That is what they call a gentleman who has more than one wife."

"Bigamist," Gabriel said softly. He thought about the photograph of the larger-than-life man hanging on the wall of Venetia's study.

That information explained a great deal, he thought.

"Papa had another wife and some children in New York, where he went on business twice a year. We did not find out about it until after Mama and Papa were killed in the train wreck. Because Papa was a *bigamist,* it means that Venetia and Amelia and I are not his real children."

"You're wrong, Edward. Regardless of the circumstances of your parents' relationship, you are most certainly your father's real children."

"Aunt Beatrice says we are ill —" Edward stumbled over the word. "Ill something."

"Illegitimate?"

"Yes, that's it. Anyhow, after Mama and Papa died we discovered that Mr. Cleeton had disappeared with the money that was supposed to come to us. Aunt Beatrice says that was a *huge* disaster because having a comfortable, respectable income would have covered up a *host of sins,* in the eyes of the world. She says if it weren't for Venetia's skill with photography we would all very likely have wound up on the streets."

Gabriel had already concluded that Venetia was supporting the entire family, but this explained why she had been obliged to shoulder such an enormous responsibility.

"Who was Mr. Cleeton?" he asked.

"Papa's man of affairs. He stole our inheritance. Papa always told us that if anything dreadful ever happened to him, we would be *comfortably situated financially.* Only we weren't because Mr. Cleeton took our money and went far away."

"Bastard," Gabriel said.

"Yes, I know I am a bastard." Edward's lower lip trembled. "That is another word for illegitimate, isn't it? Aunt Beatrice and Venetia and Amelia don't think I know it but I overheard Aunt Beatrice tell Venetia and Amelia that people will call me that if they find out that Papa was not really married to Mama."

Gabriel crouched down in front of the boy. "I was referring to Mr. Cleeton, not you, Edward."

Edward's brow furrowed. "Was Mr. Cleeton illegitimate, too?"

"I have no idea. But it does not matter because I employed the wrong word to describe him. Being a bastard is not a bad thing; it is merely a fact. Like having red hair or blue eyes. It does not tell you the character of the person in question. Do you understand?"

"I think so."

"Pay attention now because I am going

to say something to you that my father said to me when I was your age. You are to remember it always because it is very important."

"Yes, sir."

"It does not matter whether your father was ever legally married to your mother. You are not responsible for what he did. But you are responsible for what you do. Every man must see to his own honor, and you will see to yours. That is what is important."

"Yes, sir."

Gabriel rose and put his hand on Edward's shoulder. He steered the boy toward the door. "Now that we have got that clear, we will go down to breakfast."

"Yes, let's." Edward grinned widely, looking suddenly a good deal happier than he had a moment ago. "Usually we have only buttered eggs and toast on Wednesdays but Mrs. Trench says that because there is a man in the house now, we will also have kippered salmon today. She says men need substance in their meals."

"Mrs. Trench is obviously a wise woman."

They went out the door and down the narrow attic stairs.

On the landing Edward looked up at

Gabriel. "You never told me the right word, sir."

"Right word for what?"

"For Mr. Cleeton. You said *bastard* was not the correct word to describe him."

"Right."

"What is the correct word, then?"

Gabriel reflected on his obligations as a brother-in-law. "I will tell you the proper term but you must bear in mind that a gentleman does not use it when ladies are present. Is that understood?"

Edward glowed with anticipation at the prospect of garnering secret manly knowledge. "Yes, sir. I promise I will not repeat it in front of Aunt Beatrice or my sisters."

"You must not use it in the presence of Mrs. Trench, either. She is a respectable woman and she is owed the same good manners as your aunt and sisters."

"Very well. I promise not to use it around Mrs. Trench."

"The appropriate term to describe Mr. Cleeton is *son of a bitch.*"

"Son of a bitch," Edward repeated carefully, clearly wanting to get it right. "Does that mean his mother was a female dog?"

"No," Gabriel said. "That would be an insult to female dogs everywhere."

18

"The two of you discovered Mr. Burton's body at the exhibition last night?" Beatrice put one hand to her breast and swayed in her chair. "You say he was likely murdered? Dear heaven. We are ruined."

The shock and horror in her voice caused Gabriel to look up from his kippered salmon.

He studied Beatrice, who sat at the opposite end of the long table. It had not been his idea to sit at the head of the table but Mrs. Trench had made it plain that in her view he was expected to occupy the position that Polite Society had ordained as the proper station of the master of the house. When Venetia had walked through the doorway a short time later, dressed in black, he knew immediately by her expression that he was sitting in the chair that she normally occupied.

"I don't think that will prove to be the case," Gabriel said. He looked at Edward. "Would you please pass the strawberry jam?"

"Yes, sir." Edward spoke around a mouthful of buttered eggs. He dutifully handed the jam pot to Gabriel. "Sir, what does a murdered person look like?"

"Edward," Beatrice said tightly. "That is quite enough. One does not talk about such things at the breakfast table."

"But, Aunt Beatrice, you were the one who brought up the subject."

Beatrice sighed. "Eat your eggs and do not interrupt your elders when they're talking."

Edward went back to his eggs but Gabriel knew that the boy was taking in every word of the conversation. The ghoulish subject of murdered people was not going to be ignored so easily.

"Aunt Beatrice," Venetia said firmly, "please do not fly into a panic. The situation is well in hand."

"How can you say that?" Beatrice rounded on her. "We are talking about a great scandal. Why, if it gets out that you discovered a body at the exhibition last night there will be no end of gossip."

"The word is already out, I'm afraid." Amelia walked into the room, waving a copy of *The Flying Intelligencer.* "And you will never guess who wrote the piece."

Venetia made a face and reached for the coffeepot. "Mr. Otford?"

"The very same." Amelia sat down beside Edward. "It is an exciting review, to say the least. I expect everyone will be reading it this morning. It is rather rare to find a dead body at a photographic exhibition, after all."

"We are doomed," Beatrice intoned. "We shall be forced to vacate this lovely house and give up the gallery. We will lose everything."

Gabriel looked at Amelia. "Why don't you read the article to us?"

"Certainly." Amelia cleared her throat.

SHOCKING EVENTS AT
PHOTOGRAPHIC EXHIBITION
by Gilbert Otford

The body of a photographer was discovered during the course of an exhibition of photographs on Tuesday evening. The deceased was identified as Mr. Harold Burton, of Greenstone Lane.

It is believed that Mr. Burton's lack of success in his chosen field, together with recent financial reverses and mounting debts, led him to take the sad course of drinking potassium of cyanide.

The body was discovered quite by

accident by Mrs. Jones, the well-known photographer. Her husband, Mr. Jones, was with her when they happened upon the corpse. Readers of this paper will recall that Mr. Jones is only recently returned to London and the arms of his loving bride after having been presumed dead for a year.

Needless to say, the discovery of Mr. Burton's body cast a pall of gloom over the exhibition. Mrs. Jones, whose striking pictures won admiration from all present, appeared quite distraught. There was great concern that she might faint. She was seen being tenderly escorted out of the hall by her devoted husband.

"Oh, for pity's sake," Venetia fumed. "I was nowhere near fainting."

"I think the fact that you were quite distraught and that you had to be tenderly escorted out of the hall was a nice touch," Amelia announced, putting aside the paper. "I agree with Mr. Jones. I don't think this news will create any severe problems. In fact, I would not be surprised if it attracted a few more clients. People will be more curious than ever about the mysterious widow photographer."

"Former widow," Gabriel corrected mildly.

"Yes, of course," Amelia said, scooping eggs onto her plate. "Forgive me, sir, I must not forget your miraculous return. It is, after all, the latest installment in the legend of the mysterious Mrs. Jones."

"Happy to be of service," Gabriel said.

Beatrice's brows came together in a baffled frown. "I don't understand." She looked at Gabriel. "I thought you said that Mr. Burton was murdered."

"That was certainly the conclusion that Venetia and I arrived at," Gabriel said.

"But the newspaper article clearly implies that Mr. Burton took his own life."

"Yes, it does, doesn't it?" Gabriel contemplated that information while he ate another bite of salmon. "And there is no mention of the fleeing figure that Venetia saw in the hallway. Interesting. I wonder if the police decided to keep certain details quiet in hopes of letting the killer think that his crime has gone undetected, or if they truly believe Burton's death was a suicide."

"There may be another explanation," Venetia said. "Mr. Jones, last night you and I were primarily concerned with our own situation. We forgot that there was someone in the building who had every reason to try to ensure that the exhibition hall not be tainted with the scandal a murder might cause."

"Of course," Beatrice said immediately. "Christopher Farley, the sponsor of the exhibition. Mr. Farley is a very influential gentleman both in art circles and in Society. I would not be at all surprised to learn that he was able to apply some pressure to the police to get them to announce a suspected suicide instead of murder."

Either way, Gabriel thought, he had one less problem on his hands today. The fact that the reporter had not learned that Venetia had seen someone fleeing the scene of the crime meant that in all likelihood the killer did not know it, either.

Venetia regarded him with a considering expression. "What are your plans for today, Mr. Jones?"

He wondered how much longer she intended to address him with such excruciating formality.

"I made a list, as it happens." He drew a slip of paper from his pocket and put it on the table. "First, I am going to give you the negative of the photograph of the strongbox that you made while you were at Arcane House. I would appreciate it if you would develop it as soon as possible."

She inclined her head. "Very well. What will you do with the picture?"

"I have already deciphered the encoded passage that was inscribed on the lid of the strongbox. It is merely a list of herbs that mean nothing to me or to my cousin. I cannot conceive of how it might be important. But there is a member of the Arcane Society here in London who has done a great deal of research on the alchemist's papers. Perhaps he will be able to make something of the design that surrounds the names of the herbs."

"You plan to show the photograph of the strongbox to him?" Edward asked.

"Yes," Gabriel said. "But just to be on the safe side, in the event that Mr. Montrose, who is quite elderly, loses the print or if it falls into the wrong hands, I am going to request that it be slightly retouched. I want to change the name of one or two of the herbs. Is that possible?"

"I can do that for you," Beatrice offered.

"Thank you," Gabriel said. "I will tell Mr. Montrose what is missing, of course, so that he will have the right information with which to work."

Edward beamed with admiration. "That is very clever, sir."

"I do try," Gabriel said. "But I must admit that I am not hopeful that Montrose will be able to tell me anything that my cousin and I have not already deduced. However, he may be able to assist me in another aspect of my search."

"What is that?" Venetia asked.

He looked at her. "Montrose has been in charge of maintaining the membership rolls of the Arcane Society for a number of years. The records include not only the names of those inducted into the society but also the names of their relatives."

Venetia frowned slightly. "You are expanding your investigation to include the families of the members?"

"Yes." He sat back, coffee in hand. "I am broadening the pool of suspects to include the relatives of those members who would have known about the excavation of the alchemist's laboratory. In addition, I made note of the names of some of those present at the exhibition hall last night. I am curious to see if any of them have any links to the Arcane Society."

Beatrice's expression darkened with anxiety. "You are convinced that this thief you seek has been watching Venetia, aren't you?"

"Yes," he said. "I'm sorry to say it, but I

fear that is extremely likely. That is why I felt it necessary to return from the grave."

"One thing is certain," Beatrice observed with a thoughtful air. "If the villain is hanging about in Venetia's vicinity, you will most certainly have his full attention now. He must know who you are."

"Yes," Gabriel said. "Quite likely."

Venetia put down her fork. Somber comprehension lit her eyes. "You think that now that you are here, the villain will refocus his attention on you. You hope to distract him from me."

Gabriel shrugged and reached for another slice of toast.

Beatrice suddenly cheered. "Yes, of course. That makes perfect sense. What a brilliant ploy, Mr. Jones. Why would the villain pay any more heed to Venetia now that you have reappeared? The thief will naturally assume that if anyone knows anything about the code on the strongbox, it will be you. After all, Venetia was just the photographer."

"It is a simple plan," Gabriel admitted. "But in my experience, they are usually the best."

Venetia returned her attention to her food. He noticed that she did not look at all relieved by Beatrice's conclusion. He wondered if he dared hope that meant that she was anxious about his own safety.

It had not been easy to watch her walk out of the study last night. Everything inside him had longed to keep her with him. Didn't she understand that they belonged together? Had she forgotten the vow she had made in the throes of passion that last night at Arcane House?

I am yours.

19

Harold Burton's small, shabby photographic gallery was sunk in gloom. It was almost as if the business had somehow sensed that the proprietor would not be returning and had closed its own doors.

The heavy fog did nothing to brighten the atmosphere, Venetia thought. She stood in a doorway directly across the cramped lane from the entrance to Burton's Photographic Gallery. It was early afternoon, but the vapor was so thick she could barely make out the little shop. She raised her eyes to the windows of the rooms above the gallery. There was no indication that anyone was about up there, either. Those rooms had no doubt been Burton's private quarters.

She had made the decision to come here today on impulse, leaving Amelia and Maud, the shopgirl who managed the gallery, the task of choosing the model for the next portrait in the gratifyingly successful *Men of Shakespeare* series.

The possibility that Burton had taken

other photographs of her, photographs that he had not had time to deliver to her doorstep before he died, had been worrying her since she had awakened. There was no knowing what mischief Burton might have been up to with his retouching tools before his untimely demise. She could not afford to have an embarrassing photograph fall into the hands of one of her competitors or, worse, land on a client's doorstep.

There was little activity in the lane. The shops on either side of Burton's Photographic Gallery were open but there were no customers. The few hearty souls who had ventured out in the heavy fog wandered like lost ghosts, so concerned with not bumping into walls or stumbling over the paving stones that they did not notice Venetia lurking in the doorway. She realized that, garbed in black from head to toe, her face clouded by a black net veil, she was almost invisible.

She waited until an empty hansom rattled past, moving slowly in the mist, and then she crossed the lane to the gallery.

It came as no surprise to discover that the front door of the shop was securely locked. Shades had been lowered in all of the windows. Burton would have closed for the day before taking himself off to the exhibition hall and the encounter with his killer last night.

She made her way to the corner, turned and went down a narrow walk that led to a thin alley intended to service the shops. If anything the fog seemed even denser in this narrow passage.

She found the rear door of the gallery and discovered that it, too, was locked. She removed a hairpin and went to work. One became quite handy with tools and mechanical devices when one took up a career as a photographer, she reflected. It seemed one was always having to improvise.

The door opened. She paused, taking a last look around to make certain that there was no one about to see her enter the shop. Nothing stirred in the sea of fog that had drowned the alley.

Moving quietly she let herself into the back room of the gallery and closed the door. She stood still for a moment, surveying the cluttered, gloom-filled space.

The room contained the usual paraphernalia that proliferated in a photographer's gallery. Cartons of old negatives were stacked to the ceiling. Faded backdrops of various colors and designs were pushed up against the wall. An aged, well-worn sitter's chair, one leg broken, occupied a corner. A pair of small-sized ladies' shoes was tucked under the chair. The shoes were in a style that had gone out of fashion at least two years earlier.

An unexpected pang of sympathy went through her. Poor Burton. He had either not realized how important it was to stay current with the latest fashions or else he had not been able to afford to replace the shoes when styles changed.

There were three pairs of ladies' shoes in her own gallery. They were all in the very latest style and considerably more elegant than the pair here in Burton's establishment. But they had one thing in common with Burton's shoes. They were all sized for the smallest and daintiest of feminine feet.

She was quite certain that Burton had invested in the shoes for the same practical reason that had led her to buy three pairs that were too small for anyone in her family. Delicate, elegant footwear proved extremely useful when one was confronted with a female client who desired a full-length portrait that did not display her own large feet.

One simply placed the smaller shoes in front of the sitter's real feet and arranged her skirts so that only the tiny, pointed toes of the more dainty pair peeked out from beneath the hem of the lady's gown. It saved a great deal of retouching.

On a nearby table lay two framed photographs. The glass had been shattered in each frame. Curious, she went closer to get a better look.

A single glance underlined the depths of Burton's animosity toward her.

The photographs showed scenes of the Thames. She recognized both. Burton had entered them in one of Farley's exhibitions. Her own *Views of the River at Dawn* had taken the first-place honors in that show. Burton had been furious when he left the hall that night. She could well imagine him returning to his gallery, his losing photographs under his arm. Very likely he had stormed in here and slammed the pictures onto the workbench with such force that the glass had shattered. He had never bothered to clean up the broken shards. Perhaps he had taken some perverse pleasure in looking at them every day, reminding himself just how much he hated a certain Mrs. Jones.

She turned away from the disquieting scene on the workbench. The toe of her shoe caught on an object that lay on the floor. A length of iron clattered on the wooden boards at her feet. The sound was unnaturally loud in the even more unnatural silence.

She froze, her heart pounding. *Calm yourself,* she thought. There is no way anyone outside this gallery could have heard that small noise.

After a few seconds, her pulse slowed. She glanced down and saw a long iron head clamp and stand. In the days of daguerreotypes and tintypes such devices had been widely used to secure the sitter so that he or she would not move while the picture was taken. The advent of newer, faster film mediums and improved cameras had rendered the clamps unnecessary from a technical point of view but many photographers still relied on them to keep a sitter perfectly still. It was always a great temptation to employ a head clamp when one was faced with taking the portrait of a restless little boy.

She crossed the room and opened a door. The reek of strong chemicals that had been stored too long in a badly ventilated space nearly knocked her over.

Trust Burton to ignore all of the sound advice in the photographic journals regarding the safe storage of his darkroom chemicals, she thought. No wonder he'd had that perpetual cough. He had probably locked himself in here for hours at a time, breathing the concentrated fumes in a small, confined space that had no provision for a healthy circulation of fresh air. She sighed. It was a common problem in a profession replete with hazards.

She held the door wide for a moment, letting the worst of the fumes dissipate, and then moved into the darkroom. The dim light angled into the small space, revealing the fixing tray and the bottles of chemicals.

Burton's equipment was shiny and quite new-looking, she noticed, and of the very best quality. Several of the bottles on the shelf were still unsealed.

The room was so dark that she almost failed to notice the wooden chest stored under the workbench. Crouching down, she opened it. Inside were several dry plate negatives.

She needed to examine only one to realize what she had found.

She never heard the telltale footfalls behind her. By the time a powerful male hand closed over her mouth, it was far too late to scream.

As she was hauled to her feet, she grabbed the only potential weapon that was available, a set of tongs used to remove prints from the chemical baths.

20

"Do not," Gabriel said into her ear, "make any loud noises."

She went limp with relief, nodded frantically and released her grip on the tongs.

He took his hand off her mouth and spun her around. In the shadows of the darkroom he looked very large and very annoyed.

"What the devil do you think you're doing here?" he asked in a voice that was much too soft. "I thought you were spending the day at the gallery."

She collected herself with an effort. "I should be the one asking you that question. I seem to recall that you were going to interview an elderly member of the Arcane Society this morning."

"I have already spoken with Montrose. I was on my way back to Sutton Lane when I decided to stop by this address instead."

"What did you expect to discover here?" she asked warily.

"I was curious to learn more about Burton."

"For heaven's sake, why? Surely his death is not connected to the missing formula."

Gabriel said nothing.

Something fluttered wildly in her stomach. "Is it?"

"The answer to that is perhaps not," he allowed.

She cleared her throat. "I cannot help but notice that the phrase *perhaps not* leaves some room for equivocation."

"As always, madam, you are extremely perceptive." He glanced at the wooden chest. "I see you found the negatives of the pictures he took of you."

"Yes."

"I went through them. With the exception of the cemetery monument inscribed with your name on it, they all appear to be quite innocuous. There are pictures of you coming out of a bakery and going into your gallery and chatting with a client, that sort of thing."

She shuddered. "Burton's envy must have inspired him to some sort of weird obsession with me."

"Personally, I'm starting to wonder if he really was that fixated on you," Gabriel said.

"What do you mean?"

"I find the fact that Burton had been following you about for several days and then managed to get himself murdered in close proximity to you last night troubling, to say the least."

"What?" The implications slammed through her. "Hold on, sir. Are you saying that Mr. Burton's death may be connected to me?"

"It is a possibility I cannot discount without further evidence."

"I hesitate to remind you, sir, but I am the only person we know thus far who had a motive to kill poor Burton. Given the fact that I did not do it, we must assume that someone else murdered him for some entirely unrelated reason."

"Perhaps."

"There is that word again," she said. "Where, pray tell, is the flaw in my argument?"

"Your reasoning is excellent, my sweet, but it relies upon a disturbing coincidence. I have never been fond of such explanations."

It irritated her to hear him call her *my sweet* in such an offhand manner. It was as if their association had progressed to the point where such familiarity was second nature.

He looked at her. "You have not yet told me why you chose to stop by this place and commit a small act of breaking and entering this morning."

She set her teeth together. "I didn't actually break anything. I merely fiddled around a bit with a hairpin and the door opened." She stopped suddenly. "How did you get in?"

"I did some fiddling, too." He nodded toward the door in the other room. "But I made certain to reset the lock after I was inside in order to forestall the possibility that someone might walk in on me unannounced."

"Good thinking," she said, struck by the logic. "I must remember that in future."

"In future," Gabriel said deliberately, "you will discuss any plans for this sort of activity with me before you execute them."

"Why would I do that?" she asked. "You would no doubt try to talk me out of them."

"In case you have not noticed, Mrs. Jones, this is an excellent way to get yourself arrested. That detective who interviewed us last night was not inclined to view you as a suspect in Burton's death but his view of things may shift if you are discovered in a situation like this."

"I was very careful not to be seen. In answer to your question, I came here because I was afraid that Burton might have taken other photographs of me and perhaps retouched them in ways that could prove embarrassing if they were to fall into the hands of my competitors."

"That thought occurred to me, too," he said. "Aside from the apparently harmless-looking negatives in that wooden chest, I found no other pictures of you."

"Thank goodness." She glanced up at the ceiling. "What about his lodgings?"

"Nothing of interest up there, either." He picked up the wooden chest and walked out of the darkroom. "Come, we will take these pictures with us and examine them more closely after we are both safely away from this place."

She trailed after him, intending to follow him to the back door. She stopped when she noticed the carton of dry plates standing on a nearby table. The manufacturer's name was familiar. She ordered her plates from the same firm.

"Now, that is interesting," she said half under her breath.

One hand on the doorknob, he watched her from across the room. "What is it?"

"From all accounts, Burton was barely

eking out a living with his photography, yet the equipment in the darkroom is quite new and expensive. What's more, that carton of plates is the largest size available from the manufacturer. It costs a considerable sum."

"Burton obviously took his work seriously. He no doubt invested what little money he did make in his supplies and equipment."

"From the rumors I heard, he did not command an income that would have allowed such extravagance." She tapped one toe on the floor and took another look around the room. "I wonder if he also bought a new camera?"

"There is a camera on a tripod in the other room," Gabriel said. "I did not take a close look at it."

She went into the front room of the shop. Burton had arranged a chair and a simple backdrop positioned to take advantage of what little light came through the grimy windows. One glance at the bulky camera on the tripod was sufficient.

"It is definitely an old model," she said, going back around behind the counter. "Apparently he was not making enough money to purchase a new one."

She stopped short at the sight of a hat

sitting on a shelf beneath the counter.

"Venetia, do not delay any longer," Gabriel said. "It is past time we both left this place."

"One more minute, sir, that is all I need." She picked up the hat. It was much heavier than any hat had a right to be.

"What the devil are you doing with that?" Gabriel asked, sounding reluctantly intrigued.

"On the occasions that I caught Mr. Burton watching me, he had this hat with him. But he always carried it under his arm. I never saw him put it on his head." She turned the hat upside down and smiled with satisfaction. "And this is the reason why."

"What have you got there?"

"A concealed camera." She held the hat so that he could see the device inside. "Quite new. Made by Crowder. He uses excellent lenses. This must have been very expensive."

"Damnation." Gabriel set down the wooden chest and took the hat camera from her. He examined it closely. "I've never seen anything like this."

"We in the profession refer to them as detective cameras. They are constructed in various secretive ways. I have seen cameras hidden inside vases and briefcases and other objects."

"So this was how he took those photographs of you without you knowing what he was about."

"Yes."

Gabriel set the hat camera down on the shelf, picked up the chest and started once more toward the rear door. "There is money to be made taking pictures in secret?"

"Yes," she said, following him. "Mind you, the detective camera work is still a limited sideline but I expect that, in time, it will grow into a major portion of the business."

"Who would pay to have clandestine pictures taken?"

"Only consider the possibilities, Mr. Jones. Imagine how many wives would pay to obtain pictures of their philandering husbands when the gentlemen in question are in the company of their mistresses. Then ponder, if you will, all of the suspicious husbands who fear that their wives might be meeting with other men. The financial potential is virtually unlimited."

"Has anyone ever remarked to you, Mrs. Jones, that you have a decidedly cynical view of marriage?"

"I prefer to think that I have a realistic view." She paused. "But at least I have answered the one question that was bothering me about Mr. Burton."

"You now know how he managed to purchase the new equipment and supplies."

"Yes. He went into the detective camera business."

Back in the little house on Sutton Lane, Venetia put the last of the negatives back into the wooden chest. She sat back in the chair behind the desk and looked at Gabriel.

"You were right, sir," she said. "With the exception of the one retouched negative, there is nothing remarkable about any of those photographs."

"Aside from the fact that they create a very precise record of your comings and goings and the people you have met with during the past several days," Gabriel said quietly. "Either Burton did, indeed, develop a very odd sort of obsession with your person or else someone employed him to watch you."

21

Amelia sat with Maud Hawkins, the young woman who managed the gallery, in a small room just off the main showroom. Together they studied the young man in the Roman-style toga who stood in front of them.

Maud was only a year older than Amelia. The daughter of a housekeeper and a butler, she was determined not to follow her parents into service. She had applied for the position in the Jones Gallery soon after it opened and had been hired immediately. Maud was intelligent, enthusiastic and she had a way with customers.

The man in the toga was named Jeremy Kingsley. He was the last of the three candidates who had responded to the advertisement in the newspaper. The first two had proved unsuitable but Jeremy had promise, Amelia decided. She could see that Maud felt the same.

Jeremy was tall and blond with riveting blue eyes and a strong, square jaw. He looked very handsome in the toga, if a trifle awkward. The garment revealed his muscular arms and a broad expanse of one powerful shoulder. Jeremy made his living in a livery stable. The years of pitching hay, handling large horses and maneuvering carriages had done wonders, Amelia thought.

She dragged her eyes away from Jeremy and made a note on a piece of paper. *Manly shoulders.* Venetia liked that sort of detail.

When she looked up she noticed that Maud was still staring at Jeremy as though he were a large and very tasty cream cake.

"Thank you, Mr. Kingsley," Amelia said. "That will be all for now. You may return to the dressing room and change into your regular clothes."

"Beggin' yer pardon, miss." Jeremy's noble brow creased with anxiety. "But will I do, miss?"

Amelia glanced at Maud.

"I think he'll do nicely," Maud said. "Looks very good in a toga, doesn't he?"

Jeremy gave her a grateful smile. Maud smiled back.

"I agree." Amelia put down her pencil and looked at Jeremy. "I do not see any reason why Mrs. Jones will not find you acceptable as Caesar, Mr. Kingsley. But you do understand that she will make the final decision herself, when she meets with you."

"Yes, miss. Thank you, miss." Jeremy was clearly thrilled. "I'll do my best to give satisfaction, I will."

"Very well," Amelia said, "Mrs. Jones will see you at three o'clock on the twenty-third. If she approves of you, she will photograph you at that time. The process will take at least two hours, quite possibly longer. Mrs. Jones is very particular about her photographs."

"I understand, miss."

"You must be prompt," Maud added. "Mrs. Jones is an extremely busy lady. She does not care to wait on her models."

"No need to fret on that account, miss," Jeremy said, heading toward the dressing room. "I'll be here on time."

He disappeared behind the heavy red-and-gold drapery that veiled the gentlemen's dressing room. A few minutes later when he reappeared, he was back in his ill-fitting, store-bought clothes. Amelia privately thought that the toga looked much better on him. She could see Maud felt the same.

Jeremy stammered a few more words of gratitude and rushed exuberantly outside into the street.

Amelia and Maud walked back into the showroom.

"I do believe that Mr. Kingsley will make a very fine Caesar," Amelia said.

"Yes, miss, he certainly will and that's a fact." Maud rubbed her hands together. "I expect sales will be even brisker than they were for Hamlet a few weeks ago. Something about a man in a toga, don't you agree?"

"Yes, but I must say, it will be difficult to surpass our Hamlet."

Amelia stopped in front of one of the framed prints displayed on the wall. The moody, exotically shadowed photograph was an intimate portrait of a very handsome man who looked out at the viewer with the seductive eyes of a romantic poet. His dark curly hair was tousled in a most interesting manner.

Hamlet wore a white shirt that was open partway down his chest, dark, close-fitting trousers and gleaming, high leather boots. He looked more like a dashing explorer than a doomed prince. He was shown lounging on a gilded chair, one booted leg stretched full-length in a pose that female customers seemed to find enormously affecting. One long-fingered hand was draped elegantly over the arm of the chair.

In the other hand he held a Yorick skull. It had not been easy turning up a human skull, Amelia reflected. Maud had finally managed to purchase a spare one from a small theater.

"Your notion of putting Hamlet in a shirt that was partly unfastened was nothing short of brilliant," Amelia said.

Maud smiled modestly, admiring the picture. "It just came to me out of the blue."

Amelia looked at the next portrait in line. It showed another extremely handsome young man dressed in the ancient Italian style. Locating a skull had been difficult, Amelia reflected, but finding a codpiece had been considerably more of a challenge. The effort had been worthwhile, however. Who could have imagined that female customers would find a man in a codpiece so fascinating?

"We can only hope that our Caesar does as well as our Hamlet," Amelia said. "But I expect that we will never again attain the degree of success that we've had with Romeo."

"He is still far and away our best seller," Maud agreed, studying the codpiece. "I sold twenty prints just last week alone. We shall have to make more soon."

"Well, it is Romeo, after all."

"By the way," Maud said, going behind the counter. "I got a message from a gentleman inquiring whether Mrs. Jones was available to take a photograph of his lady friend. I sent a message back scheduling the sitting for tomorrow. All of the particulars are in the appointment book."

"Thank you, Maud. Who is the client?"

"Lord Ackland," Maud said. "He wants Mrs. Jones to photograph a lady named Mrs. Rosalind Fleming."

22

"It must have come as a great shock to discover that your husband was still very much alive, Mrs. Jones." Rosalind Fleming's smile was cool and knowing. "One can only imagine the effect on the nerves of having a dead man show up on one's doorstep."

"Quite startling, certainly." Venetia pushed a small statue into a slightly different position beside Rosalind's chair and hurried back to her camera. "But one must adjust to life's little inconveniences and carry on, mustn't one?"

There was the tiniest of pauses.

"Inconveniences?" Rosalind murmured on a faint, questioning note.

Amelia, standing directly behind Rosalind with a parasol covered in a bright white fabric, made a quick, frantic little warning gesture with her hand.

Venetia got the message. Referring to the return of a spouse one had presumed gone for good as an *inconvenience* was probably somewhat inappropriate. She made a mental note to be more cautious in future.

If it wasn't one thing, it was another when one was dealing with clients. It was always difficult to concentrate on making casual conversation with a sitter when one was trying to organize the photograph. Nevertheless, it was a necessary part of the process. If one did not chat with the sitters they tended to become restive and tense.

It was not as though she did not have more than enough problems as it was, working outside of her greenhouse studio today.

Rosalind had made it plain that she was not particularly interested in having her photograph taken. She had explained that it was Lord Ackland's idea and that she was only acquiescing as a favor to him.

Nevertheless, like every other sitter over the age of five that Venetia had ever encountered, Rosalind was vain enough to want a flattering portrait. To that end, she had insisted upon being photographed in her own home, surrounded by some of her most costly possessions.

The dark blue evening gown she had chosen for the occasion was in the latest style: very French and very low at the neckline. She wore a fortune in jewelry. Diamonds glittered around her throat, dangled from her ears and glowed in her elaborately coiffed hair.

Rosalind had even selected the chair on which she would pose. It was heavily gilded and bore an unsettling resemblance to a throne.

The high-ceilinged room was as rich and elegant-looking as Rosalind herself. Antique urns and statues stood on marble pedestals. Claret-colored velvet curtains tied back with golden sashes pooled on the thick carpet.

Two hours ago Gabriel and Edward had helped load the necessary equipment, including the camera, plates, tripod, parasols and reflective shields, into a hired carriage. When the vehicle had rolled out into the street Venetia had chanced to look back. She saw Gabriel standing on the steps, looking quietly satisfied.

She had known then that he was distinctly pleased to have her occupied with her photography that morning. He had no doubt told himself that this way he could pursue his inquiries without having to wonder what she was doing. She knew that he was still annoyed about her visit to Burton's gallery yesterday.

Taking photographs in clients' homes was always a cumbersome business. Fortunately Rosalind's library was well lit with natural light. Nevertheless, it had required ages to get the illumination correct and it was clear that Rosalind was losing patience. The conversation had turned increasingly personal.

Venetia was starting to wonder if Rosalind was deliberately taunting her, perhaps as a means of relieving her boredom.

"No need to mince words with me, Mrs. Jones." Rosalind gave a throaty chuckle. "I was married myself at one time. I do not mind telling you that I am enjoying my widowhood vastly more than I did my marriage."

Venetia could not think of a suitable response to that comment so she stuck with a safer topic. "Would you please shift your right hand a degree or two left? Yes, that will do nicely. Amelia, move that parasol a little closer to Mrs. Fleming. I need more light on the left side of her face. I want to emphasize the elegance of her profile."

It never hurt to flatter the sitter, Venetia thought.

"Will this do?" Amelia asked, angling the parasol.

"Much better, thank you," Venetia said.

She looked through the viewfinder again.

This time she concentrated briefly, the way she always did just before she took a photograph.

Light and shadow reversed. Rosalind Fleming's aura flashed, pulsing with intense emotion.

Rosalind was not simmering with impatience, Venetia realized. She was simmering with rage.

Best to get this done as quickly as possible.

"Please hold still, Mrs. Fleming," Venetia said.

She took the picture. Every instinct was urging her to get out of Rosalind's house as quickly as possible but professional common sense held her back.

"It would be best to take a second picture, if you don't mind holding the pose, Mrs. Fleming."

"Very well, if you insist."

Venetia removed the exposed plate from the camera, inserted a fresh one and took another picture.

"Excellent," she said, relieved to be finished. "I think you will be quite pleased with the results."

"When will the prints be ready?" Rosalind asked, displaying little enthusiasm.

"I'm rather busy at the moment. But I

can have them ready for you the first of the week."

"I will send one of the servants for them," Rosalind said.

Venetia nodded at Amelia, who, evidently sensing the mounting tension in the atmosphere, had already begun to pack up the parasols, mirrors and reflective shields.

"I'll have the footman help you with your equipment," Rosalind said. She glided across the carpet to a dainty writing desk and tugged on the velvet bell pull.

"Thank you," Venetia muttered, removing her camera from the tripod.

"The thing about husbands is that they demand so much time and attention," Rosalind said, returning to the earlier conversation. "No matter how wealthy they are, they have an unpleasant tendency to complain about the money that one spends on such vital necessities as gowns and shoes. Mind you, they do not blink twice at the notion of purchasing expensive jewelry for their mistresses, but let a wife acquire even the smallest of baubles and there is no end of carping."

Venetia paused in the act of collapsing the tripod. "I beg your pardon, madam, but I think it would be best if we changed the subject. I'm sure you did not realize it, but my sister, Amelia, is only sixteen. One does not discuss these sorts of things in front of young ladies of that age."

Amelia made an odd, half-choked sound and pretended to be very busy with the reflective shields. Venetia knew that she was struggling to stifle a laugh.

"Forgive me," Rosalind said. She smiled her icy smile and studied Amelia as though she had not noticed her until now. "I had no notion she was so young. I must say, she seems quite mature for her age and very skilled at her work." She turned back to Venetia. "You have obviously taught her well. Tell me, Mrs. Jones, where did you learn your trade?"

Rosalind had just thrown down the gauntlet.

Venetia controlled her temper with an effort.

"Photography is both an art and a profession, as you know, Mrs. Fleming," she said smoothly. "My father gave me my first camera and instructed me in the basic techniques shortly before he died. I am fortunate in that my aunt is an excellent artist. I learned a great deal about composition and the use of light and shadow from her."

"I imagine Mr. Jones must have been

nothing short of astonished to discover that his wife had set herself up in the photography business while he was wandering around the Wild West with a case of amnesia."

"Mr. Jones," Venetia said evenly, "is a very modern-thinking sort of husband, quite advanced in his notions."

"Indeed? I did not know that there was any such creature as a *modern-thinking* husband."

The door to the library opened. A liveried footman appeared.

"Yes, madam?"

Rosalind motioned toward the stack of photographic paraphernalia. "You may convey that equipment back outside, Henry. Then summon a carriage for Mrs. Jones and her assistant."

"Yes, madam."

Henry bent to collect the tripod. Venetia put a protective hand on her precious camera.

"I'll carry the camera," she said.

"Yes, ma'am."

Loaded down with the gear, the footman started toward the door.

"One more thing, Henry," Rosalind said.

Henry paused. "Yes, madam?"

"I am aware that Mrs. Jones and her

sister were shown into this house through the front door, but you will see them out through the back entrance, the one used by the tradesmen. Is that quite clear?"

Henry turned a dark shade of red. "Uh, yes, ma'am."

Amelia's mouth fell open in stunned shock. She looked at Venetia for guidance.

Venetia had had enough. "Come along, Amelia."

She picked up the camera and went toward the door of the library. Amelia grabbed the parasols and hurried after her. Henry brought up the rear.

Venetia paused just short of the door and allowed Henry and Amelia to move past her out into the hall. When they were gone, she looked back at Rosalind.

"Good day, to you, Mrs. Fleming," she said. "It will be extremely interesting to see how your photograph turns out. My critics say that I have a gift for capturing the essence of a sitter's true character, you know."

Rosalind regarded her the way a viper regards a mouse it intends to devour whole.

"I expect nothing less than perfection from you, Mrs. Jones," she said.

Venetia smiled serenely. "Of course. I am an artist, after all."

She turned on her heel and went out into the dimly lit hall. Henry and Amelia stood waiting, uncertain and tense.

Venetia promptly turned to the right and started toward the front door. "This way, Amelia. Come along, Henry."

"Excuse me, ma'am," Henry whispered uneasily. "I'm sorry, ma'am, but the tradesmen's entrance is at the other end of the house."

"Thank you, Henry, but we are in a hurry to leave and it will be much quicker to use the front door," Venetia said. "We already know the way, you see."

Not knowing what else to do, Henry trailed helplessly after her, lugging the equipment.

At the end of the long hall Venetia paused and turned to look back along the shadowy length of the corridor. Rosalind, apparently realizing that her orders had been disobeyed, had emerged from the library. She stood in the gloom of the unlit passage.

"What do you think you are doing?" she said, tight-lipped with fury.

"Taking our leave through the front door, of course," Venetia replied. "We are professionals, after all."

On impulse, she concentrated hard for a

moment, letting her vision slide into the other spectrum again. Rosalind's aura snapped into focus, hot and erratic with the force of her rage.

She isn't just angry, Venetia thought, shaken. *She hates me.*

"There is one thing you should know, Mrs. Fleming," Venetia said, reverting to her normal vision. "We at the Jones Gallery pride ourselves on our retouching skills. Why, the most homely of persons can be made to appear stunningly attractive in a photograph." She paused for emphasis. "The process can, of course, be easily reversed."

It was a bold threat and a risky one. But she had never met a sitter who wanted to be made to appear unattractive in a photograph. Given Rosalind's lush beauty and obvious vanity, it seemed reasonably safe to assume that she would detest the idea of having a bad picture made of herself regardless of her sentiments toward the photographer.

Rosalind stiffened. "Use the front door if you must, Mrs. Jones. It does not alter the facts. You are nothing but a clever, scheming shopkeeper who has managed to capture the fancy of your betters with your photographic tricks and illusions. But the

Polite World will soon grow bored with you and turn elsewhere for amusement. Who knows? Perhaps one day you, too, will be driven to drink a glass of brandy laced with cyanide."

She whirled and stormed back into the library, slamming the door behind her.

Venetia caught her breath, aware that she was shaking. She could feel icy perspiration beneath the bodice of her gown. It took everything she had to compose her expression and walk the rest of the way into the front hall.

Amelia and Henry waited there. A maid was stationed at the door. She appeared nervous and bewildered. Venetia gave her a bright smile as she bore down on her.

"The door, if you please," she said briskly.

"Yes, ma'am." She leaped forward and yanked open the door.

Clutching her camera very tightly, Venetia sailed through the opening and out onto the front steps. Amelia was right behind her.

Henry lumbered after them, struggling with the photography equipment.

A cab stood at the end of the street, horse and driver dozing. Henry whistled loudly. The driver straightened in response and slapped the reins.

The vehicle rumbled to a halt in front of the town house. Henry loaded the equipment, handed Venetia and Amelia up inside the cab and shut the door.

The trapdoor opened in the roof of the cab. The driver looked down inquiringly.

"The Jones Gallery in Bracebridge Street, please," Venetia said.

"Aye, ma'am."

The trap closed.

There was a short, brittle stillness in the vehicle.

Then Amelia burst into a torrent of giggles. She laughed so hard she finally had to clap one gloved hand across her mouth.

"I cannot believe what you did back there," she finally managed to get out.

"I had no choice," Venetia said. "If we had allowed ourselves to be dismissed through the tradesmen's entrance the damage to our business would have been irreparable. It would have been only a matter of time before word got out that we were not considered exclusive enough to use the front door."

"I know. I must say, the way you threatened to have Aunt Beatrice retouch Mrs. Fleming's photograph to make her appear unattractive was a brilliant stroke."

"We can only hope the threat works."

"How can it fail?" Amelia widened her hands. "Even if she were to refuse to accept the picture, she would know that we possessed the negative. We could do anything we liked with it, including creating an unflattering portrait to display in the gallery for all the world to see. What a sensation that would cause."

"Unfortunately we can do no such thing. My threat was nothing but a bluff."

"What do you mean? Mrs. Fleming deserves such a fate after the way she spoke to you."

"Revenge may be sweet for a moment," Venetia said, "but it always comes back to haunt one. And in this case, it would be particularly dangerous. If we showed an unattractive picture of the obviously very beautiful Mrs. Fleming, other clients would think twice before employing me to do their portraits."

"For fear that they might end up appearing downright ugly." Amelia made a face. "Yes, I take your point. So much for revenge. Pity, though. Mrs. Fleming certainly deserves to be treated as rudely as she treated you."

Venetia looked out at the street. "The question is, why?"

"Why did she treat us rudely?"

"No. Why does she hate me? I saw her in the crowd at the exhibition the other night but we were not even introduced until today. What have I done to give her such an intense dislike of my person?"

23

Gabriel sat with Venetia and Beatrice in the small parlor that looked out on Sutton Lane.

A large pot of coffee provided by Mrs. Trench graced the table next to the sofa. Beatrice, glasses perched on her nose, was placing neat stitches in a yellow rose on an oval of linen secured in an embroidery frame.

Venetia drank her coffee in an absent manner. It was clear that the experience at Rosalind Fleming's town house had left her shaken and uneasy. The profession of photography contained a number of hazards, Gabriel thought. Well-connected clients who could destroy one's status with malicious gossip was obviously one of them.

"What I fail to understand," Venetia said, lowering her cup, "is why Mrs. Fleming agreed to be photographed by me in the first place."

"I would have thought that was quite obvious," Beatrice said. She examined the rose. “I believe that I will use a dark gold thread for the interior of the flower.”

Gabriel raised his brows at Venetia. She shook her head, very slightly, indicating she did not know what her aunt had meant, either.

He cleared his throat. “Miss Sawyer, do you mean to imply that Mrs. Fleming agreed to have her picture taken by Venetia because it was the fashionable thing to do?”

“No, of course not.” Beatrice rummaged around in her sewing bag, evidently searching for the dark gold thread. “There are a number of other fashionable photographers in London. It is obvious that Rosalind Fleming sat for a portrait by Venetia because she had no choice.”

“I beg your pardon?” Gabriel prompted.

Beatrice peered at him over the rims of her spectacles. “It was her paramour, Lord Ackland, who wanted the picture taken, if you will recall. He was the one who booked the sitting and he is the one who will pay for the finished photograph.”

Venetia’s teacup stilled in midair. Startled comprehension flashed across her face. “Yes, of course. You are right, Aunt Beatrice. I should have thought of that straight off.”

Gabriel looked at her and then switched his attention back to Beatrice. "Miss Sawyer, are you saying that Mrs. Fleming sat for her portrait merely to please her lover?"

"I am saying that she had no choice but to please him, Mr. Jones." Beatrice found her thread. "Perhaps, as a man, you do not comprehend the true nature of the relationship in which Rosalind Fleming is involved."

"There is nothing mysterious about the connection." He shrugged. "She is Ackland's mistress, according to Mr. Harrow."

"Indeed." Beatrice sighed. "A woman in Mrs. Fleming's position may pretend to the world that she has a degree of freedom that a married lady cannot dream of enjoying, but that is not the case. She is, in fact, just as constrained in many ways and certainly more vulnerable to the whims of the gentleman who is paying the bills."

Venetia looked at Beatrice with sudden understanding. "In other words, if Lord Ackland insisted upon commissioning a portrait for her, she had no alternative but to sit for it."

"To be successful as a mistress a woman must be clever, charming and fascinating at all times," Beatrice said. "She may fool herself into believing that she is the one manipulating the relationship but deep down there lurks the knowledge that if she does not satisfy her lover in every way, she can be replaced."

Gabriel raised his brows. "You make an excellent point, Miss Sawyer."

"But it does not fully explain why Mrs. Fleming took such an intense dislike of me," Venetia said, brows crinkling. "Granted, she may have been irritated by the fact that she had to take time out of her social rounds to sit for the picture. Nevertheless, her reaction seemed quite extreme."

"Not if you consider the difference in your positions," Beatrice said. "In fact, her dislike of you strikes me as eminently reasonable."

"How can you say that?" Venetia demanded. "I did nothing to offend her."

Beatrice's smile was a strange mix of wry amusement and resigned worldliness. "Don't you see, my dear? You offended her simply by being what you are, a woman who has become successful in her own right, one who does not need to depend upon a man to support her."

"Hah." Venetia made a face. "Judging by

her clothes and jewelry and the furnishings of her town house, she is doing far better from a financial standpoint as Ackland's mistress than I can ever hope to do with my photography."

"Yes, but she stands to lose it all tomorrow should Ackland take it into his head to cast her aside in favor of another mistress, doesn't she?" Beatrice said quietly. "In addition to the income, she would lose what she no doubt values most."

Gabriel folded his arms across his chest. "Her status in Society."

Beatrice nodded. "Precisely. Mrs. Fleming does not appear to have any important social or family connections of her own and no independent source of income. Society finds her beautiful and entertaining because the wealthy Lord Ackland does. But if he loses interest in her, or if he is so thoughtless as to drop dead tomorrow, the Polite World will snub her immediately. Her only hope in such a situation would be to find another gentleman who will keep her in the same style. In addition, the clock is always ticking for a woman in Mrs. Fleming's profession. She is not getting any younger, is she?"

"I suppose that is true." Venetia gave Gabriel a meditative look. "There was something else that struck me as odd, however. Mrs. Fleming spent a great deal of time taunting me about how unfortunate it was that my husband had returned from the grave. There were some rather pointed remarks to the effect that being a widow was vastly superior to being a wife."

Gabriel raised his brows. "I do hope you are not planning on doing me in a second time, Mrs. Jones. I understand from young Edward that I narrowly avoided being shot to death by outlaws and trampled by wild horses on the last occasion. Luckily, I was able to survive the fall into the canyon but if you concoct an even more diabolical plot, I may have some difficulty bouncing back."

She blushed. Her fine brows snapped together. "That is not amusing, sir. As it happens, I informed Mrs. Fleming that you were a very modern-thinking sort of husband who took an enlightened view of marriage."

He wondered how Venetia would react if she knew just how primitive his thoughts were when it came to her.

She made a face. "Unfortunately that information only served to outrage her all the more."

"Because you appear to enjoy the best of

both worlds, my dear," Beatrice said. "You have your independence and your career and a husband who is not alarmed by either of those conditions." She abruptly closed the embroidery bag and got to her feet. "Well, what is done is done. It was most unfortunate that Mrs. Fleming chose to take such a strong dislike of you, Venetia. We can only hope there will be no unpleasant repercussions."

Venetia set her cup and saucer down very carefully. "Do you think I was wrong to insist upon using the front door at Mrs. Fleming's house today, Aunt Beatrice?"

"Absolutely not." There was no trace of doubt in Beatrice's voice. "I told you when you first embarked upon a career as a photographer that if you ever once allow your clients to treat you as an inferior, the Jones Gallery would instantly lose its cachet. Now then, I must go and have a word with Mrs. Trench. I fear that since we now have a man in the house, she has gone quite mad and completely forgotten that there is a budget for food."

"My fault entirely, Miss Sawyer." Chagrined, Gabriel opened the door for her. "I should have considered that my presence here was inflicting additional costs on the household. I have been occupied with other matters. Rest assured that I will make a contribution to your budget this very afternoon."

"You will do no such thing," Beatrice said. "You are a guest and as such you are not expected to pay for your room and board."

"Ah, but I am not a guest, madam. I am well aware that I have imposed myself upon you. I will cover the costs of my lodgings."

"If you insist," Beatrice said with the air of a lady reluctantly granting a great favor.

"I do, madam."

She gave him a benign smile and swept out of the room.

It was then that Gabriel realized that the casual mention of the strains he was placing on the household budget had not been quite as offhand as it had been made to appear.

He closed the door and turned to see a small, knowing smile tugging at the corners of Venetia's mouth.

"She could have simply asked me for the money," he said dryly.

Venetia shook her head. "Impossible. Aunt Beatrice is far too proud. But I had a hunch that sooner or later she would bring up the subject of the household budget.

My aunt was a governess for many years. It is a notoriously low-paid profession that instills in one an acute awareness of finances."

He went to the window and stood looking out into the tree-shaded lane. "Discovering that Mr. Cleeton, your father's man of affairs, had run off with the money that should have come to all of you after your parents died no doubt brought back a lot of her old anxieties regarding finances."

There was a short silence behind him.

"Edward told you about Mr. Cleeton?" she asked finally.

"Yes. He also informed me that your father was a bigamist."

"I see." There was another long pause. "You and Edward appear to have become quite close in a very short period of time."

He turned back to look at her. "You must not blame your brother for confiding in me, Venetia. Edward did not mean to break any confidences. It was his understanding that in my role as your husband, I am now a party to your family's secrets. He assumes that I am another member of the cast of actors in this play that you are all performing with such grand success."

"How can I possibly blame him?" She

sighed. "Poor Edward. We have placed a great burden on his small shoulders. I know it weighs very heavily upon him at times."

"You must know as well as I do that the secrets that you have asked Edward to hold fast are not nearly as dreadful as some."

"I suppose that is true." Her mouth tightened. "Aunt Beatrice has told me some tales from her days as a governess that are the stuff of nightmares. She said that there were goings-on in some of the so-called respectable households where she was employed that were so dreadful she was forced to resign her post on more than one occasion."

"I can well believe it. There is no need to worry about Edward. He will survive his burden. But in the meantime, it might be wise to allow him a bit more freedom. He has expressed a wish to go to the park and fly kites and play games with other boys."

"I know. We do take him to the park as often as possible but Aunt Beatrice is terrified that if he makes friends with boys his own age he will inadvertently reveal the truth about Papa."

"I do not think you need be concerned on that point. There are secrets in every family and children are astonishingly good at keeping them."

She blinked as though he had said something that caught her by surprise. Her eyes narrowed very faintly in a way that he was starting to recognize.

He smiled. "Are you trying to make out my aura?"

She blushed. "You could tell?"

"Yes. You are wondering if I have a few family secrets of my own, aren't you?"

"The thought did cross my mind."

"The answer, of course, is yes. Doesn't everyone? But as my secrets do not represent a threat to you or your family, I trust you will allow me to keep them."

She turned an even brighter shade of pink. "For heaven's sake, I did not mean to pry."

"Yes, you did, but we will let that go for now. We have other, more pressing problems."

"One of which," she said, recovering her composure, "may prove to be Mrs. Fleming."

He propped one shoulder against the wall and folded his arms. "I do not think she will dare to cause you too much trouble. Not as long as Ackland is an admirer of your art. He may be a doddering old fool but he is the source of her finances. As your aunt just pointed out, no one knows that better than Mrs. Fleming."

"You did not see what I saw when I looked at her through the eye of the camera this afternoon."

"You perceived her aura?"

"Yes. I did not tell Aunt Beatrice because I knew she would only worry, but the truth is, I do not think that what Mrs. Fleming feels for me is mere envy or even dislike. She *hates* me. It is as if she believes that I am standing between her and something she wants very badly, as if she views me as a direct threat. That simply makes no sense."

He felt everything inside him tighten. "The more you explain her reaction to me, the more I am inclined to agree. Perhaps we should try to find out a little more about Rosalind Fleming. Harrow seemed somewhat acquainted with her history."

"Harrow knows a great deal about almost everyone in Society," Venetia said, brightening. "And what information he does not already possess, he knows how to uncover. I will send a message to him immediately. I'm sure he will assist me."

"Very well." This was all he needed, he thought. One more convolution in an already overly convoluted mystery.

Venetia looked at him. "Have you had any word from Mr. Montrose yet?"

"I went to see him while you were taking Mrs. Fleming's photograph. Like me, he cannot see anything unusual or meaningful about the list of herbs on the strongbox lid, or the leaf design. In addition, the names of those I found interesting at Farley's exhibition, including one in particular named Willows, have proved to be unlikely suspects for one reason or another."

"What will you do next?"

"I have asked him to concentrate on the names of those members of the Arcane Society who have died in the past few years."

"Why are you interested in members who are deceased?" she asked.

"It occurred to me today that perhaps the man I am hunting is no longer a member of the society because he is no longer among the living."

She stilled. "What do you mean?"

"I faked my own death because I wanted to create confusion in the mind of my opponent. What if he has done the same?"

"I sense more secrets, Mr. Jones."

He smiled. "You must possess psychical powers, Mrs. Jones."

24

The response from Harrow was gratifyingly swift. The note and a package arrived at the back door of the house in Sutton Lane at five o'clock that afternoon. Venetia tipped the young boy who had delivered the items and then carried the package and the note upstairs.

When she arrived on the landing, Gabriel's voice halted her in mid-stride.

"What have you got there?" he asked from the shadows of the attic stairs.

She looked up holding the box very tightly and watched him come toward her. The man did have a knack for appearing just when one wished he would be occupied elsewhere, she mused.

"I received a note from Harrow saying that he has found someone who can help me with information about Mrs. Fleming. Harrow has arranged for me to meet the person this evening."

"I see." Gabriel stopped in front of her. He, too, carried a package. It was tucked under his arm, wrapped in brown paper and oddly shaped. "What time will you be leaving?"

"Harrow says that I am to arrive at nine."

Gabriel nodded. "I will accompany you."

"It won't be necessary to change your plans," she said quickly.

"It is no trouble."

"I assure you, I will be quite safe."

"I realize that Harrow is your friend and no doubt trustworthy, but I must insist on accompanying you, especially since you are not personally acquainted with the individual you will be meeting."

She hugged her package tighter. "Sometimes you sound distressingly like a *real* husband, sir, one of those who is *not* a modern thinker."

"I am crushed by your poor opinion but I shall endeavor to carry on." He lounged against the railing and glanced casually at the box she carried. "Not that you are an expert in the matter of how real husbands act."

Anger flashed through her. "If you are implying that because my father was not legally married to my mother I do not know anything of proper husbandly behavior —"

He winced. "I meant nothing of the

kind. I was referring to the fact that you have never been married, yourself."

"Oh." She relaxed. Curiosity replaced the momentary outrage. "What of yourself, sir?"

"No, Venetia, I have never had a wife. Given our lack of mutual experience, I feel we are doing rather well at the business of marriage, don't you? Which is not to say that there are not some areas of our association that could stand improvement." He indicated the box she held. "A gift?"

"The clothes that I will wear this evening."

"A new gown? I hope it is not solid black. If you do not move out of mourning soon, people will begin to think that you are not pleased to have your husband back."

"Black has become my hallmark, sir." She looked at his package. "Where are you off to?"

"I have an appointment in the park with your brother."

25

"It is the most beautiful kite in the world, sir." Entranced, Edward gazed upward. "Look how high it is now. Higher than any of the other kites."

Gabriel studied the soaring paper wing he had purchased earlier that day. The kite had caught the wind eagerly, delighting Edward, who had quickly mastered the technique of handling the string. The boy was intelligent, Gabriel thought, like everyone else in the Milton family.

"Better reel it in a bit," he advised. "We don't want it to snag on those trees."

"Yes, sir." Edward concentrated hard on easing the kite down.

Satisfied that the kite was under control, Gabriel took the opportunity to study the lightly crowded park. Several of the benches were occupied by nannies and governesses garbed in dreary gowns. They chatted among themselves while their charges played simple games. The older boys flew kites or played hide-and-seek in the trees.

He had assumed that there would be few adult males in the vicinity. He had been right. Those who were present appeared to be older brothers, uncles or fathers who had accompanied their younger male family members.

The man in the dull brown coat and trousers stood out for the simple reason that he was alone. He occupied one of the benches, his low-crowned hat pulled down over his eyes. From a distance he appeared to be watching a group of boys play with a ball.

Half an hour later Edward reluctantly brought the kite back to earth. Gabriel showed him how to pack it up so that the string and tail did not become tangled.

"That was great fun, sir." Edward grinned. "My kite was the best one in the park today. It flew better than anyone else's and it never crashed into the trees."

"You did an expert job of controlling it." Out of the corner of his eye Gabriel watched the man on the bench get to his feet and amble slowly after them.

They all walked back to Sutton Lane, Brown Coat trailing at a discreet distance. When Gabriel and Edward arrived at the front door Mrs. Trench opened it.

"There you are, Master Edward." She

smiled at him. "Did you enjoy the kite-flying expedition?"

"Very much." Clutching the kite carefully in both hands, Edward looked up at Gabriel. "Thank you, sir. Do you think we might go back to the park again soon?"

Gabriel ruffled his hair with one hand. "I don't see why not."

"And perhaps play cards some evening? Amelia and I are very good at card games."

"I'll look forward to it."

Edward glowed brighter than a gas lamp and hurried off toward the stairs.

Gabriel looked at Mrs. Trench. "Please tell Mrs. Jones that I'll be back shortly. I have some business to attend to."

"Yes, sir. She's in the parlor. I'll let her know."

He went back down the front steps and walked along the street at a swift, purposeful pace. Brown Coat would have to hurry to keep him in sight, he thought.

At the corner, he turned abruptly to the right. In the brief time that he was certain that Brown Coat could not see him, he ducked into a narrow walk that led to the service entrance between two ranks of town houses. He flattened himself against the wall and waited.

Brown Coat dashed past the opening

looking extremely anxious a moment later. Gabriel seized him by the arm, dragged him into the narrow passage and slammed him up against the brick wall.

"Bloody hell, what do you think yer doing?" Brown Coat yelped. His eyes widened when he saw the pistol in Gabriel's hand.

"Why are you following me?" Gabriel asked.

"See here, I don't know what yer talking about." Brown Coat was unable to take his eyes off the pistol. "I swear it."

"In that case you are not of much use to me, are you?"

Brown Coat's mouth went slack. "You can't shoot me."

"Why not?"

"You've got no right. I'm an innocent man."

"Explain to me how innocent you are."

"I'm just going about my daily business." Brown Coat squared his shoulders. "I'll have you know I'm a photographer, sir."

"I don't see any camera."

"Photographers don't always walk around with a camera in hand."

"That is true enough. I have discovered that sometimes they walk around with cameras disguised as hats." Gabriel eyed

Brown Coat's low-crowned head gear. He reached up and removed it. There was no camera inside.

"Now, see here," Brown Coat squawked. "You can't just —"

A figure moved at the entrance to the walk.

Gabriel and Brown Coat both turned their heads. Gabriel felt a rush of annoyance at the interruption. Brown Coat looked pathetically hopeful of rescue.

"Mr. Jones?" Venetia walked briskly forward. The skirts of her black gown were hooked up so they would not sweep the paving stones. "What on earth is going on here? Mrs. Trench said that you had some business to see to but I had a strong suspicion that you were up to something secretive."

"You know me so well, my sweet."

Somewhat belatedly she noticed the gun. *"Mr. Jones."*

Gabriel sighed. "You really are going to have to start calling me by my given name one of these days, my sweet." He nodded at Brown Coat. "Do you know this man?"

"Yes, of course." She inclined her head graciously. "Good day to you, Mr. Swinden."

Swinden touched his hat nervously.

"Mrs. Jones. You're looking lovely, as always. You positively glow in black."

"Thank you." She turned to Gabriel, steely-eyed. "What is this about?"

"I was just asking Swinden the same question," Gabriel said. "He followed Edward and me to the park, hung around while we did some kite flying and then he followed us home. I found myself somewhat curious."

"It's all a terrible misunderstanding, Mrs. Jones." Swinden appealed to Venetia. "I happened to be in the vicinity, you see, getting a bit of fresh air, and Mr. Jones, here, evidently leaped to the conclusion that I was spying on him."

"Forgive me, Mr. Swinden," Venetia said, "but I find myself making the same assumption. You do not live in this part of town."

Swinden cleared his throat. "Client in the neighborhood."

"What address?" Gabriel asked.

Swinden's face went blank. "Uh —"

"There is no client," Gabriel said.

"Got lost trying to find the address," Swinden muttered.

He appeared decidedly braver now. Venetia's presence had given him confidence, Gabriel thought. Swinden was no doubt convinced that he was safe as long as she was around.

"In that case," Gabriel said, taking his arm, "allow me to escort you back to a more familiar part of town. I know a shortcut. It takes one through a rather dangerous neighborhood and involves some rather remote alleys and a tour of the docks, but never fear, I have my gun."

"No." Swinden was horrified. "I'm not going anywhere alone with you. Don't let him take me away, Mrs. Jones. I beg you."

"Perhaps you should just answer his questions," Venetia said gently. "If you do, I promise I will not let Mr. Jones hurt you."

Gabriel raised his brows but refrained from comment.

Swinden seemed to collapse in on himself. "I just wanted to see if you had discovered the name of Burton's new client. You cannot blame me."

Anticipation flashed through Gabriel. "What client?"

Swinden heaved a resigned sigh. "Some time back Burton decided to expand his business. He never did have much luck with the art world or portraits, you know. But a fortnight or so back he started sporting a very nice detective camera. I asked him how he'd managed that feat. Said he'd got a very wealthy client who had hired him to follow someone around and take some pictures."

"He told you about his new line of work?" Gabriel asked.

Swinden nodded. "Burton was quite proud of his new success. Bragged about it."

"Were you a friend of his?"

Swinden was briefly baffled by that question.

"Burton didn't have what you'd call friends," he said judiciously. "But I reckon I was the next best thing as far as he was concerned. Known each other for as long as we've both been in the photography business. We were partners together back at the start. Made a fair living doing spirit photography for a time."

"I understand that end of the business was once quite profitable," Venetia said.

"It was, indeed." Swinden turned wistful. "For a number of years it seemed that everyone wanted a picture of himself that showed a spirit hovering in the background. Burton and I were very good at our work, if I do say so. Never once got caught. Unfortunately there were too many inexperienced practitioners in the field of spirit photography. They were always getting themselves exposed as frauds. Gave the whole business a bad reputation and eventually the public lost faith."

"I would be interested to know some of the techniques you used to produce spirit photographs," Venetia said, turning conversational. "I have done some experimenting on my own and produced some interesting results but I have never been entirely satisfied."

It dawned on Gabriel that this was sounding less like an interrogation and more like a pair of photographers exchanging observations about the profession. He gave Venetia a warning look. She did not appear to notice.

"There are a variety of ways to put a spirit into a picture," Swinden said, metamorphosing into a Learned Expert. "The trick is to make certain that the client does not discover that the final result is an illusion, of course. Burton and I were good enough to impress even the most skeptical of psychical researchers. Had 'em lined up at the door some days."

Gabriel slid one booted foot slightly forward, putting himself between Swinden and Venetia. Both jumped back a little as though surprised to find him still present.

"Now, see here," Swinden muttered indignantly. "I was just answering the lady's questions."

"I prefer that you answer my questions, instead," Gabriel said.

Burton blinked several times and tried to press his back into the bricks. "Certainly, sir."

"What broke up your partnership with Burton?" Gabriel asked.

"Money, naturally." Swinden gave a sad little shake of his head. "Couldn't agree on how to make it or spend it. Argued day and night. Worse than being married, it was. Then Burton developed a little gambling problem. That was the end, as far as I was concerned. I went my way and he went his."

"But you kept in touch."

"Like I said, we had been acquainted a long time."

"Do you know the name of the person Burton was paid to follow?" Gabriel said.

"No," Swinden said quickly. Too quickly. His eyes darted to Venetia and then slid away.

"The subject was Mrs. Jones, wasn't it?" Gabriel asked.

Venetia stiffened. She rounded on Swinden.

"You knew that Mr. Burton was taking clandestine photographs of me?" she demanded.

Swinden started to look nervous again. "Burton dropped a few hints in that direction. Never came right out and said your name, you understand. But I took his meaning. I'm afraid the commission gave him a certain amount of satisfaction. I regret to say that he did not hold you in high esteem, Mrs. Jones."

"Yes," Venetia said through her teeth. "I was aware of that."

"Not your fault," Swinden said hastily. "Burton was very contemptuous of the fair sex, in general. Developed a particular dislike of you after you appeared on the scene and took first prize in that exhibition that he had entered."

Gabriel studied Swinden. "It did not occur to you to warn Mrs. Jones that Burton was following her around, taking pictures of her with his detective camera?"

"Didn't want to get involved," Swinden said. "None of my affair."

"Did you know that in addition to taking pictures for this mysterious client, Burton took some for his own personal use?" Gabriel continued softly. "Pictures that he used to try to frighten Mrs. Jones?"

"Uh, well, now that you mention it," Swinden mumbled, "I believe Burton did tell me that the commission had given him an idea of how to put a bit of a scare into Mrs. Jones. Said he'd taken a couple of photographs involving a cemetery theme and retouched one in particular in a way that would rattle your nerves, Mrs. Jones. But I'm sure it was just a joke as far as he was concerned."

Venetia narrowed her eyes. "Some joke."

Swinden sighed. "Like I said, he was most annoyed with you, ma'am."

Gabriel watched him for a moment. "Those two pictures had nothing to do with his work for the client?"

Swinden shook his head. "Don't think so. I gathered it was a little something he was doing to amuse himself on the side while he was following the lady around."

"Continue with your tale, Swinden," Gabriel said.

"Not much more to tell." Swinden scrunched up his face. "When I read about Burton's death in the morning papers I realized straightaway what had happened, of course. Knew he hadn't taken his own life."

Venetia frowned. "You believed that he had been murdered?"

"Perfectly understandable," Swinden assured her.

Outraged comprehension lit Venetia's face. "You think I killed Mr. Burton, don't you?"

"No, no, Mrs. Jones, I swear —"

"For heaven's sake, I did not murder the poor man," she snapped.

"Of course not, Mrs. Jones," Swinden said quickly. "Don't worry, I wouldn't dream of spreading that kind of gossip."

"A wise decision," Gabriel said. "That sort of gossip can get a man deposited into the river some dark night."

Swinden jerked back in alarm. "I say, you've no call to threaten me."

"Perhaps not, but I find it vastly entertaining," Gabriel said. "As it happens, I'm inclined to believe you when you say that you don't think that Mrs. Jones poisoned Burton, however."

"Thank you, sir." Swinden was clearly relieved.

"You think that I am the one who gave Burton the cyanide in the brandy," Gabriel concluded softly.

Swinden reddened. "It was only the merest conjecture on my part, I assure you. Wouldn't dream of mentioning it to anyone."

Venetia's lips parted in shock. "What on earth?" She glowered at Swinden. "I was the one Mr. Burton had followed around with his detective camera. Why would you think that Mr. Jones murdered him?"

"I can answer that for you, my sweet." Gabriel did not take his eyes off Swinden. "It was hardly a secret that I had only just returned to London and the arms of my loving bride. Swinden, here, naturally supposed that, upon discovering me on your doorstep, you collapsed, distraught, and confided to me that a man named Burton was causing you a great deal of distress. I, of course, immediately set out to protect you and myself from potential scandal by getting rid of Burton at the earliest opportunity. That happened to be that very night of Farley's exhibition."

"As I said," Swinden muttered, "it was just a theory."

"You then concluded," Gabriel continued, "that, after giving Burton a stiff dose of cyanide, I somehow discovered the name of Burton's mysterious wealthy client."

Swinden coughed slightly. "Perfectly reasonable thing to do."

Venetia looked at him, baffled. "Why would Mr. Jones want the name of Mr. Burton's anonymous client?"

"Because, having no way of knowing that it was the client who was the one who had hired Burton to follow you around, I would, of course be quite eager to make contact with him and offer him your services in place of Burton's," Gabriel explained patiently. "You are, after all, in the photography business, my sweet. Why shouldn't we take advantage of Burton's sudden demise to sell your professional skills to his generous new client?"

"*We?*" Venetia repeated in ominous tones.

Gabriel ignored that. He turned back to Swinden. "You decided that if you spied upon me for a while, sooner or later I would lead you to the unknown client. Once you knew his identity, you planned to go to him and let him know, for a small gratuity, that I had very likely murdered Burton and might prove quite dangerous if it got out that a certain person had hired Burton to take photographs of Mrs. Jones."

"Why, that would be blackmail," Venetia exclaimed.

Swinden cringed. "Mrs. Jones, I assure you, I never intended to blackmail anyone."

"Bah, I do not believe that for one moment," Venetia said. "Your plans to set yourself up in business as an extortionist aside, Mr. Swinden, how dare you assume that now that I have acquired a husband I am no longer capable of managing my own affairs?"

Swinden went from appearing nervous and alarmed to looking quite befuddled. "But Mr. Jones is back. Surely he will be keeping an eye on your business now."

She took a step toward him, fitting her hands to her hips. "I am the proprietor of the Jones Gallery. I make all the decisions connected with it. I assure you that I do not rely upon Mr. Jones or any other man to get rid of obnoxious competitors."

"No, no, of course not." Swinden edged sideways along the wall, trying to put some distance between himself and Venetia.

"I did not kill Burton." She gave him a charmingly menacing smile. "However, if at some point in the future it should become necessary to take such drastic action against a competitor, you must believe me when I tell you that I am fully prepared to handle matters myself. One does not require a husband for that sort of thing, sir."

Swinden paled. "I do not see us as competitors, Mrs. Jones. Indeed, we move in entirely different circles in the photographic world."

"Indeed we do, sir." Venetia swept out her arm, aiming toward the street. "Go, immediately. I do not want to ever again see you anywhere in the vicinity of either myself or Mr. Jones."

"Understood, madam. Understood."

Swinden fled down the walk.

Venetia waited until he vanished around the corner of the building before turning back to confront Gabriel.

"What an absolutely infuriating little man," she said.

He smiled. "You were very impressive, my sweet. Very impressive, indeed. I do not believe that you will have any more trouble from that quarter."

"Tell me the truth, sir. Do you think that everyone in Society is currently under the impression that because I have accidentally acquired a husband I am no longer in charge of my own affairs? That I am no longer capable of making important decisions? That I now look to you for guidance in all things?"

"In a word, yes."

"I was afraid of that."

Gabriel put the gun back into the pocket of his overcoat. "I regret to say that, in the eyes of Society, you have been transformed from a dashing, mysterious widow into a dutiful, trusting wife who, quite naturally, looks to her husband for direction in all matters of a critical nature."

She closed her eyes. "You cannot begin to imagine how maddening that is." Her lashes lifted. "Mrs. Fleming was right. There is a great deal to be said for widowhood."

"Do try to remember that I am a very *modern-thinking* sort of husband."

"That is not amusing, Mr. Jones."

"Neither is this latest development," he said. He stopped smiling. "We now know for certain that Burton was not following you around for his own purposes, at least not entirely. Someone hired him to do so."

"The thief who stole the formula?"

"I suspect that is the case." He took her arm and started toward the street. "I would remind you that he is not merely a thief. He is also a murderer who has killed at least twice."

26

"Wait until you see Venetia in her evening clothes, sir." Edward could barely contain himself. "You will be amazed."

Gabriel contemplated the boy in the dressing table mirror. Edward was fairly bursting with excitement. He and Amelia had been very secretive throughout dinner, exchanging furtive grins and once or twice erupting in giggles. Beatrice had attempted to quell them with a few admonishing looks but she had been largely unsuccessful.

Venetia had pretended to ignore the undercurrents at the table. She had excused herself to go upstairs to dress for the meeting with Harrow's friend as soon as Mrs. Trench had removed the dessert course.

Edward and Amelia had gone into the parlor to play cards, leaving Beatrice alone with Gabriel in the dining room. Beatrice had crumpled her napkin and placed it on the table.

"Perhaps we should take a moment to discuss the rather unusual situation in which we find ourselves, Mr. Jones," she said.

"You are naturally concerned about Venetia." He folded his arms on the table. "Rest assured, I will see to it that she does not come to harm because of this affair of the formula."

"It is not only the business of the missing formula that worries me, sir."

"I sincerely regret that I have brought trouble to this household, Miss Sawyer."

Beatrice frowned. "I am well aware that you are not the one who created this unfortunate situation. It was Venetia who chose to use the last name of Jones, after all."

"She had no way of knowing the risks involved. I assure you that I am doing my best to repair matters."

"And when you have finished repairing matters, Mr. Jones? What happens then?"

He rose and went down the long length of the table to pull out her chair. "I'm not sure I comprehend your question, madam."

Beatrice got to her feet. "You seem to forget, sir, that in the eyes of the world, you are my niece's husband."

"Trust me, I am well aware of that fact."

Her brows rose. "Well then, how do you

propose to fix that little problem when this business is concluded?"

"I admit that my fate is still somewhat unclear. Fortunately for me, however, there are very few herds of wild horses running around London. There is still, of course, a risk of being gunned down by a gang of Wild West outlaws but I have every expectation of avoiding that outcome as well."

"What outcome do you anticipate, Mr. Jones?"

"I am hoping that I will be able to convince Venetia to make our marriage real."

Surprise lit her expression. She searched his face. "Are you sincere, sir?"

"Yes." He smiled slightly. "Do you wish me luck, madam?"

She contemplated him for a long moment.

"I believe I do," she said eventually. "You will need it. Venetia is not inclined to place a great deal of trust in men. Her father's doing, I'm sorry to say. She loved him dearly and he loved her. Indeed, he loved all of his children. But there is no getting around the fact that when all was said and done H. H. Milton lived a double life. This family has paid dearly for his bigamous actions and his lies."

"I understand."

* * *

Edward moved closer to the dressing table to watch Gabriel knot the bow tie. "Venetia told us that we must not tell you what she will be wearing tonight because it is to be a surprise. But she did not say that you could not try to guess."

"Let's see." Gabriel slipped a black and gold cuff link through the opening of one cuff. "She has decided to wear some color other than black?"

That seemed to confuse Edward. Then his face cleared. "There will be some black in her attire."

"But not all black?"

Edward shook his head, looking sly. "There will be another color, as well."

"Green?"

"No."

"Blue?"

Edward giggled. "No."

"Red?"

Edward collapsed on the bed, laughing. "You will never guess, sir."

"Then I may as well give it up and prepare to be amazed." Gabriel turned away from the mirror and collected his evening coat and hat. "Ready?"

"Yes, sir."

Edward flew to the door, yanked it open

and pelted down the stairs. Gabriel followed at a more sedate pace, savoring the prospect of the evening that lay ahead. True, he and Venetia were going out together for the sole purpose of discussing Rosalind Fleming with Harrow's unknown acquaintance. And there was no getting around the fact that they still confronted a great deal of mystery and danger. Nevertheless, he was going to be alone in a carriage with Venetia for an extended period of time tonight and she had purchased a new gown for the occasion. The knowledge made the blood beat more heavily in his veins.

When he reached the bottom of the staircase he found Edward and Amelia in the front hall. Expectation hummed in the air. The pair darted sly glances in his direction. This family was expert at keeping secrets, he thought, amused. But evidently the mystery of Venetia's new gown was almost too much for Edward and Amelia.

"I heard the carriage at the front door," Beatrice called from the landing. "Venetia, dear, it is time to leave."

"I'm ready, Aunt Beatrice," Venetia announced from the vicinity of her bedroom.

Gabriel heard her on the stairs before he caught sight of her. He barely had time to register the fact that there was something decidedly unusual about the sound of her footsteps when she came into view.

"Good evening, Mr. Jones." She gave him an approving, head-to-toe examination. "I must say, you make your tailor proud."

He was acutely aware that Edward and Amelia were both holding their breath, waiting for his shocked reaction to the sight of Venetia.

He gave her the same deliberate examination that she had given him, taking in the excellently cut black trousers, white linen shirt, bow tie and black evening coat.

"You must give me the name of your tailor, Mrs. Jones," he said. "I do believe he may be even more skilled than my own."

Venetia laughed. "Let us be off, sir. The night is young."

She clapped her tall hat on top of her short, dark-haired wig, twirled a carved walking stick in a rakish manner and descended the remaining stairs.

Mrs. Trench appeared from the direction of the kitchen, wiping her hands on her apron. She shook her head when she saw Venetia.

"Not again," she said, sounding resigned. “I thought that now that there was a man in the house we would be done with this sort of foolishness.”

Edward sprang to open the front door. Venetia went outside and down the steps to the waiting carriage.

Gabriel started through the doorway after her.

“Were you amazed, sir?” Edward demanded eagerly.

“One of the things that I most admire about your sister is that she never ceases to surprise me,” Gabriel said.

The door closed behind him. Edward and Amelia’s muffled laughter pursued him all the way down the steps.

27

"Congratulations, Mr. Jones," Venetia said. "You dealt with the shock very well. I suspect Edward and Amelia are quite disappointed by your failure to faint dead away at the sight of a lady in gentleman's attire."

Gabriel lounged into the corner of the cushions and looked at Venetia. She was seated across from him. The carriage lamps were turned down low, cloaking them both in shadow.

"The disguise is very good," he allowed. "You even managed to alter your walk somewhat. Your hair is well concealed beneath that wig. But you cannot camouflage your scent. I would recognize you anywhere, anytime, on the darkest night."

"But I used a cologne that is blended especially for gentlemen."

He smiled. "It is not your cologne that is locked in my memory. It is the essence of you and that essence is very, very female."

She frowned. "I am quite certain that no one realized that I was a woman when I wore these clothes on previous occasions."

"How often do you go out dressed as a man?"

"I have only done so twice," she confessed. "The clothes belong to Harrow. He had them altered to fit me. He also purchased the wig and had it styled to suit me."

"The masculine attire is very interesting on you but may I ask why you felt it necessary to dress as a gentleman this evening?"

"We are going to meet Harrow and his friend at their club. I would not be admitted if I arrived at the door garbed as a lady. You know how it is with gentlemen's clubs."

He would not have described his reaction as shocked, he decided, but he was certainly surprised by that bit of information. "You have been to this gentlemen's club before?"

"On one other occasion," she said blithely. "The second time I wore these clothes, Harrow and I attended the theater together and afterward enjoyed a late dinner at a restaurant." She smiled. "The establishment was one where no respectable lady would have allowed herself to be seen. It was a very educational experience, I assure you."

"You do this for a lark?"

"I find it to be an intriguing adventure," she said. "Have you any notion of how astonishingly different the world appears when you walk through it as a man?"

"I had not given the subject much thought."

"A woman is so much freer when she goes about as a gentleman. It is not just the clothes, although you may believe me when I tell you that trousers and a coat are far less cumbersome and restrictive than even the lightest of summer walking dresses. Why, I could run quite easily in these garments if it proved necessary. Have you ever tried to run in a long gown?"

"Can't say that I have had the experience."

"Trust me, it is extremely difficult. The skirts and petticoats are so heavy. They tend to become tangled around one's ankles. And you cannot imagine how even the smallest of bustles affects one's balance when one is in full flight."

"When did you find it necessary to run in a gown?"

Her teeth flashed in a knowing smile. "About three months ago, as I recall."

He winced. "Of course. When I escorted you out of Arcane House via the concealed tunnel. Forgive me. I never considered how difficult running must have been for you that night. All I cared about was that you managed to keep up with me. You did that rather well."

"I will allow that you had other things on your mind at the time."

"Yes." He regarded her outrageous attire again, seeing it with new eyes. "You do realize that you are courting scandal and disaster. What if your secret were to be discovered by some of the club members tonight?"

She gave him a mysterious smile. "My secrets are safe at the Janus Club."

Some time later the carriage halted in the drive of a handsome mansion. Light glowed warmly in the windows. Extensive gardens afforded privacy on all sides.

A liveried footman came down the marble steps to open the carriage door.

Gabriel looked at Venetia. "This is the Janus Club?"

"Yes." She collected her hat and walking stick. "You had better let me descend first so that you do not forget and try to assist me."

"So many little things to remember."

"Just follow my lead," she said.

He smiled to himself. In spite of the seriousness of their purpose here tonight, it was obvious that Venetia was enjoying herself. He had not seen her in this bright, sparkling mood since their time together at Arcane House. The clothes and the adventure had transformed her, at least for tonight.

The footman opened the door but he did not lower the steps.

"Good evening, gentlemen," he said. "May I assist you?"

"We have an appointment with Mr. Harrow," Venetia announced in low, throaty tones. "The name is Jones."

"Yes, sir, Mr. Jones." The footman held the door wide. "Mr. Harrow told me to expect you and your companion."

Venetia jumped lightly down to the ground. She was right, Gabriel thought, following suit; she certainly did move more easily in a pair of trousers.

In point of fact, he thought, watching her go up the marble steps ahead of him, she looked quite charming in men's clothes. He wondered if she realized how well the closely cut evening jacket defined her narrow waist and accented the shape of her hips. In some odd manner the masculine garb only served to emphasize her femininity, at least in his eyes.

At the top of the steps another footman opened a large, dark green door, admitting them into a hallway lit by a massive chandelier.

Low-voiced conversation sounded from the room on the left. Gabriel looked through the doorway and saw a portion of an elegantly appointed library. Gentlemen dressed in evening clothes lounged in the gaslit room, glasses of brandy and port in hand.

"Mr. Harrow is waiting for you and your friend upstairs, Mr. Jones," the footman said to Venetia. "This way, please."

He ushered them toward a waterfall of a staircase.

Gabriel went up the steps side by side with Venetia. When they reached the landing he caught the distinct trace of cigarette smoke.

"The smoking room is just down that hall," Venetia explained. "Across the way is the card room."

"This was once a private residence," he observed, looking around.

"Yes. I believe that the owner leases the premises to the management of the Janus Club."

The footman led them down a long hall

and stopped in front of a closed door at the far end. He knocked twice.

Gabriel automatically registered the spacing between the two knocks. A subtle but distinct code, he thought.

"Enter," a low voice called from inside.

The footman opened the door. Gabriel saw a man standing in front of the fire, his back turned toward the door. Harrow was propped on the edge of a large desk, one leg hooked carelessly over the corner. Like everyone else in the establishment, both gentlemen wore black-and-white evening attire.

"Mr. Jones and his companion," the footman said.

"Thank you, Albert." Harrow smiled at Venetia and Gabriel. "Come in, gentlemen. Allow me to introduce you to Mr. Pierce."

Pierce turned around to face them. He was short, square and solid-looking with black hair that was laced with a judicious amount of silver. Startlingly vivid, dark blue eyes surveyed Gabriel in an assessing manner.

"Mr. Jones," Pierce said in a voice that suggested a daily diet of brandy and cigars. He gave Venetia an amused look. "And Mr. Jones."

Gabriel inclined his head. "Pierce."

Venetia nodded once. "Thank you for seeing us, Mr. Pierce."

"Please be seated," Pierce said. He motioned toward a pair of chairs and then sat down, himself.

Venetia sank down onto one of the velvet-upholstered chairs. Gabriel noticed that she unconsciously sat forward in a very upright manner, as though she wore a bustle that prevented her from leaning back in a more comfortable fashion. Some habits were hard to break, he reflected.

Instead of taking the chair that had been offered he went to stand in front of the fire, one arm stretched out along the carved marble mantel. It went against something deep in his nature to sit when he was among people he did not know well. One could move much more quickly if it proved necessary when one was already on one's feet.

Venetia looked at Pierce. "Mr. Harrow has told you why we wish to speak with you, sir?"

Pierce propped his elbows on the arm of his chair and put his fingertips together. "You wish to know something about Rosalind Fleming."

"Yes," Venetia said. "She seems to have conceived a great dislike of me for no apparent reason. I am curious to know why."

Harrow straightened from the corner of the desk and crossed to the brandy decanter. "In particular, Mr. Pierce, they would like to know if there is anything about Rosalind Fleming that might lead a prudent person to believe she could prove to be dangerous."

"I am almost certain that the answer to that question is yes," Pierce said.

Gabriel felt his psychical senses stir. He looked at Venetia. Tension radiated from her.

"I must tell you that I cannot offer you any evidence to support my suspicion," Pierce continued. He tapped his broad fingers together twice. A grim smile edged his mouth. "I will also admit that I would very much like to acquire some evidence that would support my conclusions."

The fire crackled in the short silence that followed that announcement.

Harrow handed the brandies around without comment. Gabriel accepted his and looked at Pierce.

"We need a little more information, Pierce," he said.

"I understand." Pierce looked at Gabriel over his steepled fingertips. "I will tell you what I know. When I first became aware of

Rosalind Fleming she had not yet become Ackland's mistress. She was using another name and she was making her living by promoting herself as a practitioner of psychical powers."

Startled, Venetia paused in the act of taking a sip from her glass. "She was a medium?"

"She offered a variety of services," Pierce said, "including séances and demonstrations of automatic writing. However, her specialty was in the private consulting line. For a fee she promised advice and guidance based on information she claimed she acquired from the Other Side."

"What name did she use in that career?" Venetia asked.

"Charlotte Bliss," Pierce said.

Gabriel studied him. "How did you come to learn so much about her?"

"A very close, personal friend of mine heard about her amazing psychical powers." Pierce gazed solemnly into the fire. "My friend did not believe in such claims but he thought it would be quite entertaining to attend one of Charlotte Bliss's demonstrations. My friend came away greatly impressed by the woman's abilities and immediately scheduled a series of private consultations."

"What did your friend consult her about?" Venetia asked.

"I'm afraid that is a private matter." Pierce picked up his brandy.

Pierce was one of those who held secrets close and tight, Gabriel thought. Anything related to him or his associates would likely constitute a *private matter.* The very fact that he was willing to speak to strangers tonight was a grim indication of just how intense his feelings were on the subject of Charlotte Bliss.

"Let me hazard a guess here," Gabriel said. "Mrs. Bliss charged your friend a hefty fee and then fed him a lot of nonsense."

Pierce looked at him. Gabriel was interested to see the cold anger that blazed in the intense blue eyes. In that moment he knew that Pierce would have had no compunction whatsoever about killing the woman who now called herself Rosalind Fleming.

"My friend was satisfied with the advice he received," Pierce said in an extraordinarily even tone that only served to intensify the impact of his icy gaze. "He made an investment based upon that advice."

"What happened?" Venetia asked.

"One month later he received the first blackmail note."

Gabriel saw the glass in Venetia's hand tremble. Harrow also noticed. He deftly plucked it from her fingers and set it on the table beside her chair. She did not appear to be aware of the small action. Her full attention was directed at Pierce.

"You believe that Mrs. Bliss was the one who sent the extortion note to your friend?" she asked.

"She was the only suspect as far as I was concerned. But I admit that I could not understand how she had come into possession of the damaging information. You see, the blackmailer alluded to certain facts about my friend that only two other people in the world could have known and one of them was dead."

"Who was the one who was still alive?" Gabriel asked.

Pierce drank more brandy and set the glass aside. "Me."

Gabriel contemplated that for a moment. "I assume that you were not the extortionist."

Pierce's jaw hardened. "No. I am very fond of my friend. I would do nothing to harm him."

And everything to protect him, Gabriel thought.

"What made you so sure that Mrs. Bliss

was the guilty party?" Venetia asked.

Pierce tapped his fingertips again. "The timing."

"That's all?"

Pierce shrugged. "It was all I had to go on. That and my . . . intuition."

An intuition honed by some experience in dangerous affairs, Gabriel thought.

"What did your friend do after he received the extortion note?" Venetia asked.

"Unfortunately, I could not convince him at first that Mrs. Bliss was very likely the blackmailer. He refused to believe it." Pierce shook his head. "Instead, he went back to her for advice."

Gabriel raised his brows. "She told him to pay the blackmail, didn't she?"

"Yes." Pierce's mouth tightened. "I was outraged. But I also knew that my friend was terrified of having his secrets revealed. I saw at once that we had only two options."

Gabriel swirled the brandy in his glass. "Pay the blackmail or get rid of the suspected extortionist."

Harrow's expression sharpened in subtle surprise. Venetia's eyes widened.

Pierce regarded Gabriel with something approaching approval. He inclined his head in a gesture of respect.

One predator to another, Gabriel thought.

"But obviously you did not dispatch Mrs. Bliss on a personal journey into the spirit world," he continued aloud. "Does that mean that your friend is paying the blackmail?"

"No," Pierce said flatly.

"What changed your mind?"

"Lord Ackland changed it." Pierce drank more brandy.

Venetia searched his face. "How did he get involved?"

Pierce looked at her. "My friend and I were attempting to formulate a plan of action when Mrs. Bliss vanished quite suddenly."

"A neat trick," Gabriel said. "Of course, she did claim to possess psychical powers. Was invisibility among them?"

"All I can tell you is that her house was vacated overnight," Pierce said. "No one knew where she had gone. It occurred to me that perhaps one of her other blackmail victims had taken effective action. It was also possible that she had become uneasy about her own safety and had decided to decamp."

"What about the blackmail threats?" Venetia asked.

"There were no more. My friend's problems went away as if by magic." Pierce snapped his fingers.

Harrow cleared his throat. "But a fortnight later a certain very mysterious, very expensive-looking widow named Mrs. Rosalind Fleming appeared in some very exclusive social circles on the arm of Lord Ackland."

"Mind you, there were a few minor alterations," Pierce said. "Her hair was a different color, for one thing. But the most dazzling transformation was in her style. As Mrs. Bliss she had conducted her consultations attired in modest, nondescript dresses made of dull, sturdy fabrics. But as Mrs. Fleming her gowns are all in the latest French mode. And, of course, there are the diamonds."

"Lord Ackland is obviously a very generous man," Venetia said thoughtfully.

Pierce snorted. "The man is a senile old fool."

"But a very rich senile old fool," Harrow amended.

"My friend and I were in a quandary," Pierce continued. "It was, after all, still entirely possible that I had been wrong in my suspicions. Perhaps Mrs. Bliss, or Mrs. Fleming, as she now calls herself, was not the blackmailer."

"What happened next?" Venetia asked.

"Nothing." Pierce moved one hand slightly. "Mrs. Fleming first appeared in Society a few months ago. To date there have been no more extortion notes. But I will confess that my friend is still on tenterhooks. The threat is always there, you see."

"How dreadful," Venetia whispered.

Pierce contemplated the fire. "My friend has been careful to avoid Mrs. Fleming as much as possible but they move in many of the same circles. Recently he came face-to-face with her at the theater."

"That must have been unnerving," Venetia said. "What did he do?"

"Pretended that he did not know her, of course." Pierce smiled coldly. "It helped considerably that she returned the favor and pretended not to recognize him. To this day we do not know if her reaction was an excellent bit of acting on her part or if she truly did not realize who he was."

"Why wouldn't she recognize one of her victims?" Gabriel asked.

"The contact was brief and the lighting was low," Pierce explained. "They passed each other in the corridor outside one of the boxes." He paused. "On that particular evening my friend happened to be attired in a somewhat different manner than when he had consulted with her. You know how it is, when one sees someone who is out of context, so to speak."

"One sees what one expects to see," Gabriel said, looking at Venetia in her gentleman's clothes.

Harrow angled himself onto the corner of the desk again. He glanced first at Gabriel and then at Venetia.

"You both seem extremely concerned about Mrs. Fleming," he observed.

"Yes," she said.

"Do you mind telling us why?" Harrow asked. "It is unfortunate that Ackland took a notion to commission you to photograph Mrs. Fleming but it is hardly surprising. He is, after all, besotted with his paramour, and you are a very fashionable photographer. It seems natural that he would want you to take her portrait."

"The unnatural aspect of the matter is that Mrs. Fleming appears to have conceived a wholly irrational hatred of my person," Venetia said. "My aunt thinks that Fleming is merely jealous because I have created a profitable career for myself while she is forced to rely on the likes of Lord Ackland for financial security. But I believe there may be more to it than that."

"What makes you say that?" Pierce asked, frowning slightly.

She shook her head. "I cannot give you a logical answer. Perhaps it is just that I find it difficult to believe someone could dislike me so much when I have done nothing to offend."

"Burton disliked you quite intensely," Harrow reminded her.

"Yes, but in that case there was some explanation. Evidently, Mr. Burton disliked all women and me in particular because I was in the same profession as himself. But Mrs. Fleming's reaction to me seemed out of all proportion."

"I take your point." Pierce put his fingertips together again. He looked at Gabriel. "For what it is worth, my advice is to be on guard at all times. In her former line of work Mrs. Fleming was obviously very adept at ferreting out a person's most closely held confidences. To this day my friend has no notion of how she acquired knowledge of his secret."

"Surely he must have some idea of how she learned it," Gabriel said.

Pierce exhaled heavily. "No. In fact, I must tell you that, although I am extremely skeptical of all those charlatans and frauds who claim psychical powers, I have sometimes wondered if Rosalind Fleming actually does possess some paranormal talent. My friend swears that the only way she could have got the secret out of him is if she really does have access to the Other Side. Or else —"

"Or else what?" Venetia asked.

Pierce shrugged his broad shoulders. "Or else she can read minds."

28

Venetia watched the dark street through the carriage window as the lights of the Janus Club disappeared into the fog.

Gabriel had spoken very little since they had left Harrow and Pierce. She knew that he was contemplating the same unsettling possibility that had sent her into a meditative mood after the disturbing conversation.

"It is obvious that Pierce is a man of logic and reason who is loath to believe that Rosalind Fleming actually possesses some psychical powers," she said slowly. "But we both know that such abilities do exist. What is your opinion?"

"I think," Gabriel said, "that what we have here is either another astonishing coincidence or a genuine clue."

She smiled wryly. "I can guess which you suspect."

He had turned the carriage lamps down very low, drenching the interior of the vehicle in shadow. She knew that he did not want to take a chance that someone in a passing cab might see her and recognize her in her gentleman's attire. There was little chance of that, she thought. The streets were so choked with fog now that she was amazed that the driver and his horses could find their way back to Sutton Lane.

A thought struck her, sending a deep, cold shudder through her entire body.

"If Mrs. Fleming does possess psychical powers, I suppose we must consider the possibility that she somehow read my mind the day I photographed her," she whispered.

"Calm yourself. Mind reading is a parlor trick, nothing more."

She wanted desperately to take comfort in his reassurance. "How can you be certain of that?"

"The records of Arcane House research are very extensive. They go back some two hundred years and they reflect decades of experiments. There has never been any indication that one person can actually read another person's mind."

"But there is still so much that is unknown about psychical matters."

He shrugged. "I suppose one must allow that anything is possible. However, in this case I think there is a much simpler explanation for Mrs. Fleming's uncanny ability to pluck secrets from a person's mind without her victim being aware of it."

"What is that?"

"She may well be a very skilled mesmerist."

Venetia thought about that. "An interesting notion. It would certainly explain a few things. If Mrs. Fleming put a person into a trance and got him to reveal a personal secret he might well have no memory of what had happened after he came out of the trance."

"Arcane House investigators have done considerable research in the field of mesmerism because some believe that it is a form of psychical talent. The art has its limitations, from what I have read, however. Not everyone is a good subject, for one thing. Some people can be put into a trance rather easily. Others are impervious to a mesmerist's powers."

"You are very knowledgeable when it comes to psychical matters, Gabriel."

"I was raised by a father who has devoted his entire life to the subject. Most of my relatives are equally immersed in the field. You might say that psychical research is the family business."

"It is an unusual line."

He smiled faintly. "Yes, it is."

"If Mrs. Fleming is a mesmerist, it would explain how she fleeces her victims of their secrets, but it does not link her to the theft of the alchemist's formula."

"I admit I can see no immediate link, unless —"

"Unless what?"

"Members of the Arcane Society frequently investigate those who claim to possess psychical powers. It is possible that a member of the society did some research on Mrs. Fleming."

She straightened abruptly in her seat as comprehension dawned on her. "Only to have himself unwittingly put into a trance during which he revealed information about the expedition to recover the formula?"

"It's an extremely remote possibility," Gabriel cautioned. "Even if Mrs. Fleming did arrange to steal the formula, it does not tell us how she expected to be able to decipher the alchemist's code. You must trust me when I say that no one outside the society has access to the founder's writings, and only a handful of members inside the society have been allowed to study them over the years."

Venetia listened absently to the rumble

of the carriage wheels and the clatter of the horses' hooves. The vehicle was making slow progress in the heavy mist.

"If Mrs. Fleming is involved in the affair of the missing formula," she said after a while, "then you may, indeed, have been correct in your notion that I caught her attention when I chose to take your last name."

"Yes."

"Now that you have appeared on the scene, her suspicions will have been confirmed. She must surely know who you are and that you are in pursuit of the formula."

"But she has every reason to think that her own identity as the thief is safe," Gabriel said. "After all, she is not linked to the society in any obvious way. She will assume that I have no reason to suspect her."

"She may be the thief," Venetia said, "but I can assure you that she is not the person I saw fleeing from the darkroom where Burton was murdered. I perceived Mrs. Fleming's aura when I took her photograph. It was not the same as that of the fleeing man."

"You are quite certain?"

"Positive."

He reflected on that for a moment. "I

would not be surprised to discover that she is using someone else to do her killing for her. It is dangerous work."

Another shiver went through her. "Poor Mr. Burton. He is dead, in part, because of me. If he had not accepted that commission to follow me about and take pictures of me —"

Gabriel moved very suddenly, catching her by surprise. He leaned forward and grasped both her wrists in his big hands, imprisoning her.

"Do not," he said evenly, "think for a single moment that you have any responsibility in that direction. Harold Burton is dead because he accepted a commission from a very dangerous person who employed him to invade your privacy. He must have known or guessed that his client did not harbor goodwill toward you. I won't go so far as to suggest that he got what he deserved but I refuse to allow you to feel any guilt in the matter."

She gave him a shaky smile. "Thank you, Gabriel."

"Do you know," he said, deceptively casual, "I believe that is the second time since we got into this carriage that you have called me by my given name. I like the sound of it on your lips."

The thrilling, seductive energy that always seemed to circulate in the atmosphere when she was with Gabriel abruptly intensified. She was acutely aware of the strength of his hands wrapped so gently yet so firmly around her wrists.

He used his grip to pull her a little closer. His mouth came down on hers. She thought she knew his kisses well enough by now not to be startled by her own response but she was wrong. She tried to control the rush of hot excitement and the deep aching heat that threatened to melt her insides. She failed.

With his mouth still holding hers captive, he freed one of her wrists to lower the carriage curtains. Then he stripped off her wig and went to work on the pins she had used to secure her real hair.

The intoxicating intimacy of the carriage was her undoing. The vehicle suddenly became a ship sailing slowly through an uncharted sea of night and fog.

This was the way it had been at Arcane House, she thought. She was free for a time. She did not have to think about the past or the future. There was no threat of Edward or Amelia accidentally stumbling onto a shocking scene of their older sister engaged in a bout of illicit passion. No concerns about alarming Aunt Beatrice or jeopardizing her career.

When her hair tumbled down around her shoulders she heard Gabriel give a low, husky groan. His arms tightened around her.

He kissed her heavily, drugging her with sensation. When she surfaced briefly from the delicious haze she realized that he had peeled off her evening jacket and tossed it aside on the seat.

He rid himself of his own coat with a few swift, efficient moves. When he came back to her he reached for her bow tie. The knowledge that his fingers were shaking a little as he undid the knot thrilled her. He truly wanted her, she thought. Whatever else this might prove to be, it was no cold-blooded seduction. They were both consumed by the fires of a mutual passion.

He got the tie undone. His hand slipped to the first stud of her crisply starched white linen shirt. She felt him smiling against her mouth.

"Do you know," he said, "I have never had occasion to undress a lady attired in a man's clothes. It is more of a challenge than one would expect. I find myself having to do everything in reverse, as it were."

The remark surprised a little ripple of laughter out of her. Wildly emboldened, she tugged at the ends of his own bow tie.

"Allow me to demonstrate," she whispered.

This time she unknotted his tie with more skill than she had used that night at Arcane House because she'd had some practice with men's clothes, thanks to her adventures with Harrow.

Gabriel responded to her every touch by quickening the pace at which he was undressing her. She did not realize that he had got her shirt undone until she felt his hand on her breast. She gripped his shoulders to steady herself. He bent his head to kiss her throat. Everything inside her tightened. Heat built.

"Gabriel," she whispered.

She slipped her hands inside his shirt and flattened her palms against his chest.

He sat back against the seat and cradled her across his thighs. Reaching down, he removed her shoes. She heard them drop to the floor of the carriage.

The next thing she knew he had her trousers undone and had worked them down over her hips. The long drawers she wore underneath were next. Both garments disappeared into the shadows of the opposite seat.

When she was left in only the unfastened white shirt, Gabriel kissed her as though both their lives depended upon it. She flinched a little when she felt his warm palm on the inside of her bare thigh. She had almost forgotten how exciting it felt to have him touch her like this. *Almost.*

He shifted his hand higher. His palm closed over her. She drew a sharp breath, intensely aware of the gathering dampness between her legs.

"You are already wet for me," he said, half awed, half exultant. "You do not know how many times I have imagined having you like this again; how many times I've dreamed about it."

His mouth covered hers once more, invading, coaxing, demanding. She was swept up in the hot whirlpool of desire. He moved her, parting her legs and turning her so that she found herself braced astride his thighs, her knees on the velvet cushions.

Startled by the strange position, she clenched his shoulders to find her balance. He curved one hand around her hip and slid the other between her legs, parting her.

He began to stroke her, probing, testing, learning anew her secrets. Every touch seemed more intimate and more unbearably exciting than the last. He concentrated most of his attention on the small nubbin at the top of her cleft, working it with his thumb until she thought she would go mad. A great coiling tension built within the core of her body. The sense of urgency was overwhelming.

"I cannot stand it," she managed, digging her fingertips into his shoulders. "It is too much."

"Not nearly enough," he said. "Not yet. I want to feel your pleasure when you come."

She realized vaguely that he was unfastening his own trousers. Then she felt the hard evidence of his fierce arousal pressing against the inside of her leg.

She reached down and curled her fingers around his heavy length. He whispered something hot and dark and dangerous in her ear. She squeezed him gently.

He sucked in a deep breath.

Bending her head, she nipped his bare shoulder with her teeth.

A shudder went through him.

"Two can play at that game," he warned.

He did astonishing things with his hand.

She had to fight for breath. The delicious tension was beyond bearing now.

Without warning the gathering storm within her unleashed itself in dazzling waves of sensation.

She would have cried out with pleasure but before the sound could emerge from her lips, Gabriel pulled her down firmly, inexorably onto his heavy erection. He filled her in a single, surging thrust.

She had been prepared for pain similar to what she had experienced the first time but there was none. Only an exciting tightness that intensified the last fading pulses of her release.

All of her senses reacted to the glorious shock of the physical and psychical connection. She did not even have to concentrate to see the dark light of Gabriel's aura flaring in the confines of the cab. It flooded the small space, infused with the energy of her own aura, creating a stunning, nerve-shattering intimacy.

When he climaxed a short time later the fierce, invisible fires leaped even higher. She felt rather than heard the beginnings of Gabriel's exultant roar. It started as a low rumble in his chest. She realized that even though the driver of the carriage probably lacked the paranormal senses needed to perceive a flaring aura, his hearing was very likely quite sound.

In the nick of time she managed to cover Gabriel's mouth with her own. The roar became a muffled growl of triumph and masculine satisfaction.

Some time later she stirred in his arms. The sound of the carriage wheels and the steady clop of hooves assured her that they were still safely enclosed in the magic world inside the cab.

Gabriel, who had been reclining in the corner of the seat with the air of a lion well satiated after a successful hunt, reached out to raise a curtain. Gaslights glowed in the fog.

"We are passing the cemetery. We will soon be in Sutton Lane," he observed.

It dawned on her that the only thing she had on was the white shirt. Panic snapped through her.

"Good heavens," she yelped. "We cannot arrive at the front door in this condition."

She extricated herself from his grasp, dove for the opposite seat and scrambled madly to collect her clothes.

It wasn't easy donning a man's attire in the cramped darkness of the carriage. Gabriel put his own clothes back together with a few practiced moves and then sat back to watch her struggles with interest.

After a moment or two of watching her fight with her bow tie, he reached out to knot it for her.

"Allow me to assist you, *Mrs. Jones,*" he said.

The emphasis on her fictional name brought her head up sharply.

"Gabriel —" she began, with absolutely no notion of what she was going to say next.

"We will talk about this in the morning," he said.

His voice was oddly gentle but the words were a command, not a suggestion. A spark of anger burned away the anxiety she had been experiencing at the thought of arriving home half undressed.

"I do hope you are not going to fret about what has happened between us," she said, stuffing her hair up under her hat. "It would ruin everything if you did."

"I beg your pardon?"

She sighed. "You must know that when we were at Arcane House, I did my best to seduce you."

"Yes, and you were quite brilliant at the business, if I may say so. I enjoyed the experience immensely."

She knew she was blushing furiously.

"Yes, well, what I am trying to say is that while we were together at Arcane House I deliberately plotted to lure you into a night of illicit passion."

"Your point?"

"My point being that things were different there."

"Different?"

"We were two people alone together in a remote, secluded place."

"Except for the servants," he said.

She frowned. "Except for the servants, of course. But they were so discreet." She was starting to ramble. This was dreadful. "It was as though we had been cast adrift on a tropical island."

"I don't recall any palm trees."

She ignored that. "I explained to you that for that brief interlude I was free for the first time in my life. I did not have to worry about creating a scandal. I did not have to be concerned with shocking my elderly aunt or setting a poor example for my sister and brother. Arcane House was a place and a time that seemed to exist in another dimension, one that was far removed from the real world. You and I were the only people in that other realm."

"Except for the servants."

"Well, yes."

"About the palm trees that I can't quite seem to recall."

"You are not taking this seriously, are you?"

"Should I?"

"Yes, this is extremely important." She was growing more annoyed by the moment. "What I am trying to say is that tonight was a similar experience."

"I'm not sure about that. For starters there were no palm trees."

"Forget the damned palm trees. I am trying to explain that what happened at Arcane House and what happened in this carriage tonight are akin to the fleeting vapors of a dream, gone by dawn and not to be recalled in the light of day."

"That all sounds very poetic, my sweet, but what the devil does it mean?"

"It means," she said coldly, "that we will not discuss this matter any further. Is that understood?"

The carriage rumbled to a halt. Venetia seized the stylish walking stick and turned quickly to peer out the window.

There was a small but distinct thud.

Gabriel cleared his throat. "You might want to watch where you swing that stick."

She realized that in her nervous agitation she had accidentally struck his leg.

"I beg your pardon," she said, utterly mortified.

He rubbed his knee with one hand and opened the door with the other. "No need to be concerned. I doubt it will result in anything more than a slight limp."

Red-faced, she followed him out of the carriage and hurried up the steps. Gabriel paused to toss some coins to the driver.

When she opened the door with her key she was relieved to discover that the rest of the household was abed. The very last thing she wanted to do tonight was confront her family and their questions about what she had discovered at the Janus Club. She needed time to recover her composure. A good night's rest would put things to rights.

The sconce in the front hall had been turned down low. She saw an envelope on the table and picked it up. It was addressed to Gabriel.

"This is for you," she said, handing it to him.

"Thank you." He closed the door, took the envelope and gave it a brief scrutiny. "It is from Montrose."

"Perhaps he has finally discovered something of interest in the membership records."

Gabriel ripped open the envelope and

removed the note. He looked at it in silence for a few seconds.

"Well?" she prompted.

"It is written in one of the private codes used by members of the Arcane Society for personal correspondence. It will take me a while to decipher it. I'll work on it tonight and let you know what it says at breakfast."

"But if it is a coded message it must be something very important."

"Not necessarily." His mouth curved wryly as he pocketed the note. "Given the obsessively secretive nature of the majority of the society's membership, virtually every message sent from one member to another is encrypted. This note from Montrose is likely nothing more than a request to meet with me tomorrow to discuss his progress."

"You will let me know immediately if it is important, won't you?"

"Of course," he said easily. "But now I think we should both take ourselves upstairs to bed. It has been a long, eventful day."

"Yes, it has." She started up the stairs, trying to think of something worldly to say. "I believe the evening was quite productive, though, don't you?"

"In a variety of ways."

The amused sensuality deepened her

blush. Thank heavens the sconce on the landing had been turned down.

"I was referring to the information that we garnered about Mrs. Fleming," she said sternly.

"In that way, also," he agreed.

She looked at him over her shoulder. "One cannot help but wonder what sort of secret Mr. Pierce's friend possessed."

"Probably best that we never learn the answer to that," Gabriel said.

"You may be right." She considered briefly and then shrugged. "Nevertheless, I think I can guess the mystery there."

"You believe that the secret has something to do with the fact that Pierce and his friends belong to a club whose members are women who enjoy dressing up as men?" Gabriel sounded amused rather than shocked.

She whirled around, grasping the handrail. "You *knew* about the Janus Club?"

"Not until we got there," he admitted. "But it wasn't hard to figure out once we arrived that things were somewhat out of the ordinary."

"But how — ?"

"I told you, women smell different. Any male who finds himself surrounded by a large group of females, regardless of how they are dressed, is going to become aware of that fact sooner or later. I suspect the reverse is also true."

"Hmm." She pondered that briefly. "Did you know Harrow for a woman when you met her at the exhibition?"

"Yes."

"You are far more perceptive than most," she said. "Harrow has passed herself off as a gentleman in Society for some time now."

"How did you come to meet her? Or perhaps I should say him."

"I always speak of Harrow as a male." She wrinkled her nose. "It is easier to keep his secret if I do that. To answer your question, he sought me out to commission a portrait shortly after I opened the gallery. He was one of my first clients, as a matter of fact."

"I see."

"In the course of the sitting I realized that he was a she, as it were. Harrow knew at once that I knew. I gave him my word that I would keep his secret. I don't think he trusted me entirely at first, but after a while we became friends."

"Harrow knows that you understand how to keep secrets."

"Yes. He seems very intuitive that way."

"I see," Gabriel said again.

She frowned. "What is wrong?"

He shrugged. "I find it interesting that Harrow went to the trouble of seeking out a new, unknown photographer who had not yet caught the attention of Society."

"I had already had a successful exhibition at Mr. Farley's gallery," she said, alarmed by the direction of his reasoning. "That is where Harrow first encountered my work. Really, sir, you cannot possibly suspect him of being involved in this affair of the formula."

"At this moment I am inclined to suspect everyone."

A strange chill went through her.

"Even me?" she asked uneasily.

He smiled. "I stand corrected. I should have said everyone except you."

She allowed herself to relax slightly. "You must promise me that if you ever again encounter Harrow or Mr. Pierce or any of the other members of the club, you will not let on that you are aware of their secret world," she said.

"I assure you, Venetia, I, too, know how to keep secrets."

Something in the softly spoken words sent another disturbing frisson across her nerves. A warning or a promise? she wondered.

She stopped on the landing.

"Good night," she said.

"Good night, Venetia. Sleep well."

She hurried along the corridor to the sanctuary of her bedroom.

Some time later she awoke quite suddenly in the way that one does when the sleeping mind registers a change in the atmosphere of a house. She lay quietly for a moment, listening intently.

Perhaps Amelia or Beatrice or Edward had gone down to the kitchen for a late-night snack.

She did not know what it was that made her shove the bedclothes aside and cross the cold floor to the window.

She was just in time to see the shadowy figure of a man drift, ghostlike, through the fog-bound garden. The moon was out but the swirling mist was too thick to allow her to see the iron gate that opened onto the alley. She certainly knew its general location, however, and she could tell that the man down below her window was moving toward it in a confident manner. *He is prowling unerringly toward his goal as though he possesses the night-hunting senses of a jungle cat,* she thought. *As if he can literally see in the dark.*

There was no need to concentrate to see his aura. She knew it was Gabriel.

A second or two later he disappeared out of the garden into the night.

Where was he going at this hour and why had he left the house in such a stealthy manner? Something to do with the message from Montrose, she thought.

Gabriel's words came back to her. *I assure you, Venetia, I, too, know how to keep secrets.*

29

Gabriel descended from the hansom and paid the driver. He waited until the vehicle had disappeared into the fog before he went back to the corner, entered the small park and stopped in the dense shadows of some trees.

He stood there for a time, watching the street. There was very little traffic at this hour in this quiet neighborhood. The gas lamps illuminated small circles of fog in front of each doorway but they offered little useful light.

When he was certain that he was not being followed, he left the park and walked through the mist to the entrance of the alley.

Moving into the narrow passage was like entering a mysterious small-scale jungle. The night and the fog were heavier here. A rush of small, scurrying sounds erupted as the local predators and prey got out of his way. Strange odors fouled the atmosphere.

He walked carefully, in part to avoid the echo of his own boot steps but also to be certain that he did not lose his footing in the noxious brew of rotting garbage that littered his path.

Mentally he counted off the iron gates until he came to the one in the middle of the row, the one that marked Montrose's address.

He studied the windows. All but one were dark. The single window that was illuminated was upstairs and covered by a curtain. If it had not been for a thin crack in the drapes, it, too, would have appeared unlit. Montrose's study.

As he watched, he saw the light shift subtly at the edge of the curtain.

He thought about the message that had been waiting for him in the hall at Sutton Lane. It had taken him a few minutes in the privacy of his attic room to decipher it. By the time he had finished the task, his psychical senses, already aroused from the heated lovemaking in the carriage, were in full sail.

I have come across some disturbing information. I think it best that we meet as soon as possible. Please come to my address at your earliest convenience, regardless of the hour. I advise you not to tell anyone whom you are meeting. It would be best for all concerned if you were not seen in my street. Use the garden entrance.

M.

Just as well he had not deciphered the note in front of Venetia, Gabriel thought. She was far too perceptive. He might have given away the secretive nature of the message, even if he had managed to keep the details to himself. She would have noticed his concern and immediately plied him with questions. Just to be on the safe side, he had waited until he was reasonably certain that she was asleep before making his way out the back door.

He felt around the top of the gate, searching for the latch. His fingers brushed against cold iron.

Energy burned through his palm and skittered erratically across his paranormal senses. The shock of sensation shafted through him. The spoor was very fresh.

Someone intent on cold-blooded violence had passed through this gate quite recently. His hunting instincts thrilled to the challenge.

When he was relatively certain that he had all of his senses back under control he took his pistol out of his pocket and grasped the latch a second time.

The gate opened, squeaking only a little on its hinges. Pistol in hand, he slipped into the garden.

The light shifted again in the single illuminated window upstairs. He looked up just in time to see the lamp go out inside the study.

If that was the killer moving around up there, it was possible that Montrose was already dead. The villain would no doubt leave by the back door. The logical thing to do was to wait for him to exit the house and try to seize him by surprise when he emerged.

But what if the monster had not yet completed his mission? What if Montrose was alive? Perhaps there was still time.

Gabriel removed his boots and braced himself for the jolt he knew was coming. He put his hand cautiously on the knob of the kitchen door.

This time he was ready for the paranormal burn. The only effect it had on his psychical senses was to heighten them. The desire to hunt was as strong in him now as the desire to make love to Venetia had been earlier in the evening.

The door was unlocked. He opened it

very slowly, praying that there would be no loud groan from the hinges.

In spite of his best efforts, there was a faint squeak but he doubted that anyone upstairs with normal hearing would have caught the soft sound.

He stood listening for a moment. There was no telltale rush of footsteps or creak of floorboards overhead. More important, there was none of the unmistakable taint of recent death. With luck, that meant that Montrose was still alive.

At this end of the hall there was only deep night. But when he looked toward the opposite end he could see the pale glow of the streetlamps filtering through the narrow panes of glass that bordered the front door. The main staircase would be at that end of the hall but to use it, he would have to put himself into the weak light that radiated through the glass. No sense making a target of himself, he thought.

He knew there was a set of servants' stairs here at the back of the house. He had seen Montrose's housekeeper use them.

With his excellent night vision he could make out the opening to the stairs next to the kitchen. He gripped the door frame cautiously, half expecting another flash of seething energy. But nothing seared his senses. The killer had not come this way. If he was upstairs, he had used the main staircase. That made sense, Gabriel thought. Why would the villain trouble himself with the cramped stairs designed for the servants?

He started up the narrow stairs, listening intently. There was someone in the house, someone who had no right to be here. He could sense it. But nothing moved in the stillness.

When he reached the top of the stairs he found himself looking into another hall. This one was weakly lit by the moon filtering through the windows of the main staircase. If there was anyone waiting in the corridor, the person was not breathing or moving.

He glided out into the hall, gun at the ready. No one leaped at him. That was very likely not a good sign, he thought. He was not the only hunter here tonight. The villain was lying in wait for him.

He knew that Montrose's study, the room that had been lit when he arrived in the garden a moment ago, was located to his right at the back of the house. From where he stood he could see that the door to that room was closed.

There was nothing for it, he thought. He would have to open the door.

He moved down the hall to the door of the study and stood for a few seconds, reaching out for information with all of his senses.

There was someone inside the room. He touched the doorknob very lightly. Another sizzling jolt of energy flashed through him.

The killer had entered the study.

The knob turned easily in his palm. He flattened himself against the side of the wall and opened the door.

There was no flash of exploding gunpowder. No one rushed at him with a knife.

Someone was inside the study, though. He was certain of it.

He crouched low and peered cautiously around the edge of the doorway. He did not need his psychical senses to make out the silhouette of a man seated in a chair near the window.

Montrose squirmed awkwardly and made muffled noises. Gabriel realized that the old man was bound to the chair. A gag muffled the sounds he was trying to make.

"Mmmph."

Relief blazed through Gabriel. Montrose was alive.

He glanced quickly around the room. Montrose was the only occupant but Gabriel's hunting intuition was riding him hard, making him intensely aware that the killer was still inside the house.

Ignoring the desperate sounds Montrose was making, he turned his attention back to the heavily shadowed hallway. He could see the outlines of at least three more doors. Toward the far end of the hall a narrow, rectangular object loomed against the wall. A table, he thought, with a pair of candlesticks on top.

"Mmmph," Montrose mumbled again.

Gabriel did not respond. Keeping his back to the wall, he edged along the corridor. When he came to the first closed door he put his hand on the knob.

He sensed nothing of the foul psychical energy that had been left on the door of the study. The killer had not entered this room.

He shifted to the opposite wall and went to the next closed door. When he touched the knob he got the all-too-familiar splash of roiling energy.

Anticipation leaped within him. He kicked the door inward and simultaneously threw himself to the floor, gun gripped in both hands.

It was the faintest whisper of sensation behind him that told him he had miscalculated badly.

The door that he had just checked and dismissed as untainted had been opened.

He barely had time to register his grave mistake when he heard the near-silent rush of oncoming death.

There was no time to get to his feet or even his knees. He twisted awkwardly onto his left side, trying to get his right arm and the gun directed toward the approaching threat.

He was too late. Like some faceless menace in a nightmare, a dark figure leaped out of the deep shadows of the other bedroom. Gabriel could see that the villain's features were obscured by a mask made of dark cloth. The weak light from the far end of the hall glinted on the blade of a knife.

There was no time to aim. Gabriel knew, even as he pulled the trigger, that he was going to miss his target. He could only hope that the shot would distract his attacker. Nothing like having a gun go off nearby to make one reconsider one's original plan.

A great roar of sound deafened his heightened sense of hearing. The acrid smell and smoke of gunpowder filled the hall.

The attacker did not waver.

It dawned on Gabriel that the villain was coming at him with great precision.

He knows I'm down here on the floor. He can see me as clearly as I can see him.

There was no time for further reflection. The attacker was upon him, kicking out violently with one foot.

The blow slammed into Gabriel's shoulder, rendering his arm instantly numb. He heard the gun clatter to the floor and slide away into the bedroom.

In the next instant the villain was slashing downward with the point of the knife, aiming for Gabriel's midsection.

Gabriel wrenched himself violently to the side, rolling to evade the strike. The blade flashed past and thudded into the floor. The attacker was forced to jerk it violently in order to free it.

Taking advantage of the second's respite, Gabriel surged to his feet. He flexed his nerveless fingers, trying to regain his sense of feeling.

The attacker got the knife out of the floor and sprang toward him.

Gabriel danced backward, putting some distance between them while he searched for a weapon. Out of the corner of his eye he caught a glimpse of the table at the end of the hall on his right.

Using his uninjured hand, he grabbed one of the heavy silver candlesticks that decorated the table.

The nightmare man was closing in again, clearly expecting Gabriel to keep retreating toward the staircase.

His only chance, Gabriel thought, was to do something unexpected.

He hurled himself to the side, instead of moving back. He came up hard against the wall. The attacker whirled with terrifying speed but Gabriel was already swinging the candlestick with all of his strength.

The heavy candlestick struck the killer's forearm near the wrist. The man grunted in pain. The knife bounced onto the floor.

Gabriel swung again, aiming for his opponent's skull. The man dodged reflexively, stumbling backward. Gabriel closed in on him.

The villain whirled and made for the main staircase. Gabriel dropped the candlestick, collected the knife and went after his opponent.

The attacker was three full strides ahead. He reached the stairs and plunged downward, one hand on the banister to keep himself from tumbling headfirst to the bottom.

He arrived at the foot of the stairs, yanked open the front door and fled into the night.

Every instinct Gabriel possessed urged him to pursue his quarry. But logic and reason surfaced through the haze of his bloodlust. He reached the bottom of the staircase and went to the door. He stood looking out into the street for a moment, trying to determine the direction in which the would-be killer had fled. But the night and the fog had swallowed up all traces of the fleeing man.

Gabriel closed the door and loped back upstairs and down the hall to the study. He turned up the lamp and removed the gag from Montrose's mouth.

Montrose spit out the fabric and gave Gabriel a disgusted look.

"I tried to tell you, the villain went through the connecting door between these two rooms." He angled his head toward the side wall of the study. "He didn't go out into the hall. He was lying in wait for you in that other bedroom."

Gabriel looked at the door that he had ignored earlier when he had done a quick survey of the room. He thought about how he had been so certain that his paranormal sense of touch would provide him with the clues he needed to determine the killer's hiding place.

"So much for relying on my psychical abilities," he said.

"Psychical senses don't replace logic and common sense," Montrose growled.

"You know, Mr. Montrose, you sound a lot like my father when you say things like that."

"There is something you should know," Montrose said. "Whoever he was, he took the photograph of the strongbox lid that you gave me. I saw him tuck it inside his shirt while he waited for you. He seemed surprised to find it but he was clearly very pleased."

30

"What did you tell the police?" Venetia asked.

"The truth," Gabriel said. He downed a healthy swallow of the brandy he had just poured. "After a fashion."

Montrose cleared his throat. "Naturally, we did not burden their inquiries with a great deal of extraneous information that would have been quite useless to them. We explained that an intruder had entered my house, bound and gagged me and was searching the place for valuables when Gabriel arrived and drove him off."

"In other words, you didn't mention the alchemist's formula," Venetia said. She did not bother to conceal her exasperation.

Montrose and Gabriel exchanged glances.

"Didn't see the need, quite frankly," Montrose said smoothly. "This is Arcane Society business, after all. There's not much the police can do."

"You didn't see the *need?*" Venetia drummed her fingers on the arm of her chair. "You were both very nearly murdered this evening. How can you say there was no reason to tell the police about a possible motive?"

Her nerves would never be the same, she thought. When Gabriel had walked into the front hall a short time ago, disheveled and bruised, the cold fires of battle still glittering in his eyes, she had not known whether to sob with relief or rail at him like a fishwife. It was only the fact that the elderly Montrose was with him that had constrained her from doing either.

One look was all she needed to understand that some great disaster had befallen them. There would be time enough for a lecture later, she told herself.

The entire household was awake and crowded into the small parlor. She was in her dressing gown and slippers. So were Amelia and Beatrice. Edward, having heard the commotion, had rushed downstairs in his nightclothes to see what all the excitement was about.

Beatrice had taken charge of administering to Montrose and Gabriel. To everyone's relief, she had announced that the damage did not appear extensive.

Mrs. Trench had rushed back and forth between the kitchen and the parlor several times, checking to see *if the gentlemen need anything else. A slice of meat pie, perhaps, to build up their strength.*

Venetia had thanked her and urged her to return to bed. When Mrs. Trench had reluctantly departed, Venetia poured tea all around, although Gabriel appeared more interested in the large glass of brandy in his hand.

"The thing is, we can't be certain of the villain's motive," Gabriel said, placating. "We can only surmise his intentions. When you come right down to the crux of the matter, there really was not much we could give to the police."

Venetia looked at Montrose. "Did the intruder say anything to you, sir?"

"Very little." Montrose snorted softly. "I didn't even know he was in the house until he surprised me in my study. Thought at first he was just a common thief. He tied me to the chair, gagged me and then set about searching the room. As soon as he found the photograph of the strongbox he appeared quite satisfied. He did make it clear that he knew that Gabriel was on his way, however."

Gabriel absently rubbed his jaw. "He must have intercepted the message you sent me earlier, sir."

Montrose's bushy brows bunched together. "What message?"

They all looked at him. Montrose became even more confused.

"You didn't send a message to Mr. Jones?" Venetia asked.

"No," Montrose said. "I haven't made much progress in my research into the family connections of the various members of the society, I'm sorry to say. Every time I spot someone who might make a possible suspect for Gabriel to investigate, it turns out that the individual is either deceased or living in some foreign clime."

A terrible dread swept through Venetia. She turned to Gabriel.

"The message was intended to lure you to Mr. Montrose's house so that the villain could try to murder you," she whispered.

Beatrice, Amelia and Edward stared at Gabriel.

"Actually, he intended to kill both Mr. Montrose and myself," Gabriel said. His tone suggested that the plan for a dual murder was somehow a mitigating circumstance that left him blameless.

Venetia wanted to pound her fists against his chest in frustration.

Montrose cleared his throat apologetically. "Among the few things the intruder did tell me was that he intended to set fire to the house after he'd dealt with Gabriel.

Planned to use the gas. Doubt if anyone would have thought twice about the disaster afterward. Certainly wouldn't have been able to prove murder. Such accidents are common enough."

Beatrice shuddered. "That is true. So many people fail to take proper precautions with the mains and the jets. Well, sir, I must say, you are fortunate that the villain did not murder you in cold blood while he waited for Mr. Jones to arrive."

"The fellow explained that he couldn't do that," Montrose said.

Amelia tilted her head slightly. "Never say he had some scruples about murdering you, sir?"

"None whatsoever," Montrose assured her cheerfully. "The villain claimed that the smell of blood and death would warn Gabriel as soon as he opened the door of the house. I think he feared that in such a situation Gabriel would do the intelligent thing and summon a policeman before he went inside to investigate."

"I think it is safe to say that it is highly unlikely that Mr. Jones would have done such an intelligent thing," Venetia muttered darkly. "It is quite probable that he would have rushed straight in to see what the matter was."

Gabriel was amused. "Just as you did the night you went into the darkroom at the exhibition hall and discovered Burton's corpse?"

She flushed. "That was another situation, entirely."

"Indeed?" he raised his brows. "In what way was it different?"

"Never mind," she said, putting as much frost into her words as possible.

Beatrice peered at Montrose over the rims of her spectacles. "I understand the villain intended to murder both you and Mr. Jones, but why did he plan to set fire to your house?"

Venetia saw Montrose and Gabriel exchange what could only be described as veiled looks. She'd had enough of Arcane Society secrets.

"What is going on here?" she demanded.

Gabriel hesitated and then an air of stoic resignation settled on him.

"It is one thing to do away with a person who has no important connections," he said. "One incurs considerably more risk when one murders someone who possesses powerful friends or relatives."

"Yes, I see what you mean," Venetia said. "If you and Mr. Montrose had been found murdered, there would likely have been an extensive investigation by the police. The killer was no doubt aware of that and hoped to cover his tracks by leaving his victims' corpses to be consumed by what would appear to be an ordinary house fire."

Montrose chuckled.

Edward watched him curiously. "What is so amusing, sir?"

Montrose bobbed his eyebrows at him. "I doubt that anyone would have paid too much attention to the murder of an elderly man who did not go out much and who had no important social connections. But it would have been quite another affair if Gabriel Jones had been found stabbed to death. Why, there would have been hell to pay and that's a fact. Pardon my language, ladies."

There was a short, startled silence. Venetia looked at Gabriel. He was even more grim-faced than he had been a moment ago.

"What," Beatrice said very deliberately, "do you mean by that, Mr. Montrose?"

"Yes," Amelia added. "We are all quite fond of Mr. Jones, of course, but I do not think that we can claim to be what anyone would call *powerful friends.* I doubt the police would have paid much attention to any of us if we had tried to insist upon an extensive investigation."

Montrose was clearly bewildered by their reaction. "By powerful friends, I was referring to the Council of the Arcane Society, of course, to say nothing of the Master himself. I assure you, there would have been an enormous amount of pressure brought to bear if it transpired that the heir to the Master's Chair had been murdered."

31

"I think," Venetia said coolly, "that you had better explain precisely who you are, Mr. Jones."

He had known that he would have to deal with this sooner or later, Gabriel reminded himself. He had hoped to put it off for a while but fate had conspired against him. The entire household was watching him. Montrose, aware that he was the one who had created the problem, was paying close attention to his tea.

"Are you really going to become the next Master of the Arcane Society, sir?" Edward asked, clearly enthralled by the notion.

"Not until after my father decides to retire," Gabriel said. "I'm afraid it is one of those old-fashioned ceremonial posts that is handed down through families."

Montrose coughed and sputtered on a swallow of tea. Beatrice handed him a napkin.

"Thank you, Miss Sawyer," Montrose mumbled into the napkin. "Ceremonial posts. Hah. Wait until your father hears that one, Gabriel."

"What will you get to do as Master of the society?" Edward continued, intrigued. "Will you carry a sword?"

"No," Gabriel said. "There is no sword involved, fortunately. For the most part, it is a rather dull career."

Montrose opened his mouth in a manner that suggested that he was going to contradict that statement also. Gabriel shot him a silencing look.

Montrose went back to his tea.

"I will conduct the occasional meeting," Gabriel explained to Edward. "Review the names of those who have been recommended for membership, establish committees to oversee various areas of research and so on and so forth."

"Oh." Edward did not bother to conceal his disappointment. "That does sound quite boring."

"Yes, precisely," Gabriel said.

Venetia did not appear entirely convinced, he noticed. But then, she had seen the collection of relics and artifacts housed at Arcane House. He knew that she had been sensitive to the residual psychical energy emitted by some of them.

Time to change the subject, he decided.

"Due to events tonight, the situation has changed," he said quietly. "I can no longer assume that this household is safe. The killer has made it plain that he is willing to use others as pawns in his scheme, and I cannot be here every minute of the day and night to protect you. I must be free to continue my investigation. Therefore, it will be necessary to take certain steps."

Venetia watched him warily. "What sort of steps?"

"Tomorrow morning everyone in this household will pack for an extended stay in the country," he said. "You will all take the afternoon train to a seaside village called Graymoor. That includes you, sir," he added to Montrose. "I will send a telegram ahead. You will be met by people I know well who will identify themselves to you. They will convey you to a safe location."

Venetia stared at him, dumbfounded. "What on earth do you mean, sir?"

"What about the gallery?" Amelia asked anxiously. "Venetia has several important sittings this week."

"Your shopgirl, Maud, will manage the gallery," Gabriel said. "She can reschedule the sittings."

Edward bounced up and down in his chair. "I like trains. We took one when we came here to London. May I pack my kite, sir?"

"Yes," Gabriel said. He kept an eye on Venetia the way one keeps an eye on a volcano that is on the verge of erupting.

"No," she said. "That is impossible. Or rather, I should say it is not possible for me to leave London. Beatrice, Amelia and Edward can be sent away for a time but I cannot cancel my sittings. Exclusive clients do not appreciate that sort of treatment. Furthermore, I have another exhibition next Tuesday night. It is the most important one to date."

He had known this was not going to be easy, Gabriel told himself.

"We cannot take any more chances, Venetia," he said. "Your safety and the safety of your family is our most important priority."

She straightened her shoulders. "I appreciate your concern, sir. And I agree completely that Edward, Amelia and Beatrice must be protected. But there is another priority that must be given equal consideration."

"What is that?" he asked.

"The future of my professional career," she said.

"Damnation, where is your common

sense? You cannot mean to put your business interests above your own safety."

"You do not comprehend, Mr. Jones," she said. "Those sittings that you want me to cancel and that exhibition are crucial to my family's financial security. You cannot expect me to walk away from my schedule. There is too much at stake."

He looked at her across the small space. "I understand the critical nature of your career. But your life is more important."

"I would appreciate it, Mr. Jones, if you would bear in mind certain facts."

"What facts?" He was very close to losing what little remained of his temper. He sensed that Venetia was struggling just as hard to hold onto hers.

"After you have found your missing formula, you will likely disappear again, Mr. Jones," she said. "Aunt Beatrice, Amelia and Edward and I will be on our own. To be blunt, sir, the profits from my photography commissions are all that stand between us and a life of desperation and poverty. I cannot put that future at risk. You must not ask me to do so."

"If it is money that concerns you, I will see to it that you do not sink into poverty in the future."

"We do not take charity, sir," she said

tightly. "Nor can we afford to be placed in the position of depending upon an income from a gentleman who has no strong connection to this family. We discovered the precariousness of that sort of situation after Father was killed."

Gabriel felt his temper flare. *I am not your father,* he wanted to shout. It took every ounce of willpower he possessed to keep his anger leashed.

"I must insist that you go to the country with the others, Venetia," he said in a tone that he knew was stone cold.

She rose to her feet, clutching the lapels of her dressing gown, and faced him in the firelight.

"Mr. Jones, may I remind you that you have no right to insist upon anything. You are a guest here, not the master of this house."

She might as well have slapped his face, he thought. Pain swept through him, mingling with the cold heat left over from the battle with the killer.

He said nothing. He did not trust himself to say one damned word.

No one else in the room stirred so much as a hair. He knew they were all shocked by the confrontation, uncertain what to say or how to react. Edward looked frightened.

The silent battle raged for what seemed like an eternity but what in reality lasted only a few seconds.

Without another word, Venetia turned and walked out into the hall. Gabriel listened to her footsteps. By the time she reached the stairs, she was in full flight. A moment later he heard the door of her bedroom slam shut.

Everyone else in the parlor heard it, too. They all turned back to him.

"Sir?" Edward asked uncertainly. "What about Venetia?"

Amelia swallowed, visibly shaken. "I know her very well, sir. If she feels she must stay here in London, there will be nothing you can do to convince her otherwise."

"She is committed to taking care of this family, Mr. Jones," Beatrice said quietly. "I fear you will never be able to dissuade her from what she views as her responsibilities, not even if her life is at risk."

He looked at each of them in turn.

"I will take care of her," he said.

The tension eased. He knew that they had accepted the statement for the solemn vow that it was.

"Everything will be all right, in that case," Edward said.

32

Gabriel slung his overcoat around his shoulders like a cloak and let himself out into the fog-shrouded garden. He needed to move, to prowl, anything to work off the preternatural awareness and the restlessness that still heated his blood.

It was as if the hunter inside him was expecting another villain to leap out of the shadows; perhaps even looking forward to another such encounter. He ached for release in the form of an act of violence or an act of passion; either would no doubt suffice. But neither was available to him so he would pace.

The argument with Venetia had only made an already untenable situation worse. He needed the darkness and the silence of the night to help him order his thoughts, soothe the savage beast and allow him to regain full control.

Behind him the household was once again abed. It was also filled to the brim. He would be sharing the attic room with Montrose tonight.

Montrose had insisted that he was perfectly capable of going home alone but he had been through an ordeal and Gabriel had been unwilling to put him at risk a second time. There was no telling what the killer would do next now that he had been thwarted.

Gabriel moved off the small stone terrace and onto the little path that wound through the tiny garden. He had known from the outset that Venetia would be difficult to handle, he reminded himself. Indeed, he had welcomed the feminine challenge she presented. But deep down he had always assumed that in a toe-to-toe confrontation between them he could impose his will on her.

It was not male arrogance that had led him to that belief, he thought; not simply the fact that he was a man and she was a woman and therefore she would, in the end, submit. On the contrary, he had been certain that in a crisis she would obey him for the simple reason that she was quite intelligent and would realize he was trying to protect her.

But he had failed to take into account the fact that she had her own responsibilities and obligations. He had blundered badly. The knowledge did not improve his mood.

The kitchen door squeaked faintly.

"Gabriel?" Venetia sounded tentative, as though she thought he might bite. "Are you all right?"

He stopped and looked back at her through the fog. He wondered if she was viewing his aura. There was no way she could see him through the heavy vapor.

"Yes," he said.

"I saw you from my bedroom window. I was afraid that you were leaving again."

Had that possibility genuinely worried her? he wondered.

"I felt the need of some fresh air," he said.

She came toward him slowly, but she did not falter. She knew exactly where she was going. She must be viewing his aura, he thought, using it as a guide.

"I was concerned," she said. "You have been in a strange mood since you came home tonight. You are not yourself. That is only to be expected after what you went through at Mr. Montrose's house."

Icy amusement flickered through him. "You are wrong, Venetia. I regret to inform you that I am, in fact, very much myself tonight. Too much so, unfortunately."

She stopped a short distance away. "I don't understand."

"It would be best if you went back to bed."

She came a little closer. He could see that she was still garbed in the cozy dressing gown she had put on earlier. Her arms were wrapped tightly around herself.

"Tell me what is wrong," she said, surprisingly gentle.

"You know what is wrong."

"I realize that you are annoyed with me because I will not agree to leave London tomorrow but I do not believe that is the only reason for your present state. Is it your nerves? Are they overwrought because of the dreadful encounter this evening?"

He gave a short, sharp laugh. "My nerves. Yes. That is no doubt as logical an explanation as any other."

"Gabriel, please. Tell me why you are acting like this."

The wall inside him crumbled without warning. Perhaps it was because he wanted her so badly or perhaps it was because his self-control had been pushed to the limit tonight. Whatever the case, he'd had his fill of keeping certain secrets.

"Damn it to hell and back," he said. "You say you want the truth? Then you shall have it."

She said nothing.

"What you are witnessing is an aspect of my nature that I have spent my entire adult life attempting to conceal. Most of the time I am successful. Tonight, however, during the battle in Montrose's house, the creature escaped from its cage for a time. It will take me a while to get it back under lock and key."

"Creature? What on earth are you talking about?"

"Tell me, Venetia, are you acquainted with the work of Mr. Darwin?"

There was a moment of acute silence. The fog grew colder around him.

"Somewhat," she finally said very carefully. "My father was fascinated with Mr. Darwin's notions of natural selection and talked about them at some length. But I am certainly no scientist."

"Neither am I. But I have studied Darwin's works and the writings of others who echo his thoughts on the subject of what he termed 'descent with modification.' There is a compelling logic and simplicity to the theory."

"My father used to say that is the hallmark of all great insights."

"Most of the members of the Arcane Society are convinced that paranormal talents represent latent senses in mankind that should be studied, researched and encouraged in our species. In cases such as your ability to see auras, perhaps they are right. Where is the harm in viewing an aura?"

"What is your point?"

"I, too, possess certain paranormal senses."

He waited for her reaction. It was not long in coming.

"I suspected as much," she said. "I sensed the energy in you when we were . . . together at Arcane House and then again in the carriage tonight. And I remembered how you could make out those two men in the woods three months ago. I noticed how you made your way out of the garden earlier this evening. It was as if you could see in the dark."

"You sensed my psychical abilities?"

"Yes. They are the talents that allow you to move through the night with the ease of a hunting cat, are they not?"

He stilled. "The phrase *hunting cat* is more accurate than you can possibly know. *Beast of prey* is a better term. When I employ my psychical senses I become another kind of creature altogether, Venetia."

"What do you mean?"

"What if the paranormal senses such as

the kind I possess are not new characteristics brought about by the forces of natural selection, but rather just the opposite?"

She took a step forward. "No, Gabriel, you must not talk like that."

"What if my ability to detect the psychical spoor of others of our kind who are bent on violence is actually some atavistic sense that is, in fact, in the process of being weeded out of our species by the great forces of natural selection? What if I am some sort of throwback to something that does not belong in this modern age. *What if I am a monster?*"

"Stop it, do you hear me?" She closed the space between them in a single stride. "You will not speak such nonsense. You are not a monster. You are a man. If possessing paranormal abilities makes one a beast, then I, too, am somehow less than human. Do you believe that?"

"No."

"Then your logic is faulty, is it not?"

"You do not understand what happens to me when I employ my psychical senses."

"Gabriel, I admit that I do not pretend to comprehend the precise nature of our metaphysical abilities. But what is so odd about that? I do not understand how it is that I can see, hear, taste or smell, either. I do not know why or how I dream nor do I know what is going on inside my brain when I read a book or listen to music. I cannot even explain why I take pleasure in my photography. What is more, the scientists and philosophers cannot give me the answers, either, at least not yet."

"Yes, but everyone can do those things that you describe."

"That is not true. Some do not possess one or more senses and certainly no two people employ their senses in the same way or to the same degree. We all know that two people may look at the same picture or eat the same food or smell the same flower and each will describe the experience differently."

"I am different."

"We are all different in some way. What is so strange about the notion that some psychical senses are merely more acute versions of the normal senses that we already possess?"

She did not understand, he thought.

"Tell me, Venetia, when you employ your paranormal senses, do you pay a price?" he asked quietly.

She hesitated. "I hadn't thought about it in quite that way, but, yes, I suppose I do."

That stopped him for a moment. "What does it cost you?"

"When I concentrate to view a person's aura, my others senses grow dim," she said quietly. "The world around me seems to lose color. It is like looking at the negative of a photograph. If I try to move it is like walking through a landscape where all the light and shadows are reversed. It is disorienting, to say the least."

"What I experience is far more disturbing."

"Tell me what it is that concerns you about your psychical senses," she said as calmly as though they were discussing an interesting bit of natural history lore.

He shoved one hand through his hair, searching for the words. He had never discussed this with anyone except Caleb, and then only in an oblique manner that had left much unsaid by both of them.

"When I encounter the fresh taint of violence it is as though I have consumed a powerful drug," he said slowly. "A predatory lust is unleashed inside me. It is as if I am compelled to *hunt*."

"You say it is the spoor of violence that arouses this sensation?"

He nodded. "I can use my psychical senses without arousing the hunting lust but when I encounter the psychical traces of another who is intent on violence, a dark passion threatens to consume me. If I had caught the man who came into Montrose's house tonight, I could have killed him without hesitation. The only reason I would have allowed him to live was because I wanted answers from him. That is wrong. I am supposed to be a modern, civilized man."

"He was the beast, not you. You were engaged in a fight for your life and the life of Mr. Montrose. It is no wonder that your strongest emotions were aroused."

"They are not civilized emotions. They come upon me like a dark passion. What if someday I am unable to control the sensation? What if I become like the man in Montrose's house?"

"You have nothing in common with him," she said, startlingly fierce.

"I fear you are wrong," he said quietly. "I think he and I may have a great deal in common. He could see as well as I can in the dark and he was very, very quick in his movements. What is more, he knew enough about my abilities to lay a clever trap for me by leaving a false trail through the house for me to follow. He and I are two of a kind, Venetia."

She reached up and caught his face between her palms. "Gabriel, tell me, after that man fled, did you feel the urge to seek another's death?"

The question made no sense to him. "What?"

"Your prey escaped. Did you feel an impulse to find another victim?"

Baffled, he shook his head once. "The hunt was over."

"You did not fear that you would harm Mr. Montrose while you were still in the grip of this predatory lust you described?"

"Why the devil would I want to hurt Montrose?"

She smiled in the shadows. "A wild beast would not distinguish between his victims while under the influence of his baser instincts. Only a civilized man does that."

"But I did not feel civilized. That is what I am attempting to explain."

"Shall I tell you why it never crossed your mind to hurt Montrose or anyone else, for that matter, after the villain escaped?"

He was off balance now, a little dazed. "Why?"

"You are called to hunt because you are compelled to protect that which is in your charge. That is why you went into the house in the first place tonight. You can be extremely stubborn and quite arrogant at times, Gabriel, but I have never, for one moment, doubted that you would put your own life at risk to protect others."

He did not know what to say so he kept silent.

"I knew that much about you from the moment we met," she continued. "You proved it the night you sent your housekeeper and me out of harm's way at Arcane House. You proved it again in your own blockheaded fashion by avoiding all contact with me because you did not want to draw me into danger. When you did deign to show up on my doorstep it was because you felt obliged to protect me. And you gave fresh evidence of that aspect of your nature tonight when you went to Mr. Montrose's rescue and when you determined to send my family away to the country."

"Venetia —"

"Your fears are groundless," she said. "You are not a wild beast that succumbs to a savage bloodlust. You are a guardian at heart." She smiled. "I will not go so far as to call you a guardian *angel,* even though you are named Gabriel, but you were most certainly born to shield and protect."

He caught her shoulders. "If that is true, why did I want to throw myself on you the moment I walked through the door of your house tonight? Why is it all I can do to not strip that dressing gown off you, put you down on the ground and lose myself in you right now?"

Her hands did not leave his face. "You did not drag me off to bed earlier because it was not the right place or time. And we both know that you are not going to make love to me out here in the garden tonight. You are in control of all of your passions, sir."

"You cannot know that."

"Yes, I do." She stood on tiptoe and brushed her mouth against his. "Good night, Gabriel. I will see you in the morning. Try to get some sleep."

She turned and walked toward the house.

As always, his body responded to the challenge she had flung down.

"One more thing," he said softly.

She paused at the door. "Yes?"

"Out of curiosity, what is to prevent me from putting you down on the ground and making love to you tonight?"

"Why, because it is ever so damp and chilly out here, of course. Not at all comfortable or healthful. We would both no doubt wake up with a severe case of rheumatism or a bad cold in the morning."

She opened the door and disappeared into the hall. Her soft laughter was like an exotic perfume. It lingered long after she was gone, warming him.

Some time later he made his way up the stairs to the small room at the top of the house. Montrose stirred slightly in the shadows of the small bed.

"That you, Jones?" he asked.

"Yes, sir." He unfolded the blankets that Mrs. Trench had left on a chair and fashioned a bed on the floor.

"No business of mine, of course," Montrose said, "but I must admit I'm a trifle confused. Mind if I ask why you're sleeping up here in the attic?"

Gabriel started to unfasten his shirt. "It's somewhat complicated, sir."

"Damnation, you're a married man. And I must say, Mrs. Jones appears to be quite fit. Why aren't you downstairs with her?"

Gabriel slung his torn shirt over the back of the chair. "I believe I explained that Mrs. Jones and I were secretly married in a hurry and then immediately separated due to the events at Arcane House. We did not have the opportunity to become accustomed to each other as husband and wife."

"Huh."

"The shock of all the startling incidents

lately has naturally had a profound effect on her delicate sensibilities."

"No offense, but she doesn't look all that delicate to me. Seems quite sturdy."

"She needs time to adjust to the notion of being a wife."

"Still say the situation is extremely odd." Montrose settled himself against the pillows. "But I suppose that's the modern age, for you. Things aren't done the way they were in my day."

"I've heard that is true, sir," Gabriel said.

He settled himself into the hard, makeshift bed and folded his arms behind his head.

All his adult life he had done his best to control and confine the psychical part of his nature out of a deep-seated fear that it meant he was something other than human, something that might someday prove dangerous.

But tonight, with only a few words, Venetia had set him free.

It was time to start using all of his abilities, he thought.

33

Rosalind Fleming leaned forward and peered more closely into the gilded dressing room mirror. Anxiety and rage flashed through her. There was no longer any doubt. Faint, fine lines were beginning to appear at the corners of her eyes.

She stared at her image, forcing herself to confront what she knew was the reality of her own future. Powder and rouge would serve for a while; at best, another two or three years. Then her beauty would slowly, inevitably fade.

She had always considered her looks to be one of her two great assets. When she had first arrived in London, she had naively believed that her beauty would prove to be the most useful and had designed her strategy accordingly.

But she had soon discovered the flaw in her plan. Catching the eye of gentlemen who moved in elevated circles had proved vastly more difficult than she had assumed. Such men had their pick of beautiful women. On the one or two occasions when she had been lucky enough to draw the attention of a wealthy man she had quickly learned that they were like small boys: easily bored with their playthings and readily attracted to newer, prettier, *younger* toys.

Fortunately she had been able to fall back on her second asset, a talent for mesmerism and blackmail. The skills had helped her earn a living as a practitioner of psychical powers, but until a few months ago they had not shown much promise in helping her obtain the fortune and the social status she hungered for.

Just as London was filled with attractive women at every level of Society, it was also teeming with charlatans and frauds who claimed to possess paranormal powers. The competition was fierce in both quarters and even a genuinely gifted mesmerist could only achieve so much in the way of results. The problem was that one had to keep renewing and reinforcing the commands given to the subjects in order to make them do as one wished. It was painstaking work that all too often went awry.

In the past few months she had begun to believe that her luck had turned at last. She seemed to have it all: access to financial resources beyond anything she had ever known and a position in Society.

But her glittering, golden dream was on the verge of collapsing into a nightmare.

She knew precisely who was to blame: Venetia Jones.

34

In spite of the fact that everyone had gone to bed quite late, breakfast was served early the following morning. Immediately after the meal was concluded Beatrice rose from the table.

"Time to pack," she said. "Come along, Edward and Amelia. There is a great deal to accomplish before we leave for the train station."

There was a scraping of chairs as they all hurried out of the room.

When they were gone, Montrose got to his feet. "I shall send word to my housekeeper. She will have arrived at my house to begin work for the day and will no doubt be wondering where I am. I'll have her pack a trunk for me. I can collect it on the way to the train station."

Venetia put down her teacup. "You may use my study to write the message to her, sir."

"Thank you, Mrs. Jones," he said.

He disappeared into the hall.

Venetia found herself alone with Gabriel.

She regarded him warily, braced for another argument.

Gabriel did not appear to be in the mood for another quarrel, however. He had a black eye and she had noticed that when he reached for the newspaper earlier, he had winced, but otherwise he appeared to be in remarkably good humor.

"How do you feel?" she asked, pouring herself a second cup of tea.

"As if I've been run over by a carriage." He helped himself to the last slice of toast. "Otherwise, quite fit, thank you."

"Perhaps you should spend the day in bed."

"That sounds rather boring," he said around a mouthful of toast. "Unless, of course, you intend to spend it there with me. I must warn you, the bed in the attic will not accommodate both of us, however. We would most likely be forced to use your bed."

"Really, sir, that is not the sort of remark one makes at the breakfast table."

"Should I have saved it for dinner?"

She glowered. "You appear to be in excellent spirits for a man who only a few hours ago feared that he was on the verge of becoming a ravening beast."

He took another bite of the toast,

looking thoughtful. "I don't recall using the word *ravening.* But you are correct, Mrs. Jones, I do feel much better this morning."

"I'm glad of that much, at least. What do you propose to do today?"

"Among other things, I intend to do some extensive research on Rosalind Fleming."

"How will you go about that?"

"I would very much like to have a chat with one of her servants. Maids and footmen always know more about their employers than most people realize. If possible, I will try to find a way to get into her house, perhaps in the guise of a tradesman."

"You intend to use a disguise?"

He smiled. "Unlike you, my dear, I do not object to using the servants' entrance."

Venetia put the teapot down hard. "That would be extremely risky."

He shrugged. "I will be cautious."

She thought about his plan for a moment. "You said that the person you confronted in Mr. Montrose's house was a man."

"Without a doubt. I've told you that I can tell the difference. But I am convinced that Rosalind Fleming is involved in this affair."

She frowned. “Given recent events, it baffles me why you are in such a jovial mood this morning. One would almost think that you have been nipping at Mrs. Trench’s gin.”

He smiled his mysterious smile and drank some coffee.

Venetia decided not to pursue the topic. There were, she reminded herself, more pressing matters.

“You suggested the possibility that Mrs. Fleming may well have employed someone to do her killing for her. That villain must have been the person you encountered last night,” she said.

Gabriel inclined his head. “With luck, he will make another attempt to conclude the business.”

She straightened, thoroughly alarmed. “Gabriel, you mustn’t deliberately make a target of yourself. You said the villain may possess psychical talents similar to your own.”

“Yes.” Gabriel’s humor faded. In its place was a cold anticipation. “And if he is, indeed, employing the same kind of psychical senses that I possess, I think I can make certain assumptions.”

“Such as?”

“He may or may not be in the pay of

Rosalind Fleming but either way it is safe to say that he will have his own private objectives and his own strategy. I think it is unlikely that he will do someone else's killing unless it serves his own purposes. It is equally unlikely that he will take orders from someone else unless it suits those same purposes."

She watched him intently. "You sound quite sure of those assumptions."

"I can also say with some assurance that he will not have taken last night's defeat well. I suspect that he now views me not just as someone who must be removed because I happen to be making things difficult for him but rather as an opponent. A challenger or competitor, if you will. He and I are, to his thinking, two rival predators who have clashed. Only one can survive."

She felt the hair on the nape of her neck lift.

"Do not talk like that," she said softly, fiercely. "I told you last night, you are *not* a predator, Gabriel."

"I will not get into another debate on the subject of whether or not I am a ravening beast of prey," he said. "But of one thing I am absolutely certain."

"What is that?"

"I can think like one."

35

Gabriel was still watching Venetia's face, waiting for her reaction to his words when he heard the carriage halt in the street. The muffled sound of the front door knocker being banged in a forceful manner came a moment later.

Mrs. Trench's heavy footsteps thudded in the hall.

"I wonder who that can be at this hour?" Venetia said.

He heard the door open. A loud male voice boomed down the hallway.

"Where in blazes is our new daughter-in-law?"

Venetia froze.

Gabriel looked toward the doorway of the breakfast room, resigned to the inevitable.

"My life used to be so simple and well ordered," he said to Venetia. "Why, there was a time when I could look forward to spending an entire morning alone with my books."

"Is that your father out there in the hall?" Venetia gasped.

"I'm afraid so. Mother will no doubt be with him. They are inseparable."

"What are your parents doing here?"

"I expect some well-meaning individual sent them a telegram."

Mrs. Trench appeared in the doorway looking bewildered.

"A Mr. and Mrs. Jones to see you, ma'am," she began.

"No need to stand on formality," Hippolyte Jones roared behind her. "We're all family here."

Mrs. Trench fell back out of sight. Gabriel got to his feet. His mother came through the doorway first. Attractive and petite, Marjorie Jones was fashionably dressed in a blue gown that accented her black-and-silver hair.

Hippolyte loomed behind her. With his craggy features, brilliant green eyes and shoulder-length, snow-white mane he never failed to make a formidable impression.

Out of the corner of his eye Gabriel watched Venetia's expression as she took in the sight of his parents filling the doorway. She looked as if she had seen a pair of ghosts.

"Good day to you, Mother," Gabriel said. He nodded at his father. "Sir."

"What on earth happened to you?" Marjorie asked, catching sight of his face. "You look as though you have been in a brawl."

"Walked into a door," Gabriel said. "In the dark."

"But you can see very well in the dark," Marjorie said.

"I'll explain later, Mother." He made the introductions swiftly, giving Venetia no time to say anything. Then he turned back to his parents.

"This is a surprise," he said evenly. "We weren't expecting you."

Marjorie looked at him with a hint of reproof. "What did you expect us to do after we got the telegram from your aunt Elizabeth informing us that you had eloped? I know you were occupied with that affair of the missing formula, but surely you could have found time to send your parents a note or a telegram at the very least."

"What made Aunt Elizabeth think that I had eloped?" Gabriel asked.

"Your cousin Caleb mentioned something to her about your plan to marry the photographer who went to Arcane House to record the antiquities," Hippolyte said with a suspiciously smug smile. "Seemed to be some confusion about the actual timing of the wedding. We decided to come straight to London to see what was going on for ourselves."

"Imagine our surprise when we discovered that you and your lovely bride had already settled down into married life," Marjorie said happily.

"Caleb," Gabriel said. "Yes, of course. I should have known. Mother, I fear there has been some confusion regarding the elopement —"

Marjorie smiled warmly at Venetia. "Welcome to the family, my dear. You cannot know how I have longed for Gabe to find the right woman. We had almost given up hope. Isn't that right, Hippolyte?"

Hippolyte chuckled and rocked on his heels. "Told you Miss Milton was the right one for him."

"Yes, you did, dear," Marjorie said.

"Hah. And you said that I shouldn't dabble in our son's personal affairs. Where the deuce do you think we'd be now if I hadn't done just that?"

Venetia appeared to be locked in a trance of some sort. She was on her feet but gripping the edge of the table as though she feared her knees would give way.

"You were absolutely right, Hippolyte," Marjorie said. She turned back to Gabriel.

"But I really must protest this runaway marriage. I had intended a proper wedding for you. Now that you have deprived me of that, you must allow me to stage a decent reception. We can't have people thinking that we aren't delighted with our new daughter-in-law."

Venetia made an odd little noise. Gabriel saw that she was staring very hard at Hippolyte.

"I know you, sir," she said, sounding dazed. "You bought some photographs from me in Bath."

"I certainly did," he agreed. "Wonderful pictures they were, too. Knew the minute I met you and saw your work that you were the one for Gabe. Took a bit of maneuvering to arrange for you to photograph the collection, mind you. The Council can be quite old-fashioned when it comes to employing modern inventions, but I am the Master, after all."

"The staff is opening up the town house as we speak," Marjorie announced. "We haven't used it in years but it shouldn't take too long to make it comfortable."

"Your mother brought a small army of servants with us on the train this morning," Hippolyte explained.

Footsteps sounded on the stairs and in

the hall. Edward arrived first, eager to see what was happening. Amelia appeared behind him, her face bright with curiosity. Beatrice brought up the rear, looking troubled.

"I didn't realize we had visitors," Beatrice said.

Marjorie turned toward her. "My deepest apologies for intruding on you at such an early hour. We took the liberty, being family. I do hope you don't mind."

"Family?" Beatrice peered at her through her glasses. "Perhaps you have the wrong address."

"Yes," Venetia said in rather desperate tones. "Wrong address. That's what this is all about. Some sort of dreadful mix-up."

Everyone ignored her.

"There's just the four of us, my sisters and my aunt and me," Edward explained to Marjorie. "We don't have any other family." He glanced quickly at Gabriel. "Not a real family, that is."

Hippolyte ruffled Edward's hair with one large hand.

"I have news for you, young man," he said. "You've got a lot more family now. And I assure you, we're very real."

36

"We have a disaster on our hands." Venetia stalked to the far end of the small study. When she found herself confronted with a bookcase, she whirled around and started back in the direction from which she had just come. "A complete disaster."

Gabriel watched her from a chair near the window, calculating how to deal with the situation. The household had quieted down now that his parents had left to return to the town house, but Venetia's mood was dangerously volatile. He elected to try reason and logic.

"Look on the positive side," he suggested.

She threw him a scathing glare. "There is no positive side."

"Only consider, my sweet. There is no longer any need to send Beatrice, Amelia, Edward and Montrose out of town. I spoke with my father when I saw the carriage off a short time ago. I explained to him what had happened. He and I agreed that we will all move into the town house and stay there until this affair of the formula is concluded."

She was aghast. "You intend for us to move into your parents' house?"

"Everyone will be quite safe, I assure you," he said. "As my father noted, there is a large staff to keep an eye on things. The servants have all been with my parents forever. They are loyal and well trained. You could not ask for better guards."

That gave her pause. He was not surprised. The safety of her family was, after all, of paramount importance to her.

"But what about us?" She clasped her hands behind her back and continued pacing. "Your parents believe that we are married. You heard your mother. She is planning a reception, for heaven's sake."

He extended his legs and regarded the toes of his boots. "I will break the news to my parents this afternoon. They will understand that the strategy of pretending to be married was necessary."

She frowned. "I'm not so certain of that."

"Trust me, my father is very keen on recovering the missing formula. He will accept whatever strategy is necessary."

"He also appeared quite keen on the notion of you getting married. So did your mother."

He shrugged. “I will deal with them.”

She did another circuit of the room and then collapsed into the chair behind the desk.

“Talk about weaving a tangled web,” she said, drumming her fingers.

He smiled. “Fortunately, your family and mine are quite expert when it comes to keeping secrets.”

37

"What the devil do you mean, you aren't married to Mrs. Jones?" Hippolyte came to a halt in the middle of the park and swung around to confront Gabriel. "You're living in her house as her husband. Your mother and I were informed that the two of you are going about in public as a respectably married couple."

In spite of the assurance that he had given to Venetia, he had known that this was not going to go smoothly, Gabriel reminded himself.

He had invited Hippolyte to accompany him on a walk in the park for the conversation. He knew his father well enough to expect fireworks when the news concerning the fake marriage was delivered. He was not disappointed. Hippolyte gave every indication of being about to burst into flames.

"I am aware of how the situation appears, sir," Gabriel said.

"I demand to know what is going on here, Gabe. Your mother will be shocked to her heels when she discovers that you are posing as Mrs. Jones's husband."

"I had hoped to have this entire affair behind me before you and Mother returned from Italy."

"Did you, indeed?"

"Allow me to explain."

He gave Hippolyte a rapid summary of events. His father's expression moved through a range of emotions, beginning with outrage and ending in astonishment.

"Good lord," Hippolyte said, reluctantly fascinated. "Didn't think that black eye you're sporting was the result of walking into a door in the dark."

"Well, it was quite dark and there were some doors."

Hippolyte sat down on a nearby bench and clenched both hands around the handle of his walking stick. "You think that this Mrs. Fleming and some unknown person with talents similar to your own are involved in the theft of the formula?"

"Yes." Gabriel sat down, leaned forward and clasped his hands loosely between his knees. "I have not been able to deduce how Mrs. Fleming and her associate learned of the formula, let alone why someone sent two men to try to steal the strongbox. I plan to continue my inquiries, but meanwhile I must be certain that Venetia and her family as well as Montrose are safe."

"We will see to that by moving them into the town house," Hippolyte said. "No need to worry on that account. Once the house is secure it will be as good as a fortress."

"I could also use your assistance, sir."

"Could you now?" Hippolyte looked pleased. "What would you have me do?"

"Mrs. Fleming must know who I am but I think it highly unlikely that she has ever met you. I was going to follow her about today, perhaps see if there is a way to get into her town house and have a look around."

"Ah," Hippolyte said, enthusiasm brightening his green eyes. "You want me to play the spy for you?"

"It would give me an opportunity to make some inquiries in another area."

"What other direction?"

"I have been doing a great deal of thinking since the encounter with the intruder in Montrose's house last night. What do you know about Lord Ackland?"

"Not a great deal." Hippolyte pondered briefly. "He moved in Society years ago, back when I was courting your mother. We met at some of the same balls and soirees and we belonged to some of the same clubs. Don't believe he ever married."

"Is there any possibility that he might have been a member of the Arcane Society or closely connected to someone who is a member?"

"Good lord, no," Hippolyte said, very certain. "The man was not at all the scholarly sort. He was a notorious gambler and a rakehell in his younger days. Last I heard he had succumbed to senility and was on his deathbed."

"People keep telling me that."

38

"Why the sudden interest in Lord Ackland?" Venetia asked.

She sat across from Gabriel in an unlit cab, watching the street in front of Ackland's mansion. The windows on the ground floor of the big house were illuminated but the curtains were drawn tightly shut. Outside, a thick fog reflected the glow of the streetlamps, creating an eerie, otherworldly atmosphere.

Venetia was dressed in the masculine attire that she had worn to the Janus Club. She and Gabriel had been sitting in the motionless cab for nearly an hour. She was quite certain that both the horse and the driver had dozed off some time ago.

"We have been assuming that he is Mrs. Fleming's unwitting dupe in this affair," Gabriel said. "A source of money and an entrée into Society. But Harrow and my father have both told me that they were under the impression that as of a few months ago, Ackland was not only losing his mind but gravely ill."

"What are you thinking?" she asked.

"In the course of the conversation in the park with my father this afternoon, it occurred to me that perhaps Ackland's newfound stamina might be due to more than Mrs. Fleming's therapeutic influence."

A chill that had nothing to do with the fog tingled across her nerves. "Are you implying that someone may be *posing* as Lord Ackland?"

"When you consider it, masquerading as a doddering old fool in the thrall of a lovely schemer is excellent camouflage, is it not?"

"But if he isn't the real Lord Ackland, who is he and how did he come to take Ackland's place?"

"One question at a time," Gabriel said. "We don't know for certain yet that the man living in that house is a fraud. That is what I wish to ascertain this evening. With any luck at all, he will leave to visit the charming Mrs. Fleming for a few hours or perhaps go to his club. If he does, I am hoping that you will have an opportunity to view his aura."

"You think I have seen it before?" she asked uneasily.

"Yes."

"One of my photography clients, perhaps?"

"Hush," Gabriel whispered. "The lights are going out inside the house. Ackland is either heading upstairs to bed or leaving for the evening."

She turned back to the mansion. The front door opened. The only remaining light was the gasolier in the front hall. Ackland was silhouetted briefly in its glare. Then he turned down the lamp and tottered out onto the steps, cane in hand. He paused to close the door before he made his slow, unsteady way down to the street.

When he reached the pavement, he blew a whistle. A hansom appeared in response. It came briskly around the corner, heading toward Ackland.

Venetia realized that in another few seconds the vehicle would be between Ackland and herself, blocking her view.

She concentrated, letting everything inside her go still. The dark, fog-bound world became a negative photographic image. Across from her Gabriel's powerful, controlled aura pulsed darkly. She was also vaguely aware of the aura of the driver of the oncoming hansom. It danced in an erratic pattern that made her suspect that he had been drinking.

She focused on the hunched figure of Ackland, who was leaning heavily on his walking stick while he waited for the hansom to stop.

Ghostly energy seethed around him; intense, disturbing shades of darkness that had no names but made her blood freeze.

"Venetia?" Gabriel said softly.

She blinked, drew a deep, steadying breath and returned to her normal vision. The hansom had halted in front of Ackland. He clambered heavily up into the narrow confines of the cab. The vehicle set off down the street.

Gabriel leaned forward and wrapped his fingers around her wrist. "Are you all right?"

"Yes," she managed. She realized she was shivering. "Yes, I'm all right."

"He's the killer, isn't he?" Gabriel asked. There was the certainty of the hunter that has sighted prey in every word. "The one you saw fleeing the darkroom where Harold Burton drank the cyanide-laced brandy."

She clasped her hands very tightly together. "Yes."

"Ackland was at the reception with Mrs. Fleming that night. The two of them left before Burton disappeared. But Ackland could easily have returned to the exhibition hall using the stairs that descend into the alley at the side of the building."

"He must have arranged to meet Burton in the darkroom," Venetia said.

"I suspect that Ackland or whoever is playing the role was Burton's mysterious wealthy client, the one who paid him to follow you about and keep track of the people you met."

"What are we going to do now? We have no proof of any of this."

Gabriel released her. He leaned back in the seat and studied the dark mansion with a thoughtful expression.

"No servants," he said finally.

"I beg your pardon?"

"We have here a very large house and an obviously infirm old man living in it; a wealthy old man, at that. Yet there is no one to see him out the door, turn off the lights or summon a cab."

She examined the big, fog-shrouded house. "Perhaps he gave the staff the night off."

"I think it is more likely that he does not allow his servants to remain in the house at night because he fears they might discover his secrets," Gabriel said.

He unlatched the carriage door.

Alarmed, she put her hand on his arm. "What are you doing?"

He glanced down at his sleeve, as though surprised to see her touching him. "I am going to see if I can get inside that house and have a look around."

"You mustn't."

"I will never get a better opportunity." He made to move past her. "I will instruct the driver to take you straight to my parents' house and see you safely inside."

"Gabriel, I do not like this."

"This business must be concluded as swiftly as possible."

He paused long enough to kiss her hard on the mouth, and then he vaulted lightly down to the pavement.

He closed the door, spoke briefly to the driver and glided away into the deep shadows of the night.

Venetia looked back as the cab rolled off down the street. She could not see any trace of Gabriel, not even his aura. He had vanished like smoke into the mist.

39

Getting inside the mansion required breaking a small, square pane of glass in the back door. He knew that when the shards were discovered the man who called himself Lord Ackland would realize that there had been an intruder but that could not be helped.

The interior of the house was drenched in darkness but virtually every surface, every doorknob and every banister held the residual taint of one who was capable of killing.

The disturbing psychical pulses excited his own paranormal abilities, heightening his senses. He was intensely aware of his surroundings. His hearing and eyesight sharpened as he moved down the hall.

His sense of smell was more sensitive, too. He caught a strong whiff of dampness underscored by an unpleasant odor of rotting vegetation. The mansion smelled like a swamp. The odor was not emanating from the kitchen. Perhaps one of the bathrooms had been allowed to grow dank and moldy.

He took a quick look around the kitchen but there was nothing of interest there or in the adjoining pantry. He went along the main hall and discovered the drawing room. The furniture was draped in dust-covers.

A short time later he discovered that the same was true of the library. There were only a handful of old books on the shelves. The drawers in the desk were empty.

It was as if Ackland lived here as a ghost.

Between the weak streetlight filtering through the windows in the stairwell and his own psychically enhanced vision, he did not need to strike a light to climb the stairs.

The unpleasant dampness and the rotting odor grew stronger as he neared the landing. He sniffed experimentally and caught the scent of earth and something else. Dead fish.

Deeply curious now, he followed the noxious vapors down the hall and stopped in front of a closed door. There was no doubt in his mind that the foul smell was coming from the other side of the door. It was vaguely familiar. A memory from his youth floated through his head.

The place smelled like a giant aquarium, he thought, one that had gone bad.

He opened the door slowly and found himself standing in what had once no doubt served as the master bedroom.

Large, elaborately designed Wardian cases stood on workbenches around the room. Through the glass domes of the cases he could see a variety of miniature landscapes. Ferns appeared to be the dominant form of plant life.

There were other things inside the cases.

Something skittered behind the glass of the nearest case. When he drew closer he caught the glint of cold, glittering, inhuman eyes watching him.

The fraudulent Ackland evidently fancied himself a naturalist.

He turned back to the aquarium. It was by far the largest he had ever seen, almost a small pond.

The heavily reinforced tank was fronted on one side by thick glass. Even with his psychical vision he could not see into the depths. He struck a light and held it aloft. Two small dead fish floated just below the surface.

No matter how he angled the light, he could not see more than an inch or so into the water because the tank was choked with aquatic plants. They formed a veritable jungle and created a leafy canopy on the surface.

He put out the light and looked around. A desk was positioned near the window. Books filled a nearby bookcase. Unlike the volumes downstairs, these were dust-free and well used. When he got closer he could read the titles on the spines. He recognized a number of natural history texts and Darwin's *On the Origin of Species.*

If Ackland had any other secrets they would be in this room, he thought. He began a methodical search for a safe or other secure hiding place.

He had just pulled up the corner of a suspiciously positioned carpet when he heard the faint sound downstairs.

Someone had opened a door.

40

Venetia stumbled through the rear doorway of the mansion. Her wrists ached from being bound so tightly behind her. She had to fight off the panic generated by the gag that threatened to choke her.

The man who had kidnapped her at gunpoint out of the carriage had identified himself as John Stilwell, but he still wore the white wig, false whiskers and old-fashioned attire that made up his disguise as Lord Ackland.

Unlike Ackland, Stilwell was a man in his prime, fit and powerful. He had used a gun to force the carriage driver to halt earlier but Venetia had also glimpsed a knife tucked away in a special sheath beneath his coat.

He pushed Venetia ahead of him into the hall. She lost her footing and sprawled on the floor.

"My apologies, Mrs. Jones. Forgot you cannot see in the dark as well as your devoted husband and myself."

Stilwell turned up one of the wall

sconces. He leaned down and pulled Venetia to her feet.

"I think we can dispense with the gag now," he said. "This house is very stoutly built. I doubt that anyone outside in the street would hear you if you screamed. Nevertheless, if you make any attempt to do so, I will slit your throat. Do you comprehend me?"

She nodded once, furious. Stilwell untied the gag. She spit it out, gasping for air.

"You have company, Jones," Stilwell called loudly. "I have brought your charming bride with me. I must say, she has an excellent tailor."

Silence echoed.

"Show yourself before I lose my patience and gut her like a fish."

His voice boomed through the big house. There was no response.

"You're too late," Venetia said. "Mr. Jones no doubt found the formula and left."

"Impossible." Stilwell gripped her arm and jerked her along the hallway. "There is no way he could have located it, not in such a short period of time."

She made an attempt at a careless-looking shrug. "Then perhaps he abandoned the effort and departed."

"Come out, Jones," Stilwell yelled, louder this time. "When all is said and done, this is merely a business matter. I want an original version of the picture that Mrs. Jones made of the strongbox. As soon as I examined the photograph that I took from Montrose's house I knew it had been retouched. Did you really think you could fool me so easily?"

"Kill me and you'll lose the only bargaining chip you've got," Venetia said, fighting to keep her voice calm. "Mr. Jones will hunt you down like the mad beast that you are."

"Silence," Stilwell hissed.

He certainly did not care to be called a beast, she thought.

"I know he is in here," Stilwell said. He pulled Venetia toward the staircase. "I saw him get out of that cab and circle around the house. I've been watching him. I knew he was getting closer to discovering that I am not Lord Ackland."

"He was here but now he's gone," Venetia said quietly.

"No. He won't leave until he has found what he came here to find. I know how he thinks. We are alike, you see."

"No," Venetia said. "You are not at all alike."

"You are wrong, Mrs. Jones. Perhaps, under the circumstances, you will be glad that you are mistaken. After all, I will soon be taking your mate's place in your bed." He laughed. "Perhaps, in the dark, you will not notice the difference."

She was so shocked, she could not find words. He truly was mad, she thought.

When they reached the top of the stairs the darkness closed in on Venetia. She stopped abruptly.

"What is that dreadful moldy smell?" she asked. "You should instruct your housekeeper to clean the drains more often."

Stilwell yanked her forward. He paused in front of a door that Venetia could hardly see in the deep shadows of the hall.

When he opened the door, the damp, fetid odors grew stronger.

"Welcome to my laboratory, Mrs. Jones."

He pushed her a short distance into the room, reached out with his free hand and turned up the gas in the nearest wall sconce.

The glary light penetrated only weakly into the darkness. The far corners of the room remained shrouded in shadows but Venetia could see well enough now to realize that Gabriel was nowhere in sight.

Perhaps he really had found the formula and left, she thought.

"Bloody bastard," Stilwell said. "I refuse to believe that he found it. Not this quickly. Not ever. It is in the very last place anyone would search."

Venetia looked around uneasily. A large, plant-choked aquarium occupied the center of the room. Most of the unpleasant odors were emanating from it. But it was the array of Wardian cases set against the walls that made her skin crawl.

She had believed that she could not possibly grow any colder or more frightened but in that moment she knew she had been wrong.

"What have you got in those cases?" she asked.

"An interesting array of small predators," Stilwell said, pushing her forward. "One can learn so much from observing creatures that have not been burdened with the strictures of civilization."

She realized that he was angling her toward one of the larger Wardian cases. It stood on an iron stand. She could see exotic ferns growing inside. Malevolent, inhuman eyes watched her through the glass.

Stilwell was pulling her past the massive aquarium. Venetia looked down and saw a veil of wide green leaves and a couple of dead fish just beneath the surface. The water was so dark she could not make out anything else.

"I find it difficult to believe, but it appears that the situation has changed, Mrs. Jones," Stilwell said. "I shall have to go into hiding for a time. You will accompany me, of course. I will need you to convince Jones to turn over the untouched photograph of the strongbox."

"What is so important about that strongbox?" she asked.

"It contains the list of ingredients required for the antidote, of course." The words were laced with frustration and rage.

"What are you talking about?"

"The damned formula works, according to the alchemist's notes, but only for a short period of time. It is, in fact, a slow poison. The founder of the Arcane Society was a devious bastard, indeed. He inscribed the ingredients for the antidote on the strongbox, knowing that whoever tried to steal the formula would in all likelihood leave the heavy box behind."

A slight movement of the water made her glance down again. She saw the canopy of aquatic plants heave. Something large was stirring beneath the surface.

She wanted to scream but there was no

time. A monstrous creature draped in dripping plants and what appeared to be primordial slime surged up out of the depths of the aquarium.

Stilwell was astonishingly quick, but he had been taken by surprise. He was still turning to confront the menace when the creature from the aquarium landed on top of him.

The gun in Stilwell's hand roared as he went down. Glass shattered in one of the Wardian cases.

Venetia reeled to the side and came up hard against the edge of the aquarium. She saw Gabriel grab Stilwell's gun arm and slam it against the heavy wooden frame.

Stilwell grunted in pain. The weapon landed on the floor and slid beneath the broken glass case.

Stilwell twisted violently to the side, reaching beneath his coat.

"He's got a knife," Venetia shouted.

Neither man seemed to hear her. They were locked in savage combat. The sickening sound of fists slamming into flesh reverberated across the room. The cold, jeweled eyes watching from inside the glass cases glittered.

Venetia circled the aquarium, hurrying toward the gun.

Just as she crouched down to retrieve the weapon from beneath the case stand something moved in the broken glass case above. She jerked back reflexively.

A dainty-looking snake dropped from the shards of glass. It landed on the floor. Acting on some elemental instinct to seek concealment, it darted under the stand and stopped when it encountered the gun. It coiled around the barrel as though seeking protection.

Venetia stepped back, shuddering, and turned around, searching for some object she could use to kill the snake so that she could grab the gun.

She realized that Stilwell had somehow regained his feet. He had the knife in his hand. He launched himself toward Gabriel, who was sprawled on the floor.

Venetia watched in horror. She was too far away to do anything.

But Gabriel was already moving, rolling fluidly to his feet. The arcing blade ripped through the air an inch from his ribs.

The missed blow left Stilwell off balance for an instant. Gabriel swept out one leg and slammed his foot against the other man's thigh.

Stilwell yelled and went down hard to his knees. The knife skidded and slid across the floor. Gabriel bent down and caught it.

Stilwell skittered backward toward the broken case, flung out a hand and groped for the gun.

Venetia never saw the snake strike. It happened too quickly in the shadows beneath the broken case. It was Stilwell's cry of horror and sudden violent thrashing that made her realize he had been bitten.

He yanked his hand out from beneath the case, shaking his fingers wildly.

Gabriel halted warily, knife in hand.

"No, *no,* it can't be," Stilwell whispered. Then he peered desperately beneath the stand. "Which one? Which one?"

Venetia saw that in his frantic flailing he had delivered a damaging blow to the snake. There was something wrong with the way it was writhing.

Gabriel moved toward the snake. In a move that seemed to Venetia as swift as that of a striking viper, he pinned the twisting creature with his heavily booted foot and used Stilwell's knife to sever the head from the body.

A shocked silence filled the room. Stilwell sat up a short distance away, clutching his hand. He stared at Gabriel, ashen-faced.

"I am dead," he said tonelessly. "You

have won. After all my planning, all my careful strategy, you have won. This is not the way it was supposed to end, you know. I was the fittest. I was the one who deserved to survive."

"I'll send for a doctor," Venetia whispered.

Stilwell gave her a scornful, enraged look. "Do not waste your time. There is no cure for the venom."

He gasped, convulsed violently and fell backward.

He did not move again.

After a moment Gabriel leaned down to check for a pulse at Stilwell's throat. When he looked up again Venetia knew from his expression that he had not found one.

A short time later Gabriel put on a pair of heavy gloves that he found on a workbench and cautiously opened the hidden panel embedded in the bottom of the Wardian case that had housed the venomous snake.

"Just in case there are any more surprises," he explained to Venetia.

He reached inside and carefully removed an old leather-bound notebook.

"The formula?" she asked.

"Yes."

41

They gathered in the library of his parents' town house the following morning to talk about the events of the past few days.

The last remnants of the hunting lust that had heated his blood had faded and Gabriel was now uncomfortably aware of the second layer of bruises he had acquired. But it was the knowledge that he had allowed Stilwell to come so close to harming Venetia that had kept him from getting any sleep. He was on his third cup of strong coffee.

"In addition to the alchemist's formula, Venetia and I also found Stilwell's journal of notes concerning his experiments," Gabriel said. "He was, indeed, a naturalist. He also possessed certain psychical abilities that were very similar to my own."

Venetia's brows snapped together in annoyance. "As I have pointed out on more than one occasion, the similarity in psychical talents means nothing. The two of you were as different as night and day."

Marjorie bestowed a smile of warm approval on her. "Quite right, my dear."

"What was Mr. Stilwell's connection to the Arcane Society?" Edward asked. "How did he learn of the formula?"

Montrose cleared his throat. "I believe I can answer that question, young man. When I heard the name *Stilwell,* certain facts fell into place. Isn't that so, Hippolyte?"

Hippolyte nodded somberly. "John Stilwell's father was Ogden Stilwell. Ogden held a seat on the Council of the Arcane Society for a time until he resigned for reasons he never explained to the rest of us. He possessed some of the same psychical gifts that his son exhibited. More to the point, he was obsessed with the founder's private codes."

"What happened to him?" Amelia asked.

Hippolyte sighed. "I regret to say that Ogden Stilwell was a noted eccentric in a society that is populated with eccentrics. Toward the end of his life he became increasingly reclusive, fearful and paranoid. He lost contact with all of his acquaintances in the society. Eventually we learned of his death and marked him down as deceased in the records."

"What of his son, this John Stilwell person?" Beatrice asked.

"That is where the tale turns complicated," Montrose said. "The records show that Ogden Stilwell had a son named John who perished of consumption nearly a year ago."

"Shortly before he followed Caleb and me to the site of the alchemist's laboratory and stole the formula," Gabriel said. "He hid his tracks very well. Caleb and I, after all, were looking for a suspect with connections to the Arcane Society who was still very much alive."

"Stilwell further muddied his tracks by murdering Lord Ackland and assuming his identity," Montrose continued.

"Why did he do that?" Amelia asked.

Hippolyte looked at her. "In part because he needed an identity that was entirely different from his own. He achieved that by becoming a doddering old man. But there was another reason why he selected Ackland as his victim."

"The oldest reason in the world," Marjorie said briskly. "Money. When Stilwell became Lord Ackland, he naturally gained access to Ackland's fortune."

"He needed the money to pursue his experiments," Gabriel said. "But he also got a dark thrill out of moving, undetected, in Society. He saw himself as a wolf in sheep's clothing. A hunter, prowling, unnoticed, among his prey."

"Why did he form a connection to Rosalind Fleming?" Beatrice asked.

Gabriel had been dreading this question. He swallowed more coffee and lowered the cup. He was very careful not to look at Venetia.

"Stilwell saw himself as a superior, more highly evolved man. He felt it was his duty to produce offspring who might exhibit his psychical talents. So he sought a worthy mate."

"Huh." Hippolyte turned thoughtful. "Perfectly natural, I suppose."

Gabriel glared at him. Hippolyte blinked a couple of times and then reddened.

"Man was insane, of course," Hippolyte said quickly.

Gabriel sighed and leaned back in his chair. "Stilwell went hunting for a suitable mate among the hundreds of females in London who claim to possess psychical powers. In the course of his search he discovered the woman we know as Rosalind Fleming. She was Charlotte Bliss at the time."

Edward's eyes widened. "Does Mrs. Fleming also possess some psychical senses?"

"We're not certain," Gabriel said. "And neither, in the end, was Stilwell. He writes that she is most certainly a skilled mesmerist, however."

"Stilwell eventually concluded that she possesses some rudimentary psychical talents that allow her to enhance the power of her hypnotic trances," Hippolyte added. "But he believed that her abilities were quite weak."

"Whatever the case," Gabriel continued, "she convinced Stilwell of her talents, at least for a while. He was very impressed by some demonstrations of her so-called mind reading and decided that she would make an excellent mate. For her part, Mrs. Fleming was thrilled to have acquired such a wealthy paramour, even if she did have to pretend that he was old and senile."

"Unfortunately for Mrs. Fleming," Hippolyte said, "Stilwell became suspicious of her claims of paranormal senses. At about the same time that he started to become disenchanted with her, he finally succeeded in deciphering the formula."

"And discovered the passage at the end of the notebook that warned that the alchemist's elixir was, in fact, a slow poison that would drive a person mad if the antidote was not taken simultaneously," Gabriel said.

"The passage in the notebook let it be

known that the antidote was etched on the lid of the strongbox," Hippolyte said. "So Stilwell sent those two men to Arcane House to steal it."

Montrose nodded gravely. "Stilwell knew the location of Arcane House and precisely where the museum was located inside because his father, as a member of the Council, had known those things and passed the information on to his son."

"I was able to prevent the theft of the strongbox," Gabriel said, "but I realized at that point that the thief was very determined and had to be stopped. So I transferred the strongbox into the Great Vault at Arcane House and then put out the word that the box had been destroyed and I had died in a fire on the premises. I thought it would cause the villain to lower his guard and induce him to come out of hiding. Instead, he remained in deep cover."

Hippolyte cradled his cup in his hands. "Stilwell records in his notes that, although he viewed the news of Gabriel's death with some suspicion, very likely because he had faked his own death and knew how easily it could be done, he nevertheless believed that he had been defeated in his quest to obtain the antidote. He decided to abandon his efforts to recover it."

Venetia wrinkled her nose. "And then a certain Mrs. Jones appeared on the London scene, a widow who happened to be a photographer. Stilwell's suspicions were aroused immediately, not only because I was using the name Jones but because he knew that a photographer had recently been hired to record the collection of antiquities at Arcane House. There was also the fact that Gabriel was supposedly dead and I was going about as a widow."

"The combination of coincidences aroused his hunting instincts," Gabriel said. "Just as they did mine. It occurred to Stilwell that if Venetia was the person who had photographed the collection, there might be a picture of the strongbox that he could use to decipher the antidote. But he also knew that the Arcane Society would never have allowed the photographer to keep copies of the pictures she had taken, let alone the negative. Still, he concluded that it might be worth his while to keep an eye on Venetia."

"So he hired Harold Burton to follow her around for a while to determine what was going on," Amelia said.

Beatrice frowned. "How did he know that a photographer had been employed at Arcane House?"

"Bear in mind that Stilwell knew the location of Arcane House," Gabriel said. "The two men he sent to steal the strongbox had watched the abbey for a day or two from a vantage point on a nearby hillside. With the aid of a spyglass they had seen Venetia taking pictures of some of the relics out on the terrace."

"I do like natural light when I can get it," Venetia said wryly.

"In any event," Gabriel concluded, "the one intruder who got away that night reported back to Stilwell that a photographer had been on the premises."

Hippolyte shook his head in disgust. "John Stilwell considered himself a modern man of science. He was fascinated with Mr. Darwin's theories because he thought that they confirmed his belief that he was naturally superior. He was sadly mistaken."

"He certainly was," Edward said, ghoulishly gleeful. "Just look at what his destiny proved to be. In the end, the mighty Mr. Stilwell was finished off by a lowly viper."

They all looked at him.

Gabriel started to laugh. "Well put, Edward. Well put, indeed."

"It was, all in all, an interesting example of the delicate balance of nature," Beatrice mused. "It would seem that this evolution business may be rather more complicated than John Stilwell believed."

Edward's expression crunched up in an attitude of serious concern. "What will happen to the insects and the fish that Mr. Stilwell kept in his laboratory?"

Gabriel made a face. "I can tell you from personal experience that there were very few, if any, fish left in the aquarium."

Venetia shuddered. "Fortunately for you, sir. There is no telling what dangerous creatures Mr. Stilwell put in that tank."

"As for the insects and snakes," Hippolyte said, "I contacted an associate of mine who is a naturalist. He took charge of the creatures. I expect most will end up in his collection."

"Well then, this affair is very nearly concluded, is it not?" Marjorie announced with satisfaction. "The villain is dead. The formula has been recovered. The only outstanding problem appears to be Rosalind Fleming."

"When you consider the matter closely," Venetia said, "she was merely another one of John Stilwell's victims. But I still wonder why she took such a great dislike of me."

"I can tell you the answer to that," Gabriel said. He folded his arms on the desk. "It is in Stilwell's journal."

"Well?" Venetia prompted.

"I believe I mentioned that Stilwell had begun to doubt Mrs. Fleming's psychical talents. But the more he learned about a certain Mrs. Jones, the more he became convinced that she might very well possess strong, genuine paranormal abilities."

Venetia started violently. "He wrote about *me?*"

Edward frowned. "You mean Mr. Stilwell decided that he wanted to marry Venetia instead of Mrs. Fleming?"

"He was just beginning to formulate such a plan when I recovered from my dreadful fall into the canyon, regained my memory and returned home to the arms of my lovely bride," Gabriel said.

"I see," Venetia said quietly. "Rosalind Fleming hated me because she feared that she was losing John Stilwell's affections. She knew he was considering replacing her with me. She was jealous."

Beatrice nodded once. "I did tell you that a woman in her position is always aware that her future hangs by a thread."

"But whatever gave John Stilwell the notion that I might have some psychical talents?" Venetia asked.

Gabriel looked very steadily at his father. "I believe I will allow you to answer that one, sir."

"Certainly," Hippolyte said. Enthusiasm lit his eyes. "Stilwell reasoned that if you were, indeed, married to Gabe, it was highly likely that you possessed true psychical gifts."

Venetia was clearly baffled. "I fail to see why he would automatically leap to that conclusion."

"Why, because everyone on the Council, including Ogden Stilwell, is aware that there is a strong tradition in the society," Hippolyte said. "The heir to the Master's Chair always searches for a bride who possesses psychical talents of her own." He smiled fondly at Marjorie. "Take my own dear wife, for example. You do not ever want to play cards with her. She can read what you hold in your hand as clearly as though it were written on the reverse side."

Marjorie smiled benignly. "It was a useful talent in my younger days, I must admit. It certainly served to attract your interest, Hippolyte."

He grinned affectionately. "Lost a fortune to you before I knew what had hit me."

"What?" Venetia was aghast. "Mr. Jones,

are you telling me that you chose me as a bride for your son merely because I can see auras?"

"I wasn't sure of the nature of your talents," he said. "But I knew that there was some psychical element in your nature that would complement Gabe's."

"I see," Venetia said grimly.

Belatedly Hippolyte appeared to realize that he might have blundered. He looked helplessly at Marjorie, seeking direction.

Marjorie looked very steadily at Venetia. "You misjudge my husband's goal in this matter," she said quietly. "Hippolyte was interested only in Gabe's happiness. Gabe's talents have caused him a great deal of private anguish over the years. He was becoming increasingly remote and isolated. He was spending more and more time with his books. My husband and I both feared that if he did not find a woman who could understand and accept the psychical aspects of his nature, he might never know true love."

"It was obvious that Gabe wasn't having any luck finding the right woman," Hippolyte said earnestly. "So I took it upon myself to do so."

No one spoke.

"I think," Marjorie said, rising to her

feet, "that we had best let Gabe and Venetia discuss this in private."

She led the way out of the library, the skirts of her gown sweeping the carpet with regal grace. Without a word, everyone except Venetia got up to follow.

The retreat was a hasty one, Gabriel noted. Indeed, it was a wonder they did not all trample one another on the way to the door.

42

Gabriel looked at her across the desk.

"Will you marry me?" he asked.

Venetia was stunned speechless. She had been prepared to launch into a forceful lecture listing all of his transgressions. But the simple question turned her world upside down.

"Before you give me your answer," he said, "hear me out. I am aware that our meeting at Arcane House was arranged by my father. But in my own defense, I can only say that I did not realize it back at the beginning. I did not deduce what had happened until I began to suspect that you possessed some psychical ability. My father, of course, sensed it immediately when he met you and purchased some of your photographs."

"Why do you say he knew it immediately?" she asked, momentarily distracted.

Gabriel smiled. "That is his particular talent. He can sense psychical gifts in others."

"I see."

"It is true that he is a great supporter of Mr. Darwin's theories and it is also true that there is a long-standing tradition in the Arcane Society which holds that the person who assumes the Master's Chair will search for a bride who also possesses paranormal talents. I, however, had made it clear that I would not be bound by that tradition."

"You did?"

"Yes. What is more, my parents supported me in that decision. But then my father found you for me. And you seduced me into a night of passion that I will remember for the rest of my life."

She looked down at her clasped hands. "I had no right to do that. But I was so sure that you were the right man and that Arcane House was the right place."

"Yes, I know. You have already explained the tropical island theme."

She knew she was turning pink. "This is very embarrassing, sir."

"The thing is, Venetia, although I was taken by surprise by my father's scheme, I have come to the conclusion that he was right."

"What?" She shot to her feet. "*You want to marry me because of my psychical abilities?* Are you implying that we are a pair

of sheep that should be bred because we each possess an unusual type of wool that may be passed on to our offspring?"

"No." He was on his feet, too, facing her across the desk. "That came out badly. Allow me to explain."

"What is there to explain?"

"I don't want to marry you because you happen to be able to see auras. Devil take it, what sort of basis would that be for a marriage?"

"A very poor one, I should think," she said.

"Your ability to see auras is akin to the color of your hair, as far as I am concerned. Interesting, to be sure, but not a reason to marry you."

"Well then? Why do you want to marry me?"

His jaw tightened. "There are a great number of reasons."

"Name one."

"There is the obvious fact that in the eyes of the world we are already married."

She was crushed. "In other words, it would be convenient for both of us to turn fiction into fact?"

"I said there were a lot of reasons. We share a mutual respect and admiration. In addition, we find each other stimulating."

"Stimulating?"

"Your word, Mrs. Jones. I would remind you that you set out to seduce me when we first met because you found me stimulating. Has that aspect of my nature changed?"

"No," she admitted.

He came around the desk and caught her shoulders with both hands. "I find you equally stimulating. I think you know that."

"Gabriel —"

"Intellectually and physically as well as metaphysically," he assured her.

"Gabriel, hush." She put her fingers across his lips to silence him. "I believe you when you say that you are not asking me to marry you to please your father or because you want to honor an Arcane Society tradition."

He smiled slowly. "Then we are making progress."

She shook her head. "I suspect that you are asking me to marry you because you feel responsible for all that has happened."

He stopped smiling. "What are you talking about?"

"The fact that, even though I seduced you first, I was, after all, a virgin. In addition, you feel responsible for the danger that developed around me and my family because I photographed the collection at Arcane House. You are an honorable man, Gabriel. A man of integrity. It is perfectly natural that you would assume a sense of duty and obligation toward me because you blame yourself for the events that transpired."

To her shock, he started to smile his secret, seductive smile.

"You've got it backwards, my sweet," he said.

"I beg your pardon?"

"I allowed myself to be seduced back at the start of this affair because I had already concluded that you were the only woman for me. I fell in love with you the night you walked into Arcane House with your precious camera in your arms."

She was shocked almost breathless. "Truly?"

"When you set out to seduce me, I realized that you were attracted to me but that you had no long-term arrangements in mind. I told myself that if I was very clever and bided my time, if I let you do the seducing, I might be able to make you fall in love with me, too."

"Oh, *Gabriel.*"

"I had a strategy. A *hunting* strategy, if you will. Then those two intruders showed up and everything spun into chaos. At least for a time. But now matters appear to have come right again. So, I ask you again, will you marry me?"

"You do understand that Amelia, Edward and Beatrice are part of the package, don't you?" she said, anxious to be clear.

"Of course. They are family. I think they like me well enough, don't you?"

She smiled. "They are all quite fond of you."

He captured her hand and kissed the palm. "What about you, my love? Are you fond of me, too?"

She felt a great lightness rise within her. It was a wonder her feet did not leave the ground, she thought.

"I love you with all my heart," she whispered.

She heard the library door open just as Gabriel pulled her into his arms. She turned her head and saw Beatrice, Amelia, Edward, Marjorie, Hippolyte and Mr. Montrose crowded in the doorway.

"Sorry to interrupt," Hippolyte said. "Thought we'd better see how things were progressing in here."

Gabriel looked at the group of expectant faces. “I am happy to report that I will soon be moving out of that attic.”

43

The next day Venetia was in the sunny studio at the back of the gallery, arranging props for a portrait sitting when Gabriel appeared.

"It appears that Rosalind Fleming, using a different name, purchased a ticket on a steamship that sailed for America this morning," he said.

"Good heavens." Venetia straightened, dusting off her hands. "Are you quite certain?"

"I spoke with the clerk who sold her the ticket. He confirmed the description of Mrs. Fleming. I also interviewed two dockside workers who assisted a lady matching Fleming's description with what was evidently a vast amount of luggage. My father went to her house today. It has been vacated. The servants said that their mistress had departed on an extended stay in America. They did not know when she would return."

Venetia thought about that. "Fleeing to America is the logical thing for her to do, when you think about it. With Stilwell dead, she has lost a great deal. She will no longer be receiving expensive gifts and money from him and she can no longer move in Society. Her only choice would have been to change her name again and return to her career as a blackmailing medium."

"Whereas in America she will be able to get a fresh start as a blackmailing medium," Gabriel said dryly.

"No doubt. Something tells me that Rosalind Fleming can take excellent care of herself."

44

The following afternoon Venetia took her customary route past the cemetery to the gallery. She had a parasol hoisted high in one hand and her appointment book tucked under her other arm. The message from Maud had arrived shortly before noon.

Mrs. Jones:

A very important person has requested to meet with you at four o'clock this afternoon at the gallery. He has booked a series of portraits of his daughters and wishes to discuss the theme of the photographs. He fancies the Inspiring Ladies of History program.

Please send word if the time is not convenient.

Venetia had found the time quite convenient. Maud's instinct for identifying Very Important Persons was unerring.

She stopped in surprise when she saw

that the shades were pulled down over the windows of the Jones Photographic Gallery. A small CLOSED sign dangled on the other side of the glass door.

It was not yet four. Maud had no doubt slipped out for a few minutes to treat herself to a cup of tea and a bite to eat before the new client arrived.

Venetia selected a key from the chatelaine attached to the waist of her gown.

Her uneasiness grew when she opened the door of the shop and walked inside. The silence should have felt normal but for some obscure reason it seemed wrong.

"Maud? Are you here?"

There was a faint stirring in the backroom. Relieved, Venetia hurried around the counter.

"Maud? Is that you?"

She grasped the edge of the curtain that separated the front room of the shop from the back and pulled it aside.

Maud was on the floor in the corner. She was bound and gagged. She stared at Venetia with wide, frantic eyes.

"Dear heaven," Venetia whispered.

She started forward.

Maud shook her head violently and mumbled something unintelligible. Too late Venetia realized she was attempting to signal a warning.

There was movement to the right. Rosalind Fleming stepped out from behind a stack of cartons containing framed prints of the *Men of Shakespeare* series.

She was dressed from head to toe in deep mourning, which, Venetia realized, made a very effective disguise. Rosalind had crumpled the heavy black veil up onto the brim of her black hat.

She had a small pistol in her black-gloved hand.

"We make an interesting pair of widows," Venetia said.

"I have been waiting for you, Mrs. Jones," Rosalind said. "I didn't want to leave town without my portrait. I do hope it turned out well."

An invisible psychical wind stirred the hair on the nape of Venetia's neck. It was not just the sight of the gun that was disturbing her senses. There was something strange about Rosalind's eyes. They appeared unnaturally brilliant; strangely compelling.

"You were reported to be on a ship that sailed for New York yesterday," Venetia said, stalling for time.

Rosalind smiled coldly. "I did, indeed,

purchase a ticket. But it is for passage on another ship, one that sails tomorrow. It was very simple to convince the clerk at the other shipping company that he had sold me a ticket for yesterday's sailing, however."

"Two dockhands helped you with your luggage."

"No, they merely believe that they assisted me."

"You mesmerized all three of them and planted memories in their heads. My goodness, Rosalind, you've certainly come a long way from your days as a small-time medium."

Rosalind stopped smiling. "I am no carnival-act mesmerist. I never was that. I possess a psychical talent for mesmerism."

"A very rudimentary talent, according to Stilwell's notes."

"That is not true." The gun in Rosalind's hand trembled with the force of her sudden rage. "He was going to marry me until you came along."

"Was he?"

"*Yes.* I was his true mate. He never doubted that until you showed up as Mrs. Jones. He only wanted you because he became convinced that Gabriel Jones had selected you as a wife. He believed that

Jones would only marry a woman possessed of strong psychical abilities, you see."

"I thought you preferred your status as a widow. You once pointed out all the benefits to me in great detail, as I recall."

"It would have been different with John Stilwell."

"Because in the guise of Lord Ackland, he could give you two things you could not obtain without marriage: a secure place in Society and access to a fortune."

"I deserved a position in Society," Rosalind said fiercely. "My father was Lord Bencher. I should have been an heiress. I should have been raised with his daughters. I should have been educated at the best schools. I should have married into the highest circles."

"But you were born out of wedlock and that changes everything, doesn't it? Trust me, I do understand your position. What will you do now that your scheme to become Lady Ackland has gone up in smoke?"

"You are the one who ruined my plans, you and Gabriel Jones. But I fought my way up the ladder of Society once and I will do it again. This time, though, I will try my luck in America, where it should be a simple matter to pass myself off as the widow of a wealthy British lord. They tell me that titles are very popular in America."

"Be reasonable. If you leave here now you can escape with no one the wiser. But if you kill me I assure you that Gabriel will hunt you down, no matter how far you run or how many times you change your name. Hunting is something Gabriel is very good at. He is better than John Stilwell ever was. You will notice which of them survived."

"Yes, I know." Rosalind's face twisted and the feverish look in her eyes intensified. "John suspected that he and Gabriel Jones shared similar paranormal talents. I assure you, I have no wish to spend the rest of my life looking over my shoulder. Therefore I have arranged to make certain that your death and that of your shopgirl will appear to be just another unfortunate photographic gallery accident. I understand they are all too common."

Maud made a distressed noise.

Rosalind ignored her. She motioned with the pistol. "Go into the darkroom, Mrs. Jones."

"Why?"

"You will find a bottle of ether in there." Rosalind smiled. "Everyone knows how dangerous it is. Why, one hears that fires and explosions happen all the time in darkrooms where the chemical is present."

"I don't use ether. It was required in the old collodion-plate-process days but not with the new dry plates."

"No one will know what chemical actually started the fire," Rosalind said impatiently.

"Ether is highly flammable and explosive. You will likely kill yourself as well as Maud and me if you attempt to ignite it," Venetia warned.

Rosalind's smile was terrifying. "I do understand that igniting a fire in a darkroom is an extraordinarily risky activity. Therefore, you will do it for me, Mrs. Jones."

"You cannot possibly believe that I will assist you in an action that will bring about my own death and the death of Maud. No, Mrs. Fleming. You will have to do this yourself."

"On the contrary. I can make you do anything I desire. What is more, you will do it willingly."

"I understand that mesmerism does not work well in situations where the subject is unwilling, and I assure you, I am not at all willing."

"You are wrong, Mrs. Jones," Rosalind said softly. "You see, I drank the formula."

Venetia's mouth went dry. "What are you talking about?"

"The alchemist's elixir, of course. John prepared a batch of it using the recipe in the old notebook. He did not know that I knew about it. I saw him store a quantity of it in a cupboard in his laboratory. When I realized that he was determined to have you, I went to the mansion while he was away and drank the stuff." Rosalind grimaced. "It tasted dreadful but I knew this morning that it was working."

"Don't you know why Stilwell didn't drink the elixir himself?"

Rosalind shrugged. "I suspect that he lost his nerve. He was afraid to experiment on himself."

"He didn't drink the formula because he discovered that it was a slow-acting poison. He wanted to be certain he possessed the antidote before he downed the elixir."

"You're lying."

"Why would I lie about something like this?" Venetia demanded.

"Because you think you can convince me not to kill you if you promise to provide me with an antidote. It is a very clever move, Mrs. Jones, but I thought I had made it clear that I am not a fool."

"Dear heaven, it seems Stilwell was secretive to the last. He didn't even confide in you. But I suppose that is only to be expected, given his nature."

"That is not true," Rosalind said. "He trusted me. He was going to marry me."

"Stilwell trusted no one. Listen to me, Rosalind. I am telling you the truth. The alchemist's brew may work for a time but soon it will drive you mad."

"I don't believe you," Rosalind said. Her eyes were hot coals now. "You are trying to manipulate me but it won't work. I will force you to admit the truth."

"How?"

Rosalind smiled coldly. "Like this."

Energy slammed across Venetia's senses, striking with such speed and force that she crumpled to her knees. Her skirts spilled around her. There was pain but it was unlike any she had ever experienced. It was as if her nerves had been touched with electricity. If this kept up for very long she would be the one who went mad, she thought.

"You will now be unable to speak anything but the truth, Mrs. Jones. You will tell me what I wish to know."

Venetia sought refuge in the only place she could think of, the paranormal plane. Still on her knees, fighting a haze of pain, she forced herself to look at Rosalind Fleming as though viewing her through the lens of a camera.

Concentrate.

The world around her became a negative image. The pain was different now. It was still intense but it was transformed into a more familiar sort of energy. She could keep this energy at bay.

An aura appeared around Rosalind's figure. It was sharper and stronger than Venetia remembered it. There was a new shade at the edges, a metaphysical color that exhibited a distinctly unwholesome aspect. The poison was already starting to affect Rosalind.

"Is the alchemist's formula a poison?" Rosalind asked.

"No," Venetia gasped.

"I thought not. That is all I needed to know. You will now rise to your feet and walk into the darkroom."

Venetia stood slowly, very nearly losing her balance. It was always awkward to move in the normal world when she was viewing it from this other dimension.

Maintaining her concentration while attempting to move about and converse in a normal fashion was next to impossible. She could only hope that Rosalind would attribute her lack of coordination and short, clipped responses to the force of a mesmeric thrall.

She reached the door to the darkroom and opened it slowly. Rosalind followed but she was careful to keep a considerable distance between them.

"You are doing very well, Mrs. Jones," Rosalind said. "Not much longer now and it will all be over. I placed an unlit taper on the workbench next to the bottle of ether. Strike a light and make a flame."

Venetia looked at the bottle. It was still sealed.

She fumbled for the taper, managing to knock it to the floor.

"Pick it up," Rosalind ordered from just outside the doorway. "Be quick about it."

Venetia stooped to retrieve the taper. When she gave it an unobtrusive little push it rolled away beneath the counter that held the sink. She crawled after it.

"Get the taper, damn you."

From her position outside the door, Rosalind could no longer see anything except the skirts of her gown, Venetia thought.

She collected the taper and struggled back to her feet. She gripped the edge of the counter to steady herself. The glass jar she used to measure some of her chemicals stood near the sink. In the eerie reversed light world in which she moved it was almost invisible. If she had not known it was there, she would not have noticed it.

Concealing the jar at her side amid the folds of her gown with one hand, the taper clutched in the other, she went slowly back to the workbench.

"Strike a light and be quick about it," Rosalind said urgently. "I want to be certain the taper is lit before I leave. I do not want any mistakes."

The blast of psychical energy that accompanied the command overrode Venetia's mental defenses. For an instant she lost her concentration. The world snapped back into focus. Pain slashed across her senses.

It took all of her willpower to shift back into the reversed-image world. Her heart was pounding so hard now she wondered that Rosalind did not hear it.

Keeping her back to the open door, Venetia set the glass jar on the counter next to the bottle of ether. Rosalind would not be able to see either from where she stood.

Venetia struck a light and lit the taper. She did not turn around.

"Very good, Mrs. Jones." An unnatural

excitement and anticipation vibrated in Rosalind's voice. "Now you must listen to me very closely. You will wait until you hear the front door of the shop open and close and then you will unseal the bottle of ether. Is that clear?"

"Yes," Venetia said tonelessly.

"You will spill the ether on the floor and then you will touch the flame to the ether."

"Yes," Venetia said again.

"But you must not open the bottle until after I am out on the street," Rosalind emphasized. "We would not want any unfortunate accidents, now, would we?"

"No."

Her back still turned toward Rosalind, Venetia picked up the jar. She hurled it to the floor at her feet. It landed hard. Glass exploded violently.

Her full skirts hid the shards from Rosalind's view but there was no mistaking the sound of shattering glass.

"What was that?" Rosalind shrieked. "What did you drop?"

"The bottle of ether," Venetia said calmly. "Can't you smell the fumes? They are very strong." She turned, the blazing taper in hand, and looked at Rosalind very steadily across the flame. "Shall I light it now?"

"No," Rosalind screamed. She edged backward. "No, not yet. Wait, wait until I am gone."

The storm of energy that had been battering Venetia's senses ceased abruptly. Rosalind had lost her control.

Venetia stooped toward the floor, lowering the taper.

"Stop," Rosalind shrieked. "You stupid fool. You must wait until I am gone."

Venetia continued to lower the flame toward the floor. "They say the fumes alone are highly explosive," she observed in the same uninflected voice. "They are quite strong. This won't take long."

"No." Fury lanced across Rosalind's face. She raised the gun in both hands.

Venetia realized that Rosalind was going to pull the trigger. She threw herself to the side. The gun roared; deafening in the small space.

Ice-cold pain slashed Venetia's arm. Already off balance, she fell to the floor, instinctively trying to hold onto the burning candle.

Rosalind whirled and fled through the curtained doorway.

Venetia heard the front door of the shop open.

"Don't rush off on my account," Gabriel

said from the other room.

"Let me go," Rosalind yelled, panic-stricken. "This place will go up like a torch at any moment."

Gabriel pulled aside the curtain. Venetia saw that he held Rosalind by the scruff of her neck. The gun was in his other hand.

He looked at Venetia. "You're bleeding."

He released Rosalind and started forward, yanking a small knife and a large, square linen handkerchief out of the pockets of his greatcoat.

Venetia looked down at her arm. The sleeve of her gown was soaked with blood. Stunned, she did the only thing she could think of that made some sense. She blew out the candle.

Rosalind stared, shaken. "You aren't in a trance."

"No," Venetia said.

Gabriel crouched beside her and went to work with the knife, slicing away the sleeve of her gown.

"The ether," Rosalind whispered.

"I would never open a bottle of ether around an open flame," Venetia said.

Rosalind whirled and ran, disappearing through the curtain.

Gabriel looked up briefly from his task.

Venetia could feel the hunting lust radiating from him in waves.

"Your prey is escaping," she said dryly.

He turned his attention back to her injured arm. "I have other priorities at the moment."

"Yes," she said, smiling a little in spite of the searing pain. "You are first and foremost a protector of those in your care."

His eyes met hers. "Nothing is more important to me than you."

He meant it, she thought. He meant every word.

She wanted to tell him that the feeling was mutual but she was starting to feel light-headed. She hoped she was not going to faint.

Gabriel surveyed the wound in her arm. "It is quite shallow, thank God. I must get you to a doctor, though. It will need to be properly cleaned and bandaged."

That information steadied her.

A thought struck her.

"Gabriel, Mrs. Fleming drank the alchemist's formula."

"That is unfortunate." He concentrated on wrapping the handkerchief around her arm.

"What about the antidote?"

"It is too late. I just finished deciphering

the last passage in the alchemist's formula. It states that the antidote only works if it is mixed with the formula and consumed at the same time."

45

Six days later Venetia and Gabriel met with Harrow in the park. Harrow had a copy of *The Flying Intelligencer* tucked under his arm.

He looked at Venetia with concern. "Are you all right?"

"Yes." She gave him a reassuring smile. "There is no sign of infection. The doctor tells me my arm will heal quickly."

"You have seen the news?" Harrow asked.

Gabriel nodded. "They pulled Mrs. Fleming's body out of the river two days ago. Suicide. Evidently she jumped off a bridge."

"We can only hope the authorities are correct and that this is not another one of her tricks of psychical mesmerism," Gabriel said.

Harrow's brows rose. "It is no trick."

The absolute certainty of the statement made Venetia go very still.

"How can you be sure?" she asked.

"Mr. Pierce made arrangements to view

the body personally. He wanted to be certain that there was no mistake."

"I see," she said.

"Speaking of Mr. Pierce," Harrow continued, "he has asked me to convey his gratitude to you and to Mr. Jones. He said to tell you that he is in your debt. If there is ever anything either of you needs and if it is within his power to obtain it for you, it is yours."

Venetia glanced uneasily at Gabriel.

"Please thank Mr. Pierce for us," Gabriel said to Harrow.

Harrow smiled his cool, ethereal smile. "I will do that. Meanwhile, I trust I will see you at the next photographic exhibition."

"We will look forward to it," Venetia assured him.

"Good day to you both." Harrow inclined his head in a graceful bow and walked off across the park.

Venetia noticed that Gabriel was watching Harrow with a meditative expression.

"What are you thinking?" she asked.

"I am thinking that the alchemist's poisonous brew worked very rapidly, indeed. According to the notebook it should have taken several days before it induced a state of madness and melancholia."

"Given the nature of the brew, I doubt if the alchemist was able to conduct many experiments," Venetia said. "The length of time it took for the elixir to turn into a poison may have been only an estimate on his part."

"Perhaps," Gabriel said. He did not take his eyes off Harrow.

She turned to follow his gaze. Harrow had almost disappeared in a grove of trees but when she concentrated she could catch glimpses of his aura. A frisson touched her spine.

"Gabriel," she said suddenly. "Do you think that Mr. Harrow is Mr. Pierce's very good friend? The person Mrs. Fleming tried to blackmail?"

"I think that is a very interesting theory." Gabriel's smile was very cold. "But one I have no interest in attempting to verify. Pierce may or may not possess psychical powers of his own but the hunter in me tells me that he is quite capable of protecting that which he values. I think we can assume that there is at least one very plausible explanation for why the alchemist's formula acted so swiftly in Mrs. Fleming's case."

"Are you implying what I think you are implying?"

"Let's just say that I would not be surprised to learn that Mr. Pierce took steps to make very certain that Rosalind Fleming jumped off that bridge."

46

Two days later Hippolyte strode into the library of the town house, waving a handful of cards.

"I just lost damn near twenty pounds to Miss Amelia and young Edward," he roared.

Gabriel looked up from the newspaper. "I did warn you not to play cards with that pair."

Hippolyte grinned, satisfaction radiating from him in waves. "Why didn't you tell me that they're both showing signs of psychical abilities?"

"I knew that you would figure it out soon enough."

"Realized it as soon as I sat down to play with them, of course." Hippolyte chuckled. "I could feel the energy around the table. It was astonishing. Miss Amelia is already quite strong. Young Edward is just coming into his own. Not sure what sort of talent he's got yet, but it will be interesting to find out."

"Guiding those two as they develop their

psychical skills will give you something to occupy your spare time." Gabriel turned the page in the newspaper. "You'll be needing a new hobby now that you've finished with matchmaking."

Venetia entered the library, a photograph in her hand. "Good afternoon, gentlemen. Would you care to see the latest addition to the *Men of Shakespeare* series? I think Caesar is going to be quite popular."

Gabriel got to his feet to greet her. He glanced down at the picture of Caesar. The man in the photograph was blond and endowed with the sort of features ladies were known to admire in men. The model was also extremely well muscled. A great deal of that muscle was on display.

"What the devil is he wearing?" Gabriel asked.

"A toga, of course," Venetia said. "What else would Caesar wear?"

"Good lord, Venetia, the man's half naked."

"That's the classical Roman fashion."

"Damnation. You actually photographed a man who was wearing nothing but a skimpy toga?"

"Remember, dear, photography is an art. Half naked, indeed, entirely naked people are quite commonly found in art."

"They are most definitely not going to be commonly found in *your* art."

"Now, Gabriel —"

Hippolyte cleared his throat. "I believe I'll leave you two alone to discuss the finer points of the photographic arts. Young Edward and I are going to take his kite to the park."

47

They spent their wedding night alone in the little house on Sutton Lane. Declaring that the newlyweds needed privacy, Marjorie Jones invited Beatrice, Amelia and Edward to stay at the town house that evening.

Venetia waited for her husband in bed, demurely garbed in an ankle-length nightgown. She felt unaccountably shy and more than a little nervous. This was ridiculous, she thought. They had been together before. Why was she feeling so anxious?

She started a little when Gabriel opened the door and walked into the room. He wore a dark dressing gown and his hair was still damp from his bath.

Her husband, she thought. She was now a wife.

He stopped halfway across the room and looked at her with his sorcerer's eyes.

"What is the matter?" he asked.

"I find it hard to believe that we are married," she confessed. "There was a time when I thought I'd never see you again. Not in this life, at any rate."

He smiled and walked the rest of the way to the edge of the bed. "How odd. I knew from the beginning that we would be together."

"Did you?"

He untied the sash of his robe. "Remember the night we made love together at Arcane House?"

"I am not likely to forget it."

"Do you recall telling me that you were mine?"

She blushed. "Yes."

He tossed the robe aside, pulled back the covers and got in beside her. "As far as I was concerned, that was our real wedding night, Mrs. Jones."

He was right, she thought. That night had sealed the bond between them.

Her bridal jitters evaporated in the warmth of that knowledge. She opened her arms to him.

"I knew you were the right man," she whispered.

"Ah, but you were thinking of only one night together. Whereas I was plotting a strategy that would last a lifetime."

He came to her then. They made love slowly at first and very thoroughly. Gabriel touched her in ways that would have shocked her in the light of day. But here in the shadows of the bedroom, she gloried in the sensual intimacy.

Gradually the tender lovemaking was transformed into a sensual battle. She grew bolder and more daring. At one point she took him into her mouth. His fingers clenched in her hair.

"Enough, my sweet." His breathing was harsh with the effort he was exerting to maintain control.

"I see no reason to stop," she said softly.

Without warning he reversed their positions, rolling on top of her. In retaliation, she sank her nails into his back.

He laughed and captured her wrists, pinning them to the bed on either side of her head.

"I carried your marks from that first night at Arcane House for two days," he said.

She smiled up at him in the shadows, aware that he could see her quite clearly in the darkness. "Did you?"

"I seem to recall telling you at the time that you would pay."

"Promises, promises."

The next thing she knew he had released her wrists and was sliding down the length of her body to her melting core.

When he kissed her there she convulsed

in shock and excitement. He covered her once more, sinking himself deep inside her.

Together they sailed the crashing waves of the climax, losing themselves in the shared fires of psychical energy, sexual passion and love.

A long time later, he lay back against the pillows and gathered her close against him. He felt perfectly sated, he thought. Happy and content. Loved and in love.

"Do you think you will mind not being a widow?" he asked.

Ventia laughed and reached up to touch his face with loving fingers. "There appear to be some advantages to being a wife, after all."

The employees of Thorndike Press hope you have enjoyed this Large Print book. All our Thorndike and Wheeler Large Print titles are designed for easy reading, and all our books are made to last. Other Thorndike Press Large Print books are available at your library, through selected bookstores, or directly from us.

For information about titles, please call:

(800) 223-1244

or visit our Web site at:

www.gale.com/thorndike
www.gale.com/wheeler

To share your comments, please write:

Publisher
Thorndike Press
295 Kennedy Memorial Drive
Waterville, ME 04901